Crash &

My Strange Life as an Astral Traveler for the CIA

Peter E. Ludvick

Copyright 2016 Peter E. Ludvick

Prologue

It is my fervent hope not to die in prison. My lawyer sends someone by once a month to collect my vain scribblings. He assures me they'll be published upon my death if he fails in his attempts to win my freedom. Fat chance of going free, you might be thinking, and I'd have to agree with you. After all, I am serving a 110 year sentence. Not technically a life sentence, but I'll never live to see the end of it. Still, I escape from prison every night, only to return to my cell each and every morning. The trick will be to die when I am away. Suicide not being an option for me, I have to hope I get lucky. I've certainly had more than my share of bad breaks over the years, so is a little good luck too much to ask for?

There are over two million people behind bars in America and every one of us has a story. This is mine. I am an astral traveler.

Chapter One

If you're like me (okay, nobody is even remotely like me but you know what I mean) you've already googled my name and found nothing. Duh. It's a pen name. A pseudonym. An alias. I guess alias is most appropriate, my being in prison. I wanted to publish this as my memoir but my lawyer convinced me it would never see the light of day as a non-fiction book. It comes before you as a novel, but I assure you, every word of it is true. Once you have finished reading my book, if you're savvy enough with internet searches you'll have enough clues to eventually track down my true name. If you happen to discover my identity then you will face a dilemma: I'm real. Ninety percent of what you read in these pages is easily corroborated once you know my true name. The question for you, then, is will you believe the other ten percent, the part our government never wants to be made public? Please believe it, not for my sake, but for your own.

I grew up on the east coast of America in a relatively small town. My family was absolutely typical for those days - Dad worked full time, Mom stayed home to raise us kids until the youngest, my sister Emily, was in third grade. After that my mother worked part time at a McDonald's restaurant, not because we really needed the money but mostly because she was bored at home all day. Life was exceedingly normal for my first eleven years, then I met the woman who changed (ruined?) everything for me - Miss Grant, my sixth grade teacher. I know, you'd think the woman who so profoundly affected my life would deserve to have her full name recorded for posterity, but honestly, I can't recall her first name. Perhaps I never knew it.

There's an old joke about the 1960s, the decade of drugs, sex, and rock and roll. Hippies. Flower children. Vietnam. The joke goes like this: "If you remember the 1960s you didn't live through them." Well, I lived through the second half of the 1960s as a very, very young boy, young enough to survive untouched by the madness of that decade and too young to remember any of it. It was the 1970s that got me. My life was changed forever in the late 1970s, but nearly fifteen years would pass before I realized it.

******

In 1978 Miss Grant was an average teacher, I guess. She was young and pretty and passionate about teaching. Life and an endless succession of mediocre, apathetic students hadn't yet ground her down. She had majored in English in college and it was no surprise her favorite teaching subject was creative writing. Unfortunately, none of the two dozen children in her class, including me, had any interest in it.

Near the end of the school year Miss Grant gave us an assignment to write about our dreams. Not our hopes and dreams for the future, but rather the actual dreams we had while asleep on any given night. Immediately upon hearing the assignment a loud chorus of groans and half dozen hands went up in protest - a good portion of the class claimed they never remembered their dreams, therefore they should be excused from the assignment. Sixth graders are pretty clever about things like that.

The 1970s were known as "The Age of Aquarius," a decade when many young people turned away from psychedelic drugs for spiritual awakening and turned instead to ancient mystical subjects such as transcendental meditation, psychic healing, auras, discovering past lives, etcetera. Uri Geller was big back then, bending spoons on TV, apparently using just the power of his mind. Shirley MacLaine was wildly popular, later writing books about her mystical life which were largely scoffed at.

Miss Grant was a "New Ager," totally into the raging mystical, spiritual movement. Looking back, I think she intentionally gave us the writing about dreams assignment so she would have an excuse to teach us what she really wanted; a method of remembering our dreams, one of many New Age fascinations. The New Age movement was never widely accepted but those who believed in it were usually zealots. Miss Grant was no exception. She was secretly trying to turn us all into little New Agers, clones of herself.

The writing assignment was put on hold while our teacher spent the next few days explaining the sleep cycle to us. Miss Grant assured us if we carefully followed her instructions then in short order we would not only be able to remember our dreams but some of us might even be able to control the content of them. To dream on demand, so to speak. Wow, to go to bed at night with the certainty of dreaming about watching Susie MacPherson skinny dipping in Salter's pond! To catch Carl Yastremski's World Series winning home run (hey, it's a dream) and then have him autograph the baseball! The possibilities for an imaginative sixth grader were endless.

With practice, she said, we might eventually progress to the point of conscious action while dreaming. I have to admit that concept was fairly blurry to me but I was nonetheless enthralled by the whole subject, because I usually couldn't recall my dreams with any specificity at all. Typically, I'd wake up in the morning knowing I had dreamt, and with a general feeling of having had good dreams or nightmares. Occasionally I'd wake up and vividly recall a dream, only to have the memory fade to oblivion before breakfast. The thought of clearly recalling my dreams was exciting, and I took careful notes on her instructions.

We had to learn the sleep cycle so we would know the proper time to set on our alarm clocks to awaken us abruptly while dreaming. I'll explain it to you the way she explained it to us.

When a person falls asleep they go into light sleep followed by deep sleep, followed by REM sleep. REM stands for Rapid Eye Movement sleep. It is only in REM sleep that dreams occur. REM sleep starts about ninety minutes after falling asleep and lasts for only ten minutes or less, then the cycle repeats. With each repeat of the sleep cycle the time in REM sleep doubles. To lay it out for you, a typical night's sleep looks like this:

90 minutes, then 10 minutes dreaming. 90 minutes, then 20 minutes dreaming. 90 minutes, then 40 minutes dreaming. 90 minutes, then 80 minutes dreaming.

If you add it all up you get eight and a half hours. If you are the typical person who gets about eight hours of sleep you almost always awaken from REM sleep, in the midst of dreaming, thus the memory of your last dream is only moments old and often quite vivid. However, your morning routine is performed on automatic pilot while your brain is focused on the events of the coming day, and the memory of your last dream is quickly lost. If you happen to wake outside of REM sleep you often have no memory of dreaming at all.

Now that we knew the sleep cycle our assignment was to set our alarm clocks to awaken us once during the night while in REM, then reset the alarm to awaken us eight hours after going to bed. If we typically got more than eight hours sleep we would have to set our alarms a third time to awaken us at our normal time for school. In order to complete the assignment we would need at our bedside an alarm clock, a memo pad of some type, pen or pencil, and a light or flashlight.

Miss Grant suggested we first set our alarm clock for five hours and ten minutes after going to bed, then, after waking up briefly and writing down any dreams we could recall, reset our alarm for eight hours after our bedtime. The first alarm should theoretically awaken us during the forty minute dreaming period, the second during the eighty minute REM period. Of course, we're talking about sixth graders here, so there was a great deal of misunderstanding, mistakes, and non-compliance.

I was motivated to get it right, though, and determined to follow my teacher's instructions to the letter. I never mentioned the assignment to my parents or siblings, as I knew my older brother and younger sisters wouldn't care and my parents would probably be upset about it. Miss

Grant never asked us to get permission from our parents; it just wasn't done back then.

My efforts at remembering my dreams using my teacher's method met with immediate success. My parentally mandated bedtime was 8:30 PM on school nights and 9:30 PM on weekends. Prior to this assignment I had set my alarm clock for 6:30 AM on school days, a ten hour sleep period. If I wasn't at the breakfast table by 6:45 AM my mom would come up to my room and blast me out of bed.

The very first night I tried this was incredible. I opened my eyes at 6:45 AM the next morning to find my mother shaking my pillow. I had slept right through the 6:30 AM alarm. No recollection of any dreams at all. Crap, I thought, I either forgot to set the alarm for the REM times or I slept right through it.

I jumped out of bed fifteen minutes behind my usual schedule and raced through my morning routine of brushing my teeth, washing my face, trying to tame my unruly hair, and scowling at any new acne pimples that had blossomed like putrid flowers during the night. My last chore before heading downstairs to breakfast was to make my bed. As I tucked in the sheets on the corner nearest my bed stand I was shocked to see a half page of writing in my dream notebook, which lay open. Before going to sleep I had simply dated the top of the page, nothing else.

I read with fascination a scribbled entry apparently made by me at 1:40 AM. It was six words: "Riding my bike on Main Street." I could only conclude I had been dreaming of that, awoke to the alarm, wrote it down, and went back to sleep. I had absolutely no recollection of it. It was of special interest to me because I was not allowed to ride my bicycle on Main Street due to the heavy traffic there. I had never done so except, apparently, in my dreams.

Scrawled below that was another entry, barely legible, in overly large letters, logged at 4:35 AM. "Fishing at the Hockanum River with Wyane and Josh. Fell in everyone laughing no fish."

Holy cow! Apparently I had executed my teacher's instructions correctly - I was looking at written proof of it. Re-reading the entry about fishing stirred vague memories of the dream. I had initially assumed I must have fallen in the river in the dream, but now, reading my notes, I recalled I dreamt it was my friend Wayne who had fallen in. Yes, his name was Wayne and I had sleepily misspelled it in my dream notebook. That wasn't important. What was important was the fact I now recalled a snippet from my dream. Miss Grant's method was working!

I read my notebook entries over and over, but no further memories of my dreams emerged. Wayne and Josh and I frequently fished together at the Hockanum River, so dreaming of that made sense to me. But why did I dream of bike riding on Main Street? I never had, and never wanted to. Main Street was mostly car dealers and clothing stores, with a grocery store on the far end. Nothing of even passing interest to me, so why did I dream of it?

My mother's strident voice snapped me out of my reverie, demanding I get down to breakfast right now or she'd toss my food in the dog's bowl. I snatched up my dream notebook and ran downstairs, eager to get to school and discuss my breakthrough with Miss Grant and my classmates.

I barely made it to school on time even though I ran most of the way. Normally it took me about fifteen minutes to walk to school, but that day I made it in less than ten. Still, just as I got in my seat the final bell rang and I had no time to discuss my success recalling dreams with my friends. I didn't know what to call the dream recalling method back then, and I still don't know what to call it now, so I'll just refer to it as Miss Grant's method.

English and writing class were always in the afternoons. Mornings were math, history and social studies. I was bursting at the seams to talk about the dream assignment with my friends but had to wait until morning recess. When recess finally came none of my friends had any interest in talking about dreams, they just wanted to play kickball as usual. My friend Wayne was the most athletic kid in our class so he was always one of the kickball captains. The captains got to pick their teams, using some incredibly complicated method involving an unwritten but well-understood hierarchy of talent. The boys (girls never played unless the teachers made us pick them) were ranked as "good," "okay" and "dorky," and each captain had to alternate picking one boy from each tier. I was in the "good" group and Wayne always picked me first. After he picked me I stood next to him and started to tell him about my dream of fishing with him and Josh. He looked at me like I was speaking Bantu and said, "Maybe you should be on the dork squad today," and that was the end of that.

Later, our game ended a few minutes before recess was over and I told Josh I had dreamed about him and Wayne. He called me a homo and threatened to tell the whole class if I didn't shut up. This dampened my enthusiasm considerably, as you might imagine. Back in sixth grade, in those days, in my little clique, that was a major insult, not to be given or taken lightly. I didn't dare bring up the subject at lunch, and no one else mentioned the dream assignment, either.

When it finally came around to writing class I was again disappointed. Most of the kids claimed they had screwed up Miss Grant's method and didn't remember any of their dreams. I was pretty sure half of them were lying, too embarrassed to talk about it. Dreams are pretty personal things, after all. A couple of the weirder girls told stories of incredible dreams of princesses and Olympic figure skating, but nobody believed them. When it was my turn I said I had written down a dream about riding my bike but couldn't remember the details. I made no mention of the fishing dream. Miss Grant nodded her approval and it got me off the hook with Wayne and Josh.

Miss Grant had cautioned us not to use her method every night because she didn't want us to disturb our sleep too much, but I paid no attention to her warning. When I went to bed that night I set my alarm in accordance with her schedule, my dream notebook and flashlight at the ready, then again the next night, and the next, for many weeks to come.

******

June came and my days in elementary school ended. I earned only a B- in creative writing for Miss Grant, but in my mind I got an A+ for learning her method of recalling dreams. Each day for the first few weeks my dream notebook filled up with more dreams and more details. Some mornings I'd awaken to find notes on as many as five different dreams logged in. Each successive day also brought greater clarity in my recollection of my dreams. I was thrilled with my progress; it was just as Miss Grant had predicted. I looked forward anxiously to the next stages, hoping my teacher was right about them as well. Not wanting to incur the wrath and derision of my friends I never again spoke to them about my dreams, and none of them ever broached the subject with me.

That summer of 1978 I did what I always did - played baseball, went fishing, and hung out with my pals. Girls were becoming more and more of interest but with school out of session I seldom got the chance to meet any and I really didn't try very hard. My parents moved my mandatory lights out time to 10:00 PM, it being summer and me now almost twelve years old.

Shortly after the fourth of July I decided to see if I was ready for the next step in Miss Grant's method. Going to bed that night I did not set my alarm clock. The next morning I awoke after a full night's sleep, grabbed my dream notebook and quickly wrote down the details of three dreams. Success! I remembered some of my dreams without the aid of the alarm clock. I had entered phase two of Miss Grant's method, recalling details of my dreams the next morning without waking during the night and taking notes.

By that time, about two months into this, I was recalling some dreams with great specificity. Writing down my recollections would usually dredge up even more details. It wasn't long before I had filled my first notebook and needed a second.

One night at dinner my mom told me she had found my notebook while dusting my room. From the way she said it I knew she must have read through it. I immediately flushed a deep red, because I was of the age where I was starting to have some pretty sexually explicit dreams, and had dutifully recorded them in my notebook. "These are just dreams you're writing about, aren't they, Pete?"

I got it instantly - my mother was worried I was writing about actual sexual experiences. I wish! Was she really expecting we were going to discuss this in front of my siblings? "No, Mom," I said, sarcasm dripping from my voice like maple syrup overrunning a plateful of pancakes, "everything I wrote in *my private notebook* in *my room* is real, even the ones about monsters on the moon."

My mom gently responded, "Well, Pete, I must have missed those, but I was concerned about…"

My father put down his fork and caught my mother's eye before she could totally embarrass me. "Peter," he interrupted, "first of all, *your private notebook* and *your room* are in *my house*, and no one will speak to your mother in that tone of voice in *my house*. Is that clear?"

"Yes, sir."

"Good. Now, if you don't want your mother going through your things then put them away. Better yet, keep your room clean, and that includes dusting. You're not in grade school anymore. It's time you took on additional chores and gave your mother a break."

My brother chuckled and started to say something snarky but one stern look from Dad silenced him. I had no intention of stopping my dream experiment and certainly didn't want my mother reading from my notebooks, so after that I kept my room clean.

******

After a couple of weeks of recalling and recording my dreams without the aid of an alarm clock I felt I was ready to move on to phase three. Phase three was somewhat confusing to me so I broke out my classroom notes and studied them. The goal in the third phase of Miss Grant's method, according to my notes, was to master the ability to be awake while dreaming. I told you it was confusing! How can someone be awake while dreaming? What she meant was we were to learn how to be conscious of the fact that we were dreaming while still remaining in the dream state. In order to do that, she had said, we first had to learn to wake ourselves up during a dream. That part actually made sense to me after I gave it some thought. If I could learn to wake myself at will while dreaming then perhaps I could also realize I was dreaming and choose not to wake up.

Thank God it was summertime and I could sleep as late as I wanted. After a couple of frustratingly long, peaceful nights' sleep I had a breakthrough. I was riding my bike down Main Street one afternoon and suddenly realized I was dreaming! I had to be. Main Street was off limits to me on my bicycle, yet there I was, having that same dream again. I pedaled a few more times and woke up. My bedside clock read 11:45 PM. Having gone to bed at 10:00 PM, I was in the first, shortest REM interval. It was probably my first dream of the night. I recorded it in my dream notebook and went back to sleep.

Uncle Bernie lit up another cigarette and asked me if I was old enough to drink coffee yet. It was early morning and we were sitting on his porch overlooking a small pond. Was that an alligator there on the far shore? Wait a minute. Uncle Bernie? He lived in Florida and I had never been to his house. Mom and Dad had been talking at dinner about maybe going down to see him for Christmas this year. I was dreaming, I knew it, and woke myself up. I duly recorded it was 1:23 AM, scrawled some notes about Uncle Bernie and the alligator, and rolled over. I woke myself twice more that July night of 1978, and four or five times a night each of the next five nights. On the sixth night I slept like a rock for twelve straight hours. If I dreamt at all I didn't recall it. If I kept on waking myself up each night I'd be a wreck. It was time to try *not* waking up.

******

Once I learned to recognize when I was dreaming, not waking up while dreaming proved to be much more problematic than I had anticipated. I had another bad week of frequently interrupted sleep. My mother noticed my "raccoon eyes" and became concerned. She suspected I was sneaking out of the house at night and running around causing trouble with my friends. After a long lecture about the evils of sex, drugs and alcohol (the big three, in order of badness, for a boy who had just turned twelve years old) she let me convince her I was staying up late watching television after 10:00 PM. My parents had gotten me a portable TV for my birthday and there it sat, in my bedroom, silently agreeing with me. I'm not sure she bought the lie but I knew darn well she'd never believe the truth.

Two nights later I finally did it - I was dreaming, knew it, and rode it out without waking up. Another dream followed immediately, then another, like TV shows without all the advertisements. Suddenly my dreams had a completely different texture, for lack of a better word. It was wonderful. I was in the dream but I was also watching myself at the same time, like I was looking over my own shoulder. I awoke in the morning and wrote down details from six different dreams. Best of all, I felt completely rested. The next night it got even better, when I unexpectedly jumped from Miss Grant's phase three into phase four, consciously controlling my actions while dreaming.

It was midnight. I was in the basement of an old house, trying to find a dead body. Okay, truth be told, I was hoping *not* to find a body. My friends Wayne, Josh and David had dared me to go into the old Sullivan house, an abandoned house a few blocks from my own. Rumor had it old man Sullivan had died in the basement and his body had not been discovered until weeks afterward. All us kids believed it was haunted and we often hung out near the place, because it was cool. Once in a while, on a dare, one of us would go up and ring the front doorbell, then run like hell. Steve Simmons, who was stone crazy, even sat down in the old glider on the porch one time and pretended to read a comic book.

In the dream, there was a chalkboard in the basement. Every kid who ever dared to go down there had written his name on the board. Wayne, Josh and David all said they had been down there and I would see their names if I ever had the guts to go down there myself. David swore he had seen the old man's body, or maybe it was his ghost. Well, there I was, and the chalkboard had only two names, neither of which I recognized. Those liars!

Suddenly, an eerie noise issued from a dark corner. I bolted up the cellar stairs, but couldn't get to the top, the stairs were endless. The noise kept getting louder, closer. Terrified, I ran as fast as I could but couldn't reach the door. Then it hit me - I was dreaming, and I could wake up anytime I wanted. But I didn't want to wake up; I wanted to write my name on the damn board!

Knowing it was a dream and no longer afraid, I stopped on the stairs and confidently strode downwards. Eight steps later I was back in the dank basement, the noise fading to nothing. I walked to the chalkboard, picked up a piece of chalk and wrote "Pete was here" in bold strokes. Then for good measure I lined out the two names above mine. A door I had somehow overlooked was right behind the chalkboard. I opened the door and stepped out of the basement into bright sunlight and a completely different dream.

I had done it - I was dreaming; knew I was dreaming, and took conscious action in my dream, all without waking up. I made conscious decisions in several more dreams that night, and even in my dreams I knew I was in phase four. There was only one phase left in Miss Grant's method - dreaming on demand.

******

Dreaming on demand - it was the ultimate goal of Miss Grant's method, or so I thought at the time. A few years later I discovered there was another step, one Miss Grant apparently felt was not appropriate for sixth graders. I took that step on my own, but I'm getting a little ahead of myself.

I'm sure many of you reading this are familiar with the techniques I have been describing. Perhaps you have even had some success with them yourself. I know now they are similar to something called Wake Induced Lucid Dreaming, or WILD for short. Miss Grant's method is different enough that I can't say I was practicing WILD, and if I was I eventually moved beyond it to something more. Anyway, back to dreaming on demand.

By this point, August of 1978, I was well into my third dream notebook. Reviewing the notes on hundreds of my dreams I saw they fell into two broad categories: reality-based dreams and fantasies. Of course there was overlap from one to the other but it was useful to make the distinction.

My fantasy dreams seemed to occur at random. Less than ten percent of all the dreams I had recorded were fantasies. I re-read my notes about being on some far planet, or deep in the bowels of the earth, or time traveling. I attributed fantasy dreams to a teenager's active imagination. Oddly, they held little interest for me, perhaps because I knew they could never happen in real life.

As I reviewed my notes on the reality-based dreams I began to see a clear correlation - I dreamt most frequently about subjects I enjoyed or hated, things I was curious about, and things I was worried about. In short, if it was on my mind during the day it was often in my dreams at night. Looking back through my meticulous notes on Miss Grant's method, this corresponded exactly with what she had told us in class.

The trick, then, I thought, was to concentrate on a subject I wanted to dream about as I lay in bed waiting to fall asleep. It worked about half the time for me, but when it did, it would represent only one dream out of the dozen or so I had each night. Either Miss Grant had not made this technique clear in class or my notes were lacking some key information.

Like many aspects of my life as an astral traveler, I simply cannot explain how some things came about. I'd like to think I logically and systematically progressed from one stage to the next. But honestly, some things just happened, and to this day I have no explanation for them. Late in

August of that year I was dreaming of Fenway Park, the home of the Boston Red Sox. I was there at a game with my family. It was an okay dream, but I thought how much better it would be if I was there with Wayne and Josh instead of Mom and Dad. Suddenly, there they were, walking down the aisle towards our seats! They each carried a plastic cup of beer in their right hands, and Wayne held another beer for me. Oh boy, I thought, my parents will go nuts over this. We were only twelve years old! I cringed as I turned towards them, but they were gone, their seats empty. I realized I had consciously changed the dream. This marked a turning point for me - I was now able to not only consciously control my own actions in my dreams, but actually change the content of the dream as well. I had achieved Miss Grant's fifth phase.

Chapter Two

The fall of 1978 found me in junior high school. I was totally into dreaming now. I went to bed each night knowing I could dream about whatever I wanted for as long as the REM sleep period lasted. If I had a dream I wasn't enjoying I'd just change it. If I was loving some dream and slipped out of it I'd just will myself back into it. It was pretty freaking fabulous, I have to tell you.

It was around that time I stopped writing in my dream notebooks. My recollection of my dreams was phenomenally good and I saw no need to write them down anymore. I could recall virtually every moment of every dream when I woke up, and still remember even minute details days later if I concentrated. Best of all, my memory of everyday life was getting better by the day. Incredibly so. By Christmas I was able to recall conversations almost word for word. Teachers' lectures came back to me nearly verbatim. I could recite entire pages from textbooks. Miss Grant never mentioned anything like this, but I am convinced it was a side effect of her dream recalling method. Somehow it had rewired my brain. Or, perhaps the human brain is just another muscle. The more you exercise it the bigger and better it gets. Because of my conscious dreaming my brain was now working out in a 24 hour fitness center. Maybe it was all just a coincidence, but I don't believe that. Whatever the reason, it was awesome! I was hardly putting forth an effort and yet I was getting straight A's in all my classes. Even math, which had always been kind of difficult for me, was much easier. Life was good.

******

I won't bore you with tales of my junior high school years. Honestly, they were pretty normal, at least outwardly. I got straight A's in all my classes and was coerced by my parents and the school guidance counselor into enrolling in the honors courses, where the A's kept on coming. My memory was virtually photographic. Eidetic memory is the scientific term for it. A miniscule percentage of all humans have it, and I was now one of them.

As good as most things were for me back then, I still had to deal with all the usual teenage problems. I dated some girls but never got laid. Okay, to be perfectly honest I never got past "second base," if that means anything to you. Wayne and Josh and I, best friends in grade school, kind of drifted apart. Wayne was a star athlete and hung out with the jocks. Josh got into punk rock, which I detested, and I was stuck by default with the nerds in my honors classes. We stayed friends, though, and once in a blue moon we'd all go fishing together, but it wasn't anything like grade school when we had been inseparable.

The one constant that stayed with me throughout junior high school was my dreaming. Every night I dreamt about whatever I wanted, whenever I wanted, making conscious decisions all through the night. It became such a normal part of my existence I almost forgot how unique I was. A couple of times in those years I told someone, a girl usually, about my dreaming ability. I'm pretty sure no one ever believed me. I thought about going back to my elementary school to discuss it with Miss Grant, to thank her for changing my life, but I never did. Now I don't know whether to thank her or curse her.

In the summer of 1981 I was fifteen years old and waiting to start my sophomore year of high school. My days, like every summer since I stopped wearing diapers, were filled with baseball and fishing. Wayne and I were hanging out again. Josh was totally punked out by then and too weird for us. Imagine me of all people, thinking that!

One hot August night I lay in bed asleep, the covers thrown off due to the heat. We had no air conditioning in our house. Open windows and a small fan helped, but not much. I entered REM sleep and began dreaming. As usual, I was conscious in the dream, with the feeling and perspective of looking over my own shoulder. All these years later I don't recall the dream I was having, and it's not important anyway. During the dream I suddenly came to the realization I was no longer looking over my own shoulder within the context of the dream. Instead, I was looking down on my body lying asleep in bed. Whatever dream I had been having had been replaced.

This was a completely different feeling than my usual dreams. I almost wrote "my normal dreams" but then I realized there is nothing normal about them. I was floating above my body, in my room. There was enough moonlight coming in the open windows for me to see around the room. Everything looked real and I didn't have my usual dream feeling, but it couldn't possibly be real - I was floating above my bed, looking down at my own sleeping body! The thought of my body caused me to shift my focus closer to myself. I made an attempt to look at my hands and feet, but I had none. My body in bed was intact but the "me" above the bed had no body at all, simply consciousness. I tried to grasp the situation I was in and felt a twinge of panic. Instantly I was back in bed and woke up. I remembered everything clearly, as I always did, but I was so shaken up I turned on my bedside light. I lay awake for over an hour that night, sweating from the heat and from the mental calories I was burning trying to figure out what exactly had happened. Eventually I nodded off, to awake the next morning, my bedside light still on. I didn't realize it then, but I had just had my first out of body experience.

******

A couple of nights later I again found myself floating above my sleeping form. I was not comfortable and tried to consciously change the dream, willing myself to the banks of the Hockanum River with Wayne and Josh. Nothing happened. I tried for my old standby, riding my bicycle down Main Street, a dream I had had a million times before. Nothing. I was left with two options: wake myself up or deal with what was happening. Curiosity won out over my trepidation and I looked around my room. I had the distinct feeling of slowly turning clockwise around the room, but I had no body, only consciousness. My body lay below, inert.

There was some kind of mask on my face, that is, the face lying in bed. I moved closer to get a better look at it and saw it was merely a deeper shadow. Huh. I was moving, and in control of my movements. I had spun in a circle and moved closer to my body, but I was unable to say how I had accomplished it. I moved over to one of the windows and looked out into the night. It was the same view that had been there forever, nothing dream-like about it at all.

I decided to explore the house, moving out of my room and into the short upstairs hallway. The doors to my siblings' rooms were closed, as usual, so I floated down the stairs to the living room. It was difficult to see as the downstairs windows had the curtains drawn, but from what I could make out everything looked normal. Our dog Zoe was sleeping on the couch, as always. She was not allowed on the furniture during the day, but all of us knew she slept on the couch at night. It was impossible to miss all that dog hair.

I moved out of the living room, through the kitchen, past the downstairs bathroom and down the hall to my parents' bedroom. They always kept their bedroom door open, a legacy of days past when they would be alert for any sounds of nightmares from us children. At the threshold to their room I hesitated - it didn't seem right for me to peer in on them. In the end, I took a hasty peek at their sleeping forms and quickly backtracked to my room. Finding myself once again hovering above my sleeping form I quickly grew bored with it and tried to transition into another dream, without success. Another minute or so was all I could take before I woke myself up. A few minutes later I drifted off to sleep again and almost immediately felt myself starting to leave my body. I was able to fight it, however, and shortly I was dreaming in my usual manner.

For the next few nights I left my body for brief periods and hovered about my room. I found I was unable to return to my body without waking myself first. Now that I recognized the feeling of leaving my body I was able to resist it if I chose to do so. Although I was intrigued with this new type of dreaming (I still hadn't realized I was actually leaving my body) it was pretty boring and severely limited by the walls and doors of the house. If I could somehow manage to slip out of the house and go exploring, that sounded like fun. To that end, one afternoon I unlatched the screen to one of my bedroom windows and propped it open. Now there was nothing between me and the great outdoors. If I went into that strange new dream state tonight I could just slip out the open window and see the sights.

Sure enough, that evening I felt myself disengaging from my body and went with it. After hovering a few moments above my bed I moved toward the open window and slipped through it into the night. I was outside!

There was plenty of ambient light from streetlights and nearby homes. I was a little disconcerted because I was about twenty feet off the ground, having gone out a second story window. In kind of a knee-jerk reaction against falling I willed myself upward. To my great surprise I shot thousands of feet higher in an instant, then overcorrected and swooped precipitously down towards the ground. With the earth rushing up at me I panicked, and in far less than the blink of an eye I was back in my bed, awake and shaking from the mental equivalent of an adrenaline rush.

I lay awake in the dark, contemplating what had just happened. I had no idea how I returned to my bed - it all happened too fast. It took me quite a while to relax again, affording me a lot of time to think. Just before falling back to sleep it struck me: did I really need to open the window to leave the house? After all, I was just dreaming; my body never left the bed. Why couldn't my consciousness simply go through the tiny holes in the window screen? I decided to test this theory the next chance I got.

******

August became September and I started school as a high school sophomore. My experiments at floating through the window screen holes were successful. Thinking it over, I realized there are no truly solid objects - wood, steel, rock, they are all made up of molecules, and at the atomic level there's plenty of space in between. In short order I was simply floating out through the roof or walls.

I also learned to control my speed and altitude, and after that there seemed to be no limit to where I might go or what I might see. As time went on I found the out of body experience had become my default protocol - as soon as I entered REM sleep I would start to leave my body. Only by intentionally resisting going out of body was I able to fall into my usual conscious dreaming state. One thing remained constant: the only way for me to end an out of body experience was to wake myself up. Another odd thing was the total lack of noise when I was out of body. My usual dreams were not only full color they were surround sound, just as in real life. In my out of body experiences I never heard a peep. A freight train would come roaring through town and I could watch it from ten feet away without hearing a thing. Very strange.

School was a breeze, even though I was in the honors program and taking a couple of advanced placement courses for college credit. I had plenty of spare time to explore the limits of my out of body experiences, if any boundaries existed. I was flying around town one night ("flying" was how I thought of it by then) and decided to see if I could zoom down to Florida. Our family had driven down two years previously to visit my father's brother. Uncle Bernie's place had been nothing like I first dreamed of. In fact, he lived in a condo and did not have a porch overlooking a pond as in my dream, but rather a small deck with no view of anything.

I had no idea at that point how fast or how far I could travel in my out of body state, but I wanted to find out. Florida was a distant, known point of reference for me. I thought about going to Uncle Bernie's and within moments I was there! And by there, I mean inside his condo. Holy cow! 1400 miles virtually instantaneously. I had an extremely brief feeling of… *shifting*. I don't know how else to describe it. There was a moment of transition, like stepping out of a building into a heavy rain, or vice versa. It was only one step but you knew something significant had changed.

I took a quick look around Uncle Bernie's place. I hadn't expected to actually end up inside his home, and I was kind of embarrassed. My uncle was there, sound asleep, of course, and everything else was pretty much as I remembered it from our visit. It was exceedingly strange. How could this be happening?

I left Bernie's place and moved out over the town of Sarasota, which was also as I remembered it. Then I flew to parts of town unknown to me. I had no idea if what I was seeing was real or just my imagination. It was an incredibly odd feeling.

On the spur of the moment I decided to visit the Kennedy Space Center. I had never been there but knew it was on the Atlantic coast of Florida, northeast of me. Instead of instantly arriving there I found myself flying over the Florida countryside at a relatively modest clip. How come I went from my house to Uncle Bernie's in a flash but I'm going across Florida at driving speed? Before I could ponder that further I was suddenly yanked back to my bed, where I awoke.

******

It took me a while to figure out what happened that night. In all my previous OBEs (Out of Body Experiences) I had willed myself awake and instantly returned to my bed. That night I was precipitously jerked back to my body without warning. Why? The answer was quite simple - I could only be out of body while in REM sleep and my REM sleep period had ended. I eventually got a feel for how long I could fly around, but on occasion I still got abruptly and rudely returned to my bed.

The other mystery took longer to resolve. Why did I instantaneously *shift* to Uncle Bernie's condo 1400 miles away but fly at low speed towards a destination less than 200 miles up the road? I got a hint to the answer when I decided to fly to France.

I had never been to France but I was still trying to determine the limits, if any, of my flying ability. France seemed like as good a place as any. Hovering in my bedroom I thought of France and expected to feel the telltale *shift* of a long jump. Nothing happened. Thinking perhaps I needed a more specific destination I thought of the Eiffel Tower. Nada. Could it possibly be that I could not fly over the ocean? I tried to go to California, the farthest spot I could think of without crossing an ocean. No *shift*, but I left the house in a westerly direction at about the speed of an airliner. I'd never make it there before my REM phase ended. What the heck was going on? I thought myself back to my bedroom and tried to reason it out. To test myself, I went to Uncle Bernie's. In a *shift* I was there and just as quickly I brought myself back. I decided the best thing to do was to wake myself up, fall back to sleep, spend the night enjoying some regular dreams, and tackle the problem the next day. Real life intervened, however.

The next day was a school day. That evening after dinner I decided to attend an honors program study group at the school library. Not because I needed to study but rather I wanted to get to know some of my classmates better. I had never had a bunch of friends, never needed many, I guess, but I was basically down to none. Wayne and I hung out a lot in the summertime but once school started he stuck with his fellow jocks and wouldn't be caught dead hanging with me, one of the nerds. I never thought of myself as a nerd, but that's how everyone else in school classified me. Was it fair? Of course not, but it was high school and I was stuck with it.

To be perfectly candid, most of the kids in the honors program *were* nerds, or geeks, or whatever your term is for brainiacs with no lives outside of school. Hmmm… maybe I was a nerd, after all.

The study group that night consisted of seven girls, three boys, and me. I knew everyone there but none of them well. After only about five minutes of social chit chat (man, were they serious about studying!) they decided to break into pairs to go over the latest calculus assignment. Naturally, as a newcomer to the group I was odd man out, but was invited to join with any of the pairs. Before I could decide who to join Melissa Gabriel walked in, apologizing for being late. She was in most of my classes, which made her a serious nerd in the opinion of the rest of the student body. But oh, what a body she had! In addition to being intelligent she was extremely athletic, and had the hard body you would expect of a cheerleader. Remember, this was 1981, and high school girls' sports were practically non-existent. Cheerleading was one of the few options for athletically inclined girls.

Melissa and I were acquainted but had hardly spoken more than ten words to each other since school started. She paired up with me since I was the only person without a partner, and we spent the next hour discussing calculus. When a ten minute break was called I expected her to leave me and socialize with some of the others, but she shocked me by suggesting we go outside.

It was late October and pretty cold outside, and I wondered what we were doing out there. She answered my unspoken question by pulling out a half pack of cigarettes and asking me if I had a light. Hiding my surprise, I told her I did not smoke. She rooted around in her purse looking for matches. Finding none, she put her cigarettes away with a sigh. Ten minutes later we knew a lot more about each other and were a lot colder, but I would gladly have stayed out there for hours.

At the end of the night she surprised me again by asking me to walk her home. Even though she lived almost a mile away from me I immediately agreed. Things progressed quite nicely after that, and by the Christmas break we were an item, as we said back in the day. For the remainder of our sophomore year we were not formally going steady but neither one of us was seeing anyone else. A couple of times I told her about my dreaming and even talked about my out of body experiences. She listened politely and asked a few questions, but I could tell she didn't believe me. It was disappointing, but I probably wouldn't have believed me, either.

We saw each other every day at school and two nights a week to study together. After a few weeks we left the group and studied together either at her house or mine. I didn't really need the study sessions but it gave me more time with her. We also got together at least once every weekend for a date. As I said, we were an item.

You probably think Melissa was the classic all-American girl next door, a cheerleader and a brainiac, but she had a rebellious streak, as you might have guessed from her smoking. In the spring of 1982 she asked me if I wanted to have a couple of beers with her. Of course I said yes, even though if I drank two with her it would effectively double the total beer intake of my life to that point.

Because of her good looks it was nothing for her to obtain beer, even though she was a month shy of sixteen years old. She'd just hang out at a 7-Eleven store, light up a cigarette, put on that certain look, and ask some young man to buy her a six pack. With visions of getting into her pants the guys quickly agreed, but they were always disappointed. When they came out with the beer she would hand them a couple of bucks (beer was cheap back then), say thanks, and walk away. I was loitering nearby to bail her out if there was ever any trouble, but there never was.

The first time we did this set the stage for the future. We took the beer and went to one of our secret spots, a relatively remote area of a county park. Melissa gulped down her first beer like cold water on a hot day, even though it was a cool evening. I was just finishing my first when she cracked open her third. I think we both assumed we would each have three, but I was having a hard time finishing my second, so Melissa stepped up and started on her fourth one. That was fine by me until thirty minutes later when she was snot-slinging drunk and right on the edge of puking. She weighed about one hundred pounds soaking wet and four fast beers were an awful lot for a fifteen year old girl. In the future I made sure to gag down my half of the six pack. That way we both got buzzed but she didn't get sloppy drunk.

Chapter Three

You're probably saying to yourself, "I thought you were going to explain why you couldn't fly to Paris but instead you went off on this tangent about your girlfriend."

You're right, and I apologize. Let me take the opportunity to remind you I am writing this in longhand in my prison cell. I am not allowed access to computers and once a month I give whatever I've written to my attorney, for fear my jailers or an inmate might one day take my manuscript and destroy it. I've already had another prisoner filch a few completed pages and use them for toilet paper. If you think that's unlikely you've obviously never been in prison. Such indignities and much, much worse are inflicted and endured here on a daily basis, simply for the sport of it. I'm telling you this to explain why what you're reading may at times seem disjointed. It's an awful lot of work to go back and make changes. My lawyer says he'll have an editor go through the finished product and make it readable, but I'm not about to blame some editor I never met. Again, my apologies.

Anyway, Melissa indirectly played a large role in solving the problem, so it actually all ties together. I was falling head over heels in love with her, if teenagers can actually be in love. Unraveling the idiosyncrasies of astral traveling, and everything else for that matter, took a distant second to our relationship.

Melissa turned sixteen years old in May of 1982 and got her driver's license shortly afterwards. She and I both being honor students; her parents had no qualms about letting her use their family car on occasion for a date. In July of 1982, Melissa got permission to take the car to Misquamicut Beach in Rhode Island so we could celebrate my sixteenth birthday there. Neither one of us had ever been there so we carefully mapped out our route the day before. No GPS navigators back in those days. A Tom Tom was only a drum.

That night when I fell into REM sleep I felt myself leaving my body and before I even drifted to the ceiling I *shifted* and found myself over the parking lot at Misquamicut Beach. How could this be? I had never been there before but I *shifted* there. Then it hit me - I had studied the route earlier in the day so I knew exactly how to get there. Was it as simple as that? It turned out it was. I had been unable to fly to Paris because I didn't really know where it was located. I started for California at moderate speed because I knew it was west of me, but not precisely how far. A few days later I spent some time in the local library studying world maps. With my eidetic memory it was a piece of cake. That night I *shifted* from my bedroom to Paris and back, then to Hawaii, where I actually island hopped.

I was so pumped up I later told Melissa all about it. She smiled and said my imagination was one of the things she really liked about me. Oh yeah, our trip to Misquamicut Beach? It never happened. When we got to the interstate she turned north instead and we spent the day on Cape Cod, where we celebrated my birthday with a six pack of beer. I told you she was a rebel.

******

The summer of 1982 was a very special time for me. Looking back on it now from the perspective of my prison cell, it was surely the best year of my life. My world got much larger. I got my driver's license. With both Melissa and I licensed to drive and our folks letting us have their cars frequently we drove somewhere fun and different several times a week. We also reached the point in our relationship where we were sexually active. Everything short of actual intercourse was on the menu and our experimentations were rapidly expanding.

My dream world was also broadening. I became a flat-out expert in world geography. Name the continent and I could tell you the precise location of every country in it. Name the country and I could locate two dozen cities in it. My eighty minute long REM period started just after 5:00 AM if I fell asleep at 10:00 PM the night before. That meant I could fly anywhere in Europe, Africa or the Middle East and explore those regions in full daylight. I could only visit Hawaii and Alaska in daylight for short periods during my early REM phases. Once in a while I got a few quick glimpses of California around sunset but explored it extensively at night. Ironically, while astral traveling I had never seen my own neighborhood or the U.S. east coast during the day. I tried taking daytime naps for that purpose but I was never able to stay asleep long enough to go into REM.

I had been astral traveling for a year now. The longer I did it the more I became convinced I was actually traveling, not just having extremely vivid dreams. In my gut I knew what I was seeing was real. On the other hand I think I was afraid for it to be real. I spent many hours in libraries reading everything I could find about astral projection, astral traveling, astral anything and everything. Ninety percent of it was garbage. The remaining ten percent seemed to somewhat accurately reflect what I was experiencing, but as far as I could ascertain it was all just speculative; nothing had been conclusively proven. I read of a handful of cases where high profile self-proclaimed astral travelers had been scientifically tested. The scientists declared them all to be bogus.

About six months into my astral traveling I had figured out a foolproof way to determine if I was actually traveling or just dreaming, but I wasn't sure I really wanted to know. If I was just dreaming, well that was pretty awesome. If I was actually traveling, my consciousness leaving my body and seeing the real world, it was pretty freaking scary. According to my research I might be the one and only person in the whole world who could do it. What did that make me? I was having so much fun in the summer of my sixteenth year that I didn't want to know.

Summer ended, as it always must. The leaves turned color and dropped away. Snow fell. Melissa and I were inseparable and I was breezing through school. Life was very good, but at night things were changing. I was still having vivid, conscious dreams but I was having fewer and fewer out of body experiences. Something was changing within me. I could feel my flying ability slipping away.

I decided the time had come to finally prove whether my astral traveling was real or not. I had to know, before I lost the ability forever. On my next OBE I immediately *shifted* to Times Square in New York City. I was in my long REM phase, hovering in front of a newsstand. A clock read 5:47 AM. I moved closer to a large stack of New York Times newspapers and spent some time reading the front page above the fold. I committed everything I read to memory. Not just the headlines, but the sub-heads, the bylines, and every word of the stories I could see. Then I *shifted* back to my bedroom, woke myself up and wrote down every word of it.

By car, my town was about four hours away from New York City. Our libraries all carried the New York Times but it didn't arrive until mid-afternoon. I went to school as usual that day. After school I went to the library, the notebook page with the proof carefully folded in my pocket. In the periodicals section I hesitated. Once I knew the truth I could never un-know it. Finally, I picked up a copy of the New York Times and folded it to the top half of the front page, just the way I had seen it in Times Square. I took the notebook page out of pocket, even though with my photographic memory I didn't need it. I had to be absolutely sure I wasn't fooling myself. I had written down these words in the privacy of my bedroom hours before anyone in my state could possibly have seen that day's New York Times. The words I had written matched precisely with the newspaper. It was irrefutable now - I wasn't dreaming. I actually was an astral traveler.

Chapter Four

My junior year of high school went by in a blur. Melissa and I were together constantly - honors classes, study sessions a couple of nights per week, and every weekend. I often went to watch her cheerleading practices and I attended every football and basketball game. One evening I arrived home after a basketball game and my dad asked me who won. To my great embarrassment I was unable to tell him. I had paid no attention to the game. He laughed out loud, because he knew the reason. My dad was pretty cool.

In the winter of 1983 Melissa introduced me to marijuana. We drank beer pretty regularly but by unspoken agreement never more than a six pack between us. Occasionally we'd split a bottle of sweet wine but neither one of us did well with it. Melissa usually puked and I always got a bad hangover. She had smoked marijuana a few times and seemed to like it. When she asked me to try it I went along because, well, you know why. The first few times I tried it nothing happened, then, the third or fourth time I smoked I got totally stoned. It was horrible! I absolutely detested the feeling of not being in complete control of my own mind. I was in such a state of panic Melissa had to hold me tight for over an hour. She told me later my reaction was so bad she seriously considered taking me to the emergency room. After that we stuck to beer and I never smoked marijuana again. If Melissa did, it wasn't with me.

I continued to have out of body experiences throughout my junior year but they occurred with less and less frequency.

In the early days of my flying I would go out of body in every REM period, every night. Now it happened maybe once a week, sometimes less.

Near the end of my junior year I was getting a lot of pressure from my parents, some of my teachers and the school guidance counselor about my college plans. Melissa and I had already taken the scholastic aptitude test. She earned a 1200 on her test and I was just a handful of points from perfect. She was carrying a B+ average in the honors program and I had straight A's.

Melissa was taking the shotgun approach to college admissions: apply everywhere then choose from the ones that accept you. Hopefully a couple of schools would offer her a scholarship, but there were no guarantees. Our families were middle class and even back then college wasn't cheap. A scholarship offer would be huge.

Everybody seemed to know exactly what was best for me - my parents wanted me to go to Harvard or Yale or one of the other Ivy League schools. My science teacher was pushing hard for MIT. Everyone assumed wherever I chose to go it would be with a full ride academic scholarship. My brother Stan, a few years older than me, was in his sophomore year at the University of Connecticut and my younger sisters had already indicated they wanted to attend college as well. My parents were counting on me to save them some tuition money.

To be completely honest, I had very little interest in going to college and had no idea what I wanted to do with my life. Inside my head I was still trying to understand what it meant that I was flying around the world in my sleep. And I wasn't really some super brainiac, it just seemed that way because of my eidetic memory.

I already knew where I wanted to go to college, I just hadn't told anyone except Melissa. It was a no-brainer. I would attend college wherever she did. We'd graduate together, get married, have a bunch of children and live happily ever after. At least that was how I pictured it. I hadn't yet gotten up the nerve to tell her about the marriage part.

An incident in the summer after my junior year of high school had a profound effect upon me. I was having OBEs only once or twice a month now. When I fell into REM and felt an OBE coming on I eagerly pushed myself out of body and *shifted* to some far off daylight locale. Daylight flying was so much more enjoyable, and I wanted to relish the experience before it was lost forever. I knew I was rapidly growing out of whatever allowed me to fly. Returning to my room from the Bavarian Alps I was flabbergasted to feel the presence of another person there with me! It had never happened before but I instantly and unmistakably knew another astral traveler was present. I was far more excited than afraid. I wasn't the only one in the world who could do this! I wasn't some one-of-a-kind freak.

I looked about my room and saw no one except my own body, but I sensed the other traveler was in the corner by my east window. I meant to move that way slowly but in my excitement I raced across the room and bumped hard into something. Bumped into something? Until that moment, in my astral state I had effortlessly passed through everything. I experienced a split second of childlike wonder, an indescribably intense feeling of oneness with the other person, then woke up in my bed, alone.

******

Not long after the incident with the other astral traveler Melissa and I made love for the first time, then we started having sex on a regular basis. My love for her deepened and I began to talk of our future lives together after college; marriage, careers, children. She was flippant about the idea of marriage, saying it was old fashioned and unnecessary. If our love was strong enough marriage was superfluous. If it wasn't, then being married wouldn't save us and we'd end up having to deal with the unpleasantness of divorce. She refused to even talk about having children, telling me we could have that discussion in ten years or so if we were still together. If? Yes, of course I should have seen the warning signs, but I was seventeen years old and madly in love.

In the fall of our senior year everyone was shocked when Melissa received an early scholarship offer from Radcliffe College, an elite all girls college in Cambridge, Massachusetts. She had never expected to be accepted there, let alone get a scholarship. She had applied only to appease her mother, whose own grandmother had graduated from there at the turn of the twentieth century.

I immediately applied to Harvard University. In those years Radcliffe and Harvard were in the early stages of merging. Harvard eventually absorbed Radcliffe, which no longer exists as a separate university. Back then the two schools were walking distance apart and even shared a few buildings and commons. If I got a scholarship to Harvard Melissa and I could be together every day, perhaps even live together off campus. It was perfect! My parents were thrilled with my choice.

With a scholarship to Radcliffe in her pocket Melissa became wilder than ever. She never smoked marijuana around me but sometimes I could smell it in her hair. A couple of times I suspected she was high on some harder drug but she laughed off my questions, insisting she was just enjoying life.

As the school year progressed I began to wonder if she was dating someone else. We were still studying together two nights a week but she was not always available on weekends. She claimed her parents wanted to spend more time with her before she left for college. Ditto for her girlfriends. Sometimes she simply said she needed her space, almost daring me to argue with her about it.

I was accepted at Harvard but to my great dismay I was not offered a scholarship. My father made it crystal clear he expected to me to win a scholarship somewhere and he was not prepared financially to pay my way, especially to one of the priciest schools in America. When I told him perhaps I might not attend college at all he went ballistic. I was a straight A honors program student. I had already earned a handful of college credits in advanced placement courses. Harvard University wanted me. Surely hundreds of other fine schools would as well. If I threw all that away then on my eighteenth birthday he would kick me out of his house. He wasn't about to support his idiot son.

When my dad calmed down he sheepishly started over, strongly suggesting I cast a wider net. With my academic record there had to be dozens of colleges across the country willing to give me a scholarship. Screw Harvard! Get away from home, see a different part of the country, he said. Oh, if he only knew! I told him I wanted to attend a college near Melissa and anything else was out of the question. He frowned deeply at that, started to become angry again, then caught himself when an idea came to him. "Maybe you should consider a military scholarship," he said. "ROTC or NROTC. I'm pretty sure Harvard has some kind of ROTC program."

That stopped me cold. I never would have thought of looking for a military scholarship. My dad could see I was wavering and he pressed his advantage. "I was drafted into the army," he said, "and it wasn't too bad. I served a couple of years in Germany and it was pretty cool living in Europe as a young man. You'd be an officer coming out of ROTC and the officers have it easy. They lived like kings compared to us enlisted guys."

I had no desire to join the military, even as an officer after college, but an ROTC scholarship to Harvard would solve my father's financial concerns and allow me to remain close to Melissa. The U.S. Army has many bases in Europe, a place I had enjoyed tremendously in my astral travels, and being stationed there in the army actually sounded kind of neat. It certainly wasn't ideal but I thought it could work. I told my father I would give it some serious thought.

When I broached the subject with Melissa she was ambivalent about it, eventually saying it was my life and I should do whatever I felt was best for me. Blinded by my love goggles, all I could see was an ROTC scholarship to Harvard would give me four more years to convince her to marry me. I sent off an application.

******

Over Christmas break of my senior year in high school my family again went to visit my Uncle Bernie in Florida. My brother stayed in Storrs, Connecticut where he was working a temporary full time job between semesters to help pay for school. I loved Florida and it was great to bask in the sun in December, but my heart was aching for Melissa. The twelve day trip felt like twelve years. It was scheduled to be a full two weeks but a big winter storm was forecast for the mid-Atlantic seaboard. My dad didn't want to get caught in it so we headed north two days early. I was dialing the phone to tell Melissa the good news when I changed my mind and decided to surprise her. Big mistake, as you probably already guessed.

We arrived back in town around 6:00 PM the following day. Everyone was hungry but after the long drive mom had no interest in cooking, so we stopped in a family restaurant just off the interstate. As we were being seated my dad tapped my arm, pointed across the room and said to me, "Hey, Pete, isn't that your friend Wayne over there?"

Sure enough, it was. Wayne and I were still friends, I guess, but not very close anymore. We hadn't been for quite some time, especially since he got a football scholarship to Boston College. His scholarship was a big deal and he became a minor celebrity, getting a lot of play in the newspaper and on local television. After that he hung out exclusively with the jock crowd, where he was king of the roost.

Seeing he was sitting alone I walked over to his table to say hello and ask him if he wanted to join my family for dinner. He seemed shocked to see me and turned beet red. Before I could ask what was wrong I saw Melissa walking to his table from the ladies room.

She was as cool as a cucumber, giving me a kiss on the cheek and saying, "Hi, Pete, you're back from Florida early."

My blood was boiling and I wanted to scream at her. She smelled of both alcohol and marijuana and was obviously stoned. She managed to look me straight in the eyes, though, silently daring me to make a scene, knowing my parents were just across the room. Somehow I managed to contain my anger, mumbled something inane, and stumbled away to the men's room to get myself under control before rejoining my family.

Back at our table my mom, ever the clueless one, innocently asked me what Melissa and Wayne were doing here. I bitterly snapped at her, "They're having dinner, Mom, isn't it obvious?"

My dad got the picture, though, and empathizing with my anger, for once he didn't berate me for my tone. Later, as I listlessly pushed my food around my plate without eating it I miserably blurted out, "They're just friends. He's a football player and she's a cheerleader. It's perfectly natural."

That was so lame one of my sisters actually snorted out some partially chewed food, causing both my sisters to convulse in gales of laughter. It was more than I could take and I rushed out of the restaurant, totally humiliated.

At home that night I waited by the phone until nearly midnight for Melissa to call, but in vain. Eventually sleep overcame me. If I dreamt I don't recall it. I certainly didn't fly anywhere.

Near noon the next day I was ready to swallow my pride and call her when there was a knock on our door. It was Melissa! I opened the door and she rushed into my arms. "Welcome home, Pete!" she gushed. Gesturing to her parents' car parked out front she said, "Let's go for a ride."

I tried to talk to her in the car but she turned the radio up loud and shook her head. Ten excruciatingly long minutes later she parked in one of our favorite spots, shut off the radio, and explained herself.

First, she apologized for embarrassing me in the restaurant. She said she understood why I was angry and knew how things must have looked to me, but she swore it was not a date and she and Wayne were just friends. She must have seen the skepticism on my face because she hastened to add that Wayne was her source for marijuana, something she had long refused to tell me. She had bought some from him earlier in the evening and they smoked together, then the munchies struck and they ended up in the restaurant. She insisted that's all it was and anything else was in my imagination. She told me she loved me and thought it was sweet I became so angry at the thought of her going out with someone else. She said a few other things but after she said she loved me the rest of it was all background noise. It was the only thing I needed to hear. Love is not only blind, but deaf as well.

The week or so before we started our final semester of high school was lost in a haze of sex and beer. I hardly slept at all, and when I did I did not dream.

******

In February of 1984 I was notified the United States Army had granted my request for a Reserve Officer Training Corps scholarship to Harvard University. Harvard had booted the military off campus many years earlier but ROTC scholarship students still attended there. Their military classes and drills were conducted on the campus of the Massachusetts Institute of Technology just a few miles up the road. The ROTC cadets could not wear their uniforms on Harvard grounds. None of that mattered to me. What did matter was I was going to attend Harvard on a full scholarship and spend the next four years with Melissa.

In May I had the last out of body experience of my life, or so I thought for many years to come. It was only my fourth OBE in five months and after that they just stopped. It was not a surprise as I had felt it slowly slipping away for quite some time. A few days later Melissa and I celebrated her eighteenth birthday in grand style. So grand, in fact, I can't actually recall all we did together. Even now the non-memories bring a smile to my face. Astral traveling is wonderful but some earthly delights are even better.

High school graduation is a turning point in most people's lives and I was no different. Unfortunately, a few weeks later my life turned again and quickly spun completely out of control.

I got a phone call early on a Sunday morning in late June. The girl's voice on the other end was muffled, as if she was holding a handkerchief over the mouthpiece to disguise her voice, and she might have been crying. Still, I thought I recognized her voice from some of my classes - Jill Armstrong - a girl who always went out of her way to be nice to me. She spoke non-stop after I answered the phone.

"You're too nice and too smart to ruin your life chasing after a drugged up slut like Melissa Gabriel. She was screwing half the football team and all of the basketball players. Get over her and get on with your life, Peter. Some people truly care about you. She's not one of them."

I sat there dumbfounded in my bedroom, staring at the telephone handset. After a while the annoying buzzing noise it was making shook me out of my funk and I hung it up.

My first instinct was denial, of course. And my second, and my third. Rationalizations were easy. It was Jill Armstrong on the phone, I was sure of it. She was sweet on me, I could see that now, and she was jealous of Melissa. Jill was plain-looking and flat chested while Melissa was a classic

American beauty. That's all it was. I wouldn't even give Jill the satisfaction of asking Melissa about it.

Naturally, I immediately brought it up with Melissa when we got together that afternoon. Not in an accusatory way, because I didn't believe a word of it. More like an informational way - "Melissa, did you know there's a rumor going around…" That kind of way, making it clear I thought it was all baloney, but I thought she should know what people were saying behind her back.

Melissa looked me in the eye. She was still clear eyed this early in the day. "What difference does it make, Pete?" she said softly. "There's sex and there's love. They're not the same thing, right? You can love someone without sex and you can have sex with someone without love, can't you?"

Huh? I had been anticipating a lot of possible reactions from her, but that one wasn't even on my radar. By way of coping, I tried to keep the discussion on an intellectual plane. "I guess you're correct, on a philosophical level. I'm just speaking hypothetically, of course. I'd never even consider being with someone other than you, Melissa."

She stared at me for a long time, her silence speaking volumes. In the end she never denied any of it. I made a complete fool of myself, naturally, telling her it didn't matter. I still loved her, I could forgive her, we could start over. She just sat there mutely shaking her head.

It wasn't like the storybooks. It ended ugly, with me yelling, screaming, cajoling, crying and ultimately, begging. Yes, begging. Now, all these years later, I can finally admit that, but not without tasting the bitter dregs that still accompany it. Life really sucks sometimes.

Chapter Five

I was heartbroken and deeply despondent. My parents threw together an elaborate party for my eighteenth birthday, hoping it would help draw me out of my blue funk, but it had the opposite effect. Fortunately, my brother Stan was home from UConn and between summer jobs for a couple of weeks. He never really had time for me when we were kids, but now, sensing I was at a crossroads in my life, he went into full-on big brother mode. We spent every day together, pretending to be fishing but actually just sitting there on the river bank, talking about life and slowly getting drunk. Once in a while we'd even catch a fish. It was precisely the therapy I needed. Stan returned to Storrs knowing he had done me a world of good.

After weeks of introspection I came to a decision. I was in no mood to argue about it with my father, but knew the fight was inevitable. Fearing he would succeed in talking me out of it I took irrevocable action to make it happen. That way, we'd still have the argument but even if he won it would change nothing. I was already committed to my new situation and all that remained was to force my father to accept it.

I chose to tell him near the end of dinner one night. By prearrangement my sisters were out with friends, so it was just me and my parents. I wanted my mom there not only because this was a big deal, but also because I knew her presence would prevent my dad from going totally off the deep end. Yes, mom would be upset as well, but in her quiet way. My father was slow to anger but once he reached his boiling point he erupted like a volcano. I was hoping not to be consumed by the molten lava.

"Dad, Mom, you know how much it hurt me breaking up with Melissa. I had some long talks with Stan about it, which really helped to clear my head. I mention that because I don't want you to think I made this decision in haste or while still mooning over Melissa. I'm beyond that now."

Both my parents put down their forks and looked at me. If ever there was a pregnant pause this was it. I cleared my throat and plunged ahead. "I can't go to Harvard. With Melissa right next door at Radcliffe I'd be way too distracted to focus on my studies. All my friends from high school know how badly I was humiliated, what a complete fool I made of myself. Many of them will be going to college around here and it will take a long time for me to live this down. The ROTC scholarship is transferable to any school in the country with an ROTC program. I need to get away from here, far away."

I shoveled some food in my mouth to give them time to absorb my words. My mom was blinking rapidly, like her brain was trying to process too much too quickly. Dad, however, had no such problem. "You're going to Harvard, Peter, it's a done deal."

"Dad, I'm still going to attend college and I'm still in the ROTC. You're the one who told me to cast a wider net, and you were right. Harvard is just a name. There're plenty of good colleges around."

My mom rescued me, but not in the way I expected. "He's right, dear. That Melissa Gabriel did a terrible thing to our son, stringing him along for years while dating other boys behind his back. I've heard all about it from some of the other mothers."

Holy crap! The neighborhood moms were talking about me and Melissa! Things were far worse than I thought. My mom went on. "All the Ivy League schools are pretty much the same these days. As far as prestige, one's as good as another." Turning to me she said, "Pete, I'm sure you'll do just fine at Princeton or Yale. Do they have ROTC units?"

We batted that around for a bit while I waited for my dad's blood pressure to fall a few notches. Things seemed to be going fairly well, so I dropped my next bomb. "You know I was going to major in business management at Harvard. Well, I found a place with an ROTC program and a very highly regarded business school."

My father said, "Wharton? That's part of the University of Pennsylvania, isn't it? And Penn is still Ivy League." He nodded his head thoughtfully, warming to the idea. "Not too far from home, but far enough for you to forget all about your girlfriend."

Uh oh. This wasn't going as well as I wanted. Still, my dad seemed to have come to grips with me not going to Harvard. It was progress. I loosed another bomb. "Actually, I was thinking of a university a little farther away, someplace I've always wanted to visit - San Diego."

My mother seemed confused. "San Diego? California? That's three thousand miles from here! We'll never see you."

My dad was having none of it. "Peter, it's one thing to want to switch from Harvard to Princeton, or even Penn. But San Diego? There are no Ivy League schools on the west coast, and as your mother said, it's three thousand miles away. It's out of the question."

I was ready for that one. "Since when did our family put on such airs that it's the Ivy League or nothing? Stan's at UConn, and that's perfectly fine with both of you. You know how much I hate the winters here. It's a frozen wasteland half the year. I loved it at Uncle Bernie's in Florida. I looked into schools there with ROTC units but they just didn't have the programs I wanted. San Diego State is perfect for me."

Dad was nearing his boiling point. He stood up so abruptly he knocked his chair over. "San Diego State?" he yelled. "You want to leave Harvard and attend a state school on the other side of the country? Not gonna happen." The volcano was emitting plumes of steam. Anyone with common sense would run for safety now, while there was still time.

No one ever accused me of having common sense. I stood up to face him and dropped my final bomb, the nuclear one. "It is going to happen, Dad. A while ago you threatened to kick me out of the house when I turned eighteen. Well, I'm over eighteen now, and I'm an adult in the eyes of the law and the army. I don't need your permission. I've already dropped Harvard and getting into San Diego State is just a formality. I'm leaving for San Diego in three weeks, unless you kick me out now."

That was all my mother could take. She burst into tears, stood up and threw her arms around me, sobbing at the thought of her youngest son leaving home and moving across the country. My father, red in the face, fists clenched, mumbling incoherent threats, no longer had a clear target for his anger, so he stalked out of the room.

******

It took several days, but eventually my father calmed down and grudgingly accepted the situation. It was a good thing, too, because I had failed to think things through, as my dad was quick to point out. It was his way of salvaging a partial win and letting me know he was still the alpha dog in the Ludvick family.

"Pete, are you borrowing a car and driving to San Diego, or are you going to sprout wings and fly there?" My dad was not above being snarky when the mood struck him.

We were at the dinner table with my mom and sisters present. It was a good sign. I knew my father wouldn't mess with me too badly in front of my sisters. "Well, Dad, I uh…"

"Yeah, why don't you just sprout wings and fly there, since even if you borrowed a car you don't have any money for gasoline."

I had another one of those "oh, if he only knew" moments as I thought about all the times I actually had flown to San Diego on my own "wings." I bit my lip and kept silent, hoping he wasn't going to make me ask him what I didn't want to ask him. He didn't.

"Peter, you know I think you're making a big mistake, throwing away a once in a lifetime opportunity to attend an elite university. However, your mother has made me see this from your perspective, so I'm going to respect your decision.

"I'll foot the bill for your airfare to San Diego and pay for your first year's living expenses. Food, housing, text books, whatever you need. I did the same for Stan so it's only fair I do it for you. After the first year, you're on your own, just like your brother. That means you'll have to get some kind of a job to support yourself. It's the best I can do, son, I'm not made of money."

I was elated! In my haste to get as far away from Melissa as possible such mundane things as paying for food and housing never even crossed my mind. As I've mentioned before, an eidetic memory fools people into thinking you're a genius but it doesn't actually make you one. California here I come!

Chapter Six

Four years at San Diego State flew by in the blink of an eye. Their business school actually was very good and their reputation as a party school was equally well deserved. I excelled at both academics and partying, spending many a day and quite a few nights at the local beaches. It was especially satisfying to spend a warm winter day at the beach knowing everyone back home was freezing their butt off.

Shortly after arriving in San Diego I started tutoring other students for money. Not only was it legal, the university encouraged struggling students to hire tutors. It was rather unusual for a freshman to be tutoring other freshmen, but I had already completed several freshman level courses while still in high school. I was only an average performer in military drill but academics were a snap for me. My class advisor, an army captain, could have made an issue of it, but decided to wait and see my first semester grades. I made the dean's list my first semester and every semester until I graduated with high honors.

I went home for Christmas that first year with a fellow army cadet from Rhode Island who owned a car. We split the driving and gas money each way and may have set a record for cross country travel. We made the coast to coast crossing in less than three days, one of us sleeping while the other was driving. We were young, and anxious to get home to our families. It was fun once, but I'm not recommending it.

Every summer the corps of cadets had to complete four weeks of intensive military training at various army posts throughout the country. To my great surprise I actually enjoyed it and started to look forward to serving as an army officer. Among the various military skills I learned that first summer, how to play poker turned out to be by far the most valuable. Okay, playing poker is not actually a military skill, but it is an essential part of barracks life on every military base in the world. One of the first rules of soldiering is "hurry up and wait." While waiting, some soldiers play poker. Once I understood the game, with my photographic memory winning followed as surely as night follows day. Every so often I'd misread someone and lose on a bluff or a freak great hand, but poker is all about odds and the laws of probability, and odds are a memory thing.

Before and after our military training we were free the rest of the summer to do as we pleased. My first summer's training was completed and I was half-heartedly looking for a summer job when I learned that San Diego had card rooms. Not casinos, those came a couple of years later, when the Indians were allowed to build them on their reservations far out in the desert. Card rooms were small storefront joints right in town. Some of them had been around since the days of the forty niners. Yes, that's the 1849ers of California gold rush fame. The house collected a small table fee from each player every fifteen minutes, set the rules and dealt the cards. There were small stakes tables and high stakes ones. I quickly learned the best players gravitated to the higher stakes tables. I wasn't interested in making a fortune, just enough money to live on, so I always played the low stakes tables. Still, it wasn't uncommon for me to win fifty dollars in a couple hours of play. I played three or four times a week at various clubs and in short order I was making steady deposits into my newly opened bank account.

I was making so much money playing poker I no longer needed to tutor students, but I continued to tutor a couple so as to explain the source of my income. I didn't feel comfortable telling anyone, let alone my parents, I was making a living at poker. In fact, I was pretty sure you had to be twenty one years old to play in a poker room in California. I never asked and no one ever asked me. San Diego was home to the U.S. Navy's pacific fleet and tens of thousands of sailors, many of whom frequented the card rooms. With my ROTC haircut I fit right in.

In the second half of my junior year of college I had to choose which army career field I wanted to serve in. Technically, I requested a field and the army decided, but with my stellar grades my advisor assured me I would get my first or second choice. By that point in my life I had finally gotten completely over Melissa and was dating other girls. Enough time had passed that I was coming to regret my impulsive decision to turn down Harvard and attend San Diego State. Yes, I could see now my decision had been impulsive, regardless of what I had told my parents back then, although I would never admit that to them.

As a subtle way of making amends with my father I listed armor officer as my first choice. He had been stationed in Germany when he was in the army. In the 1980s the U.S. Army had most of its tanks stationed in Germany, waiting for the day the Soviet Union rolled through the Fulda Gap to attack Europe. I wanted to be stationed in Germany just like my father, to honor him in my own way. Being an armor officer would virtually guarantee it. Besides, I had visited Germany extensively back when I was astral traveling, and I loved the place.

In early June of 1988 I graduated summa cum laude from San Diego State University and was commissioned a second lieutenant in the United States Army. My mother and father flew out for the ceremonies. I spent a week happily acting as their personal tour guide for their San Diego vacation, then it was on to Fort Benning, Georgia for armor officer training. Melissa and astral traveling were four years behind me. I was in the army now.

Chapter Seven

I've spared you the details of my college years since I know you're reading this book primarily because of your interest in astral traveling. For that same reason I'm going to gloss over my four years in the army.

I bounced around a bunch of different army posts, or forts, as they are called, in honor of the early days of the army. If nothing else, the army is big on tradition. I spent a couple of years in Germany and traveled extensively around Europe, which I very much enjoyed. My unit deployed to Operation Desert Storm, also known as the first Gulf War. I did nothing heroic, but I was there for all one hundred hours of actual ground warfare, and spent a few months in the desert before and after, waiting. It's what soldiers do most of the time. Yes, I played a great deal of poker and won a lot of money.

One thing worth mentioning about my time in the desert: I started to have lucid dreams again. They began some weeks after my unit arrived and lasted until about a month after we returned home. Not only was I able to recall my dreams in great detail but I was once again able to control my actions while dreaming. Several times I even managed to dream on demand. In case you are wondering, yes, I admit I dreamt of Melissa a time or two. I was in the middle of a Godforsaken desert, bored out of my mind, and needed a distraction. At least that's what I tell myself.

A few times I felt as if I was right on the cusp of going out of body, but it never quite happened. Shortly after returning from the Middle East my lucid dreaming became less frequent, then faded away altogether.

My four year commitment to the U.S. Army was up in June 1992. Although I enjoyed my time in the service I had no desire to make a career of it. Plus, the military was downsizing rapidly. The first Gulf War had merely delayed it a few months. The Cold War was over and the Soviet Union no longer existed. The tanks were coming home from Germany and armor officers like me were being shoved out the door to civilian life. The army might well have forced me out even if I had wanted to stay.

My last official assignment as an army officer was to attend a week long class at Fort Benning for officers transitioning to civilian life. To get us accustomed to the idea we were ordered to attend in civilian clothes.

The week was largely a waste of time but there was a big job fair at the conclusion of the class. Companies large and small from all over the country were there; hoping to cherry pick from some of America's best and brightest. All of us mustering out of the army where about to undergo a major life change, but none would be bigger than mine.

******

I was hoping to land a job with a huge multi-national company such as General Electric, one of the oil companies, or even Coca Cola. My eidetic memory allowed me to pick up foreign languages rapidly. I was fluent in German and my French was passable. I thought I had a lot to offer a company with European branches or subsidiaries and liked the idea of returning to Europe to live there as a civilian.

I received no immediate offers of employment but several multi-national firms seemed quite interested in me. I filled out employment applications for some and in return I was promised they would contact me soon. One company, Dharma Pharmaceuticals, practically guaranteed me a job if my college transcript and army record was as good as I said. The company was headquartered in Switzerland and had facilities all over the world. I was excited by the prospect.

As I was walking back to the post officers' quarters a late-middle aged African-American man in a suit and tie hurried over to me. He said he had been busy with other officers and didn't get a chance to speak with me at the job fair. Handing me his business card he introduced himself as Thomas Jefferson. "Yes, just like our third president. What can I say? We don't get to pick our names, do we?"

I looked at his business card. "Mulvaney & Proust, International Business Consulting. I've never heard of your company, Mr. Jefferson. And I didn't see you at the job fair."

"Perhaps you didn't notice me, Lieutenant Ludvick. It was a rather large room and there were a lot of people there."

"There were only three black male recruiters in the room, sir. You were not one of them."

The man smiled broadly, revealing coffee stained teeth. "Excellent! Your powers of observation are quite keen.

You're right, I wasn't there. But I do want to speak with you about working for our company, and I wanted to do it privately."

I stopped and took a good look at the man, then resumed walking towards my quarters. "I enjoyed my time in the army, Mr. Jefferson, but I want to try my hand in the private sector now. I have no interest in working for the government."

He looked only mildly surprised. "Very good, Lieutenant, very good. Tell me, how did you surmise that?"

"An easy guess. Our instructors told us there would probably be recruiters from federal agencies at the job fair. The FBI was there, but I didn't see any others. And you called me by my name and rank, even though I never told it to you. How would someone from a civilian company know my name?"

I started walking faster, hoping he would get the message, but he didn't seem to notice. "Lieutenant, can't we just talk a few minutes? You haven't heard my offer. And aren't you even curious which agency I work for?"

"Another easy guess. If you were with one of the regular government agencies your business card would say so. Since you presented me with a fake business card I assume you work for an agency with a clandestine branch. The CIA, the State Department, any of the defense intelligence agencies. I'm sure there are others. The cloak and dagger routine is your way of piquing my interest.

"Well, it didn't work, Mr.Jefferson, or whatever your name really is. Although I did enjoy your little joke about not getting to pick your name when you so obviously did exactly that. I was an armor officer, a tank driver. You should be talking to the snake eaters over at the Ranger school."

"No, Peter, I'm talking to the right guy. My boss sent me down here to speak to you. Only you. I'm just asking you to hear me out, nothing more. Give me a half an hour of your time, then at least I can go back and tell my boss I made my pitch. I'll buy you dinner at the officers club and we'll talk. What do you say?"

******

The Fort Benning officers club was fairly crowded on a Friday afternoon. I didn't see how we were going to have a private conversation, but then again I really didn't care. I'd enjoy the free dinner and call it a night.

Jefferson had to use the restroom and said he'd meet me at the bar. I was just tasting a cold draft beer when he returned with a young woman who turned out to be the club manager. She escorted us to a far corner table in one of the private VIP rooms, normally reserved for general officers or visiting political dignitaries. There was no one else in the room. She gave us a couple of menus and stood nearby, then took our orders and left.

I looked around the room, admiring the expensive décor. "Pretty nice. I've never been in here before, of course.

Junior officers don't rate such luxury. Lucky for you it was available. The main room is pretty crowded."

Jefferson shook his head. "Luck had nothing to do with it. My boss reserved this room before I left Langley. Speaking of Langley, here's my identification card. Your first guess was correct - I work for the Central Intelligence Agency."

I examined his ID card closely. "Holy cow, your name really is Thomas Jefferson!"

He smiled and said, "Yup. Jefferson is one of the most common surnames for American blacks. It actually does go back to President Jefferson. It's a slave name."

"But how do I know it's your real name? Or even that your ID card is real?"

Jefferson sighed in exasperation. "Well, I managed to get on a military base and into a private VIP room of the officers club. If that's not good enough for you then pick up the telephone over there and ask the operator for the CIA main switchboard number. Ask for the duty officer, then give him my name and have him describe me. Will that satisfy you?"

I handed him back his credentials. "Nah, I'm satisfied. Go ahead and make your pitch." I sat back in my chair, sipping my beer.

We spent the next ten minutes discussing the Boston Red Sox. A waiter delivered our food and closed the doors to the room behind him on his way out. "Okay," Jefferson said, "now that we won't be interrupted, I can begin. I hope you don't mind if I eat while we talk. This steak looks delicious."

I dug into my own piece of medium rare beef and told him, "Go right ahead, it's your dime."

The CIA man dabbed the corners of his mouth with a napkin and said, "You are an ideal candidate for the CIA, Peter. Do you mind if I call you that?"

"I prefer Pete."

"Okay, Pete it is then. As I stated earlier, I came down here, not for the job fair, but specifically to recruit you. Knowing that, you might infer we have already done a good deal of research into your background, and you'd be correct.

"We reviewed your high school and college transcripts, both of which are stellar. We know you speak German and French and spent two years in Europe. Your army record is excellent and you are a combat veteran. All these are precisely the attributes we look for at the CIA. There is no doubt you have the intelligence to be an analyst and your military record, especially your performance under fire shows you could be a successful field agent. We are not looking to hire you for either of those positions, however."

Jefferson turned his attention to his food for the next few minutes, apparently baiting me to ask the obvious question. When I did not, he went on. "The CIA runs a number of highly classified special projects, Pete, and we want you to work with us on one of them. Special projects are mostly temporary in nature, although some have gone on for years. Usually they involve nothing more than pure scientific research. Occasionally they spill over into field operations. The project we want you for relates to a special ability you have. Do you know what I am referring to?"

"I haven't the foggiest idea."

Jefferson scoffed. "Oh, come on now. I told you we did a good deal of background research on you. Humor me and take a guess."

"Okay. I have an eidetic memory. Eidetic memory is found in less than one out of every twenty million people. There may be fewer than a dozen people like me in America. You want to study my brain. No thanks, I'm not interested in being your lab rat." I pushed my food away and stood up to leave, disgusted at the thought of performing endlessly boring feats of memory for a bunch of scientists in some windowless room.

Jefferson held up his hand like a traffic cop. "Please, Pete, it's not about that, I promise you. Yes, you have an amazing memory, we know that, but as you pointed out, so do a number of others. We want you for another reason - your ability to leave your body while dreaming."

His words hung in the air like the smell of a roadkill skunk. I was so shocked I sat down suddenly, snagging the end of my fork, which flipped through the air and clattered to the floor. I didn't bother to pick it up. For years when I was flying no one believed me, not my closest friends, not even Melissa. Now, a complete stranger, a government agent whom I met an hour ago, was talking to me about something I haven't spoken about or even experienced in over eight years.

******

I quickly morphed from stunned to enraged, my voice rising in step with my anger. "How could you possibly know that?"

"Look, Pete, it doesn't matter how we know. What's import…"

"Baloney!" I yelled. "The *only* thing that matters is how you know. I haven't had an out of body experience since I was seventeen years old. The freaking CIA was spying on me when I was a kid, talking to my friends. How else could you know?"

Jefferson's tranquil demeanor didn't waver. "We never spied on you and we never talked to your friends. Yes, we kept track of you once we discovered your ability, but I wouldn't call it spying."

"Of course you were spying on me!" I was boiling mad and couldn't contain myself. Like father, like son. "I told three or four people back then. My closest friends, my girlfriend. No one else. You had to learn it from one of them."

Unruffled, Jefferson shook his head. "Your gift is exceedingly rare, Pete, almost unique. *Almost*. There are others who are astral travelers, and some of them work for us. One of them found you."

I flashed back to the time when I bumped into another astral traveler in my bedroom, and my anger fizzled away like a tropical sun sinking into a cool blue sea. I would never forget that moment. It was thrilling to know I was not alone in the astral world. Now I knew that meeting had been no accident. "Tell me about the person who found me."

"We call her the hitchhiker. She is very limited in her ability to travel. Her talent lies in finding other travelers. Somehow she sees or senses them, even from great distances. She once told us she perceives the astral plane as an endless stretch of empty freeway. Once in a blue moon a car appears, sticking out like a sore thumb in its singularity. The 'car,' of course, is another astral traveler. We know she doesn't detect every traveler every time, but we don't know why. There's a lot we don't understand. No, that's a gross overstatement. Truth be told, we know virtually nothing.

"As I said, she's unable to travel very far on her own, but once she detects someone she tags along with them wherever they go, riding in the 'car' so to speak, hence her nickname. She found you in May, 1983 but for some reason she wasn't able to tag along with you until later that year. When she did, she was able to trace you right back to your house, and once we knew who you were and where you lived, we kept an eye on you."

Even as I grappled with Jefferson's mind-boggling admission I began to get angry again, at the thought of my own government spying on me. I wanted to learn more about the other astral travelers, however, so I kept my anger in check. "You said other astral travelers work for you.

How many are there? How long has the government been doing this? What do the travelers do? Did this hitchhiker find them all?"

Jefferson pushed away his nearly empty plate and took a sip of water. "The project has existed in one form or another for decades. We've never had more than six travelers working for us. Their levels of ability vary greatly and most are of very limited utility."

"Limited utility," I thought disgustedly. Like trying to use a flathead screwdriver on a Phillips head screw. Tools. That was how the CIA thought of astral travelers. I wanted to slap the man sitting in front of me.

Blithely unaware of my thoughts Jefferson went on. "Over the years, most of our travelers have been self-referrals. They walk in the door of a university science department or make a small splash in the local media and eventually come to our attention. Most are of no use to us. The hitchhiker has found a few good ones.

"You asked what they do, Pete. We use them as remote viewers." Jefferson must have seen the offended look on my face because he started more carefully choosing his words. "We *employ* them as remote viewers. Spies. Wherever they travel to they simply report what they have seen. Only two of our travelers have been able to direct their travel to some extent, to pre-select where they will go. Obviously, they are of the most value to us. We believe you have that ability. Coupled with your eidetic memory you may well be the most important traveler we've ever come across."

I was far less than enthused by what I was hearing but felt compelled to learn as much as I could. "And what makes you think I could direct my travel?"

"The hitchhiker. Once she started accompanying you clear patterns of your travel emerged. You went to the same areas over and over again - mainly Europe and Hawaii. Based upon our experiences with other travelers it could not possibly be random, you had to be willing yourself to go to those places."

"Yes, I was. The key word being 'was.' I told you, I haven't had an out of body experience in more than eight years. Even if I was interested in working for you, which I'm not, it wouldn't matter. Whatever ability I may have had is long gone. To put it in your terms, my utility is zero."

Jefferson softened his tone. "Pete, I'm sorry if my choice of words has offended you, but I think you're taking them the wrong way. We employ astral travelers because they have a special talent we value, just as the Boston Red Sox only employ star baseball players. They don't recruit untalented players, or even mediocre ones, only the top notch, elite athletes who can help their team win ball games. Ninety nine point nine percent of people in the world will never play professional baseball, simply because they don't have the ability. Those who do are very richly rewarded, as you would be if you work for us.

"All employers are the same in that regard. An office manager needs a secretary who can type, not one who can't. That person would have very limited utility for the job and would not be hired. Surely you see my point."

"Okay, I get your point, but you're still missing mine - I can't fly anymore."

"Flying? Is that your term for it? I like it, it fits. And I think you're wrong when you say you can't fly anymore. Just because you haven't had an OBE in years doesn't mean you'll never have one again. Let me explain.

"I told you this project has been ongoing for many years. Our research indicates most astral travelers start lucid dreaming at age five or six, are astral traveling by age ten, and lose the ability forever during or shortly after puberty. Those who continue to have out of body experiences after going through puberty generally retain the ability for the rest of their lives.

"We don't know when you started to fly, but we do know you were still flying at the age of seventeen, years beyond puberty. We're reasonably certain your OBE ability is not lost, but merely dormant, and we think we know why."

Although I wasn't willing to admit it to him I was very intrigued by what Jefferson was saying. I had always assumed my flying ability was related to childhood and I had simply outgrown it. "I'm still listening, Mr. Jefferson. You'll know when I'm bored because I'll walk out the door."

"Our research has shown alcohol and/or depressant drug use inhibits OBE ability. Huge majorities of adults regularly partake of alcoholic beverages. That may explain why we don't see much larger numbers of adults who have OBEs. If you started drinking alcohol or taking drugs as a teenager it might explain why you lost the ability. With your straight A high school transcript it's hard to believe you were a regular drug user, so we're guessing, like many teens, you used alcohol fairly frequently, and you continued to do so during your college years and in the army." Jefferson not so subtly nodded his head towards my now empty beer stein.

Wow, could it be as simple as that? Stop drinking and start flying again? I thought back to my time in the desert, almost five months without alcohol. I started lucid dreaming again, but had no OBEs. "I went without alcohol for months during Desert Storm and never had an OBE. I think you're barking up the wrong tree."

Jefferson looked intently at me. "And you noticed nothing different? No lucid dreams?"

"Yes, I had some lucid dreams, and my share of nightmares, too. So what? We may not have been in combat all those months but it was still pretty stressful, with the enemy only a few miles away and us waiting to attack across the border any minute. Having unusual dreams sounds perfectly normal to me under those circumstances."

The CIA man nodded. "And that same stress may well have prevented you from having OBEs. Our scientists believe given time in a low stress environment without alcohol your flying ability will return."

"How much time?"

"No one can say. Weeks, certainly. A few months, perhaps. It's not as if we have reams of data to support our theory, Pete. At best it's an educated guess."

"Wait a minute. Can we back up a second, because I'm missing something here? Your hitchhiker found me way back in 1983. Why didn't you approach me then?"

Jefferson smiled. "I asked my boss the exact same question. I wasn't assigned to the project back then, so I didn't know the answer. I told you most travelers discover the ability around age ten and lose it at puberty, age twelve or thirteen at the latest. In the early days of the project we conducted research on such children, always with parental consent. We operated on university campuses and never revealed to the participants it was actually CIA scientists testing them. No harm ever came to any children and most of them actually enjoyed their time with us. Not to mention the kids were all compensated with trust funds for college. Regardless, a congressional oversight committee learned of it and went ballistic, threatening to pull our special projects funding. Most congressmen thought it was a huge waste of money anyway. As often happens in large bureaucracies the people at the top overreacted. The CIA instituted a strict prohibition against anyone under the age of eighteen being involved in the project. You were only seventeen when we found you.

"You turned eighteen in 1984, but by then it was too late. President Reagan was funneling every defense dollar and every other dollar he could get his hands on to develop his

Strategic Defense Initiative. Whatever was leftover went to build new warships for his dream of a six hundred ship navy. The CIA's special projects funding completely evaporated and everything was put on hold.

"In 1989 the Berlin Wall fell and by 1990 the Soviet Union had collapsed. Suddenly we were awash in money for special projects again. By the time we got back up to speed the Gulf War was about to kick off and you were right in the middle of it. We decided it was best to wait for your army commitment to end before approaching you, and here we are."

I sat there silently for a long while, trying to absorb everything Jefferson told me, and he seemed content to let me ponder things. After a time I realized it was like trying to drink water from a firehose. Way too much, way too fast. I needed time to think, and told him so.

"That's a great idea! Why don't you take a vacation? You'll be officially discharged from active duty on Monday morning. Take some time off, go somewhere and unwind, and think about what you've learned."

"So that's it? No hard sell, you're just asking me to think about your offer?"

"I haven't made an offer yet. I've merely informed you of the existence of our project. Would you like to hear our offer?"

"Actually, no. I don't need to hear your offer because I'm not interested. I've got plenty of prospects and I'm looking forward to a normal civilian life. But thank you for dinner."

"Pete, you want a vacation, and we want you to consider working for us. How about a compromise? We'll cover the cost of your vacation and all we ask in return is for you to think about working for us."

I laughed. "You'll pay for my vacation? I haven't told where I want to go, or for how long."

"Go anywhere you want. The Bahamas, the French Riviera, New Zealand. Anywhere in the world, and take a month. We'll cover all your costs: airfare, lodging, rental car, food, incidentals."

I smelled a rat. "What's the catch?"

Jefferson chuckled. "Yes, there's always a catch, isn't there? All we ask is during your month long vacation you refrain from drinking any alcohol, and when it's over let us know if you had any OBEs or lucid dreams."

"Forget it! What kind of vacation would it be without alcohol? No beer at the beach? No wine at sunset? That's what people do on vacation."

"I know it's an inconvenience, but we'll make it worth your while. In addition to covering all your costs we'll pay you five thousand dollars at the end of the month if you go without alcohol."

"And you'll just take me at my word? Or will you have people watching my every move?"

"Pete, if we didn't trust you, you could never work for us anyway. Yes, we'll take you at your word. If you can't abstain from alcohol for a month given the incentives we're offering then you've got a serious drinking problem you've managed to hide from everyone. Is that the case?"

That irked me. "No, of course not! Just because I like to drink beer and wine doesn't make me an alcoholic." I took several deep breaths to calm myself down. "You really think I'll be flying after a month?"

"Maybe, but we'd be happy with you having lucid dreams. If you start having them then OBEs won't be far behind. Let's take things one step at a time."

I sighed, wanting to take the deal but knowing I couldn't. "I'm inclined to take you up on your vacation offer. Who wouldn't be? But I'm almost certain I'll be getting a job offer from Dharma Pharmaceuticals in the next few days, and I'm not going to pass it up just to finish my free vacation. Sorry."

"That won't be a problem, Pete. If they make you an offer tell them you won't be available for sixty days, and let me know right away. Like all big companies Dharma does a lot of business with the United States government. We'll talk to them, let them know you're involved in a short term government project and we'll make sure it doesn't affect them hiring you."

"Sixty days? My vacation is only for one month."

"If you're making progress after the first month we'd like the option to extend it one more month. The same terms would apply. At any time if you decide you want out of the deal then just tell us and we'll part ways. There's no contract here. If you aren't a willing participant it's never going to work anyway. What do you say?"

I smiled for the first time since meeting Thomas Jefferson. "It's June. The salmon must be running right about now up in Alaska." I extended my hand. "You're on."

Chapter Eight

I left the United States Army on June 15th, 1992 and arrived in Juneau, Alaska a week later. I spent the interim at home with my mother and father. The next day I was flown by a bush pilot to Baranof Island, a heavily forested island on the Inland Passage. The seaplane taxied up to a dock where the pilot helped me unload my gear. A fifteen foot fishing boat with a small outboard motor was tied up there for my use. Wishing me good luck, he shook my hand and told me he'd return to the island several times per week with additional supplies and to make sure I was still alive. He said it only half-jokingly. Alaskan fisherman must compete for the salmon with the grizzlies and black bears, and every year a foolish angler or two tangles with one of nature's fishermen, and loses.

Once I had selected Alaska for my vacation spot the CIA did the rest. My waterfront log cabin was richly appointed and well stocked with dry and canned food and drink, including, to my surprise, a selection of hard liquor and wines. Either the CIA was unaware of it or perhaps it was their way of testing my resolve not to drink alcohol. The spacious cabin had a master bedroom with a king sized bed and a separate bunkroom with four bunk beds. No electricity, but it did have a wood stove for heat and Coleman lanterns for light, if needed. In June in Alaska the sun didn't set until well after midnight. An elevated water tank provided gravity fed running water. A large propane tank fueled a cook stove and hot water heater. No refrigerator, which may have explained the lack of beer. It was not a place I'd want to live year round, but as a vacation getaway it was ideal. I loved it.

There were half a dozen other cabins scattered around this remote part of the island, all of which were occupied. In addition, there was a multi-room lodge with generator-provided electricity, currently occupied by a party of eight anglers and a fishing guide. The same plane that dropped me off also serviced the other cabins. For those of us staying more than one week the travel company provided overnight laundry service. Sitka, the main population center on the island, was on the Pacific side and may as well have been a million miles away. I had all the solitude anyone could want. There was an unwritten rule that the occupants of the outlying cabins were not to be disturbed. On the other hand, if I got lonely all I had to do was wander over to the main lodge any evening and socialize. There was even a small all-terrain vehicle for my use if I was too lazy to walk. It was pretty obvious this was not some bargain basement vacation, but rather an exclusive, high end resort where the rich came to get away from it all. If the CIA was trying to impress me it was working.

Halfway through my planned four week stay I was as mellow as a cow in clover. I spent the evenings reading by lantern light from a surprisingly eclectic collection of books. I always drew the blackout curtains across the windows in an effort to stay on my normal sleep routine, thus the lantern was necessary. The soft hissing sound it made was as soothing as a distant waterfall. It took quite an effort to get up out of my easy chair by the woodstove and drag myself to bed. A couple of nights I didn't even bother, sleeping comfortably in the big chair by the stove, lulled into a stupor by the radiant heat. It was even more of a challenge to roust myself out in the morning. Only the thought of the superb salmon and halibut fishing was sufficient to lure me outside. My days of waking up to reveille on a busy army post already seemed distant, almost dreamlike.

Speaking of dreams, near the end of my third week on the island I had my first lucid one. A few nights later I was once again consciously controlling my actions within my dreams. The bottles of liquor and wine remained untouched in their cabinet, although there were times I nearly faltered in my resolve. The great books, easy chair and woodstove were like an ice cream sundae for my mind. A glass of wine would have been the cherry on top, to make it perfect, but I had given my word. In fact, my last taste of alcohol had been the draft beer I had over dinner with Jefferson at the Fort Benning officers club. His intimation that I might be an alcoholic had bothered me more than I wanted to admit.

With five days remaining on my thirty day vacation I was motoring back to my dock when a seaplane buzzed low overhead, dipping its wings. It was Spencer, the resupply pilot. I quickly veered out of his landing area and two minutes later we were both tied up to my little pier.

"Hey Pete, no fish today? I checked out your boat on my first pass."

"Oh no, I caught three beautiful halibut. The big one probably topped a hundred pounds. I gave up keeping them two weeks ago. There's only so much I can eat and I didn't want to waste them."

Spencer said, "Well, I've got the last of your supplies, unless you're going to extend your vacation. Mister Jefferson from your company called me and said he had reserved the cabin for another month."

"No, as much as I love it here, I'm ready to get back to civilization."

"Okay. Mister Jefferson anticipated that. I have a satellite telephone in my plane. He asked for you to call him if you decided not to extend your stay here." Spencer gestured toward his airplane. "The phone's right there on one of the rear seats. I'll stay out here on the dock."

After a few moments hesitation I climbed inside the float plane and found the phone, punching in Jefferson's number from memory. He answered immediately. "Mulvaney & Proust. How may I direct your call?"

I laughed out loud. "Seriously? I recognize your voice, Jefferson."

"Just pulling your chain a little bit, Pete. How's the fishing?"

"You know exactly how the fishing is. You probably know the length and weight of every fish I've caught, and all the ones that got away as well."

Sounded abashed, Jefferson actually stuttered a bit. "P-P-Pete, I assure you no one's been keeping tabs on you. Yes,

I get a weekly update from Spencer, but that's simply to confirm you didn't become bear bait. I most strongly deny your implica…"

Laughing again, I said, "Hey, one good chain pull deserves another. I'm joking. The fishing's been fabulous. The whole set up here is fabulous, but I'll be ready to go next week when the month is up."

"Did it bring back memories of your childhood, as we hoped?"

Jefferson was obviously being circumspect. Sure, satellite phones are the easiest to listen in on, but did he really think someone was listening? If so, who? Whatever, I'd play along. "In some respects, yes, it did."

"Good, good!" The CIA man's elation was plain, even over the static of the sat phone. "Pete, if you want to renew our agreement for another month it would help if I had a few days' notice to set it up."

I figured this was the reason for the call, but I didn't yet have an answer for him. "I'll have to give it some more thought, Thomas. Whatever I decide, it can wait until I finish up here. I'll let you know then."

I thought Jefferson would argue about it, but he did not. "Okay, fine. I'll meet your flight when it gets into Seattle. Bring me a nice halibut steak, if you can manage it. Goodbye."

I climbed out of the plane. Spencer stubbed out his cigarette, carefully putting the butt into his shirt pocket.

Patting his pocket he said, "I'd hate to dirty up this pristine place. There's nothing on earth quite like it. See you Thursday about noon, Pete."

******

Thomas Jefferson met me at Seattle's SeaTac airport and steered me over towards one of the VIP lounges. A uniformed United States customs officer met us at the lounge door and escorted us a short distance further to an unmarked door. He unlocked the door, waved us inside and closed the door after we entered. Jefferson and I were alone in a small office, probably belonging to a mid-level manager in the U.S. Customs Service. Jefferson seemed to have a knack for securing private rooms in unlikely places.

A fresh pot of coffee, cream, sugar and clean cups sat on a side table, along with a platter of pastries. Jefferson helped himself and with a wave of his hand indicated I should do the same. When we were settled in he started to speak but I cut him off. "Let me save you some time. I've decided not to go any further down this road, Thomas. As you know, Dharma Pharma has offered me a managerial position in their Bonn office and I've decided to take it." I watched his face closely, staring at him, looking for the tell, that oh so subtle change of facial expression I had learned to read well playing poker. Jefferson didn't even blink. The CIA man must have been a formidable card player.

"All right, Pete. I'm disappointed, of course, but it's your choice and we'll honor it. Would you mind telling me how far your dreaming progressed? You indicated over the sat phone you had made some progress. Our researchers are chomping at the bit to know if their theory was correct."

I nodded my head. "I started having lucid dreams on day nineteen on the island. That would have been day twenty eight without alcohol. I stopped drinking right after we first spoke at Fort Benning.

"Three days after that I was able to consciously control my actions within a dream, and a couple of days ago I found I'm again able to dream on demand. Just last night I felt as if I was about to leave my body. It didn't happen, but I'm fairly certain I'll be having OBEs any night now. It seems your theory about alcohol inhibiting OBEs is correct."

Jefferson took it all in, showing no emotion, not speaking. After a silence of several minutes he seemed to come to a decision, nodding to himself. He slapped his hands on his knees and stood up. "Well, I guess that's it then. Just for our records, please call me when you actually have your first OBE. The phone number you have will remain active for two more weeks. After that, if you change your mind or wish to speak to me you'll have to go through the main switchboard."

He stood still, staring at the wall for an uncomfortably long time, then shook himself out of his reverie. "Oh, I almost forgot." He reached into his breast pocket and handed me a thick envelope. "Your five thousand dollars. Cash keeps your name off our books, and the IRS will never know about it so that's a little bonus for you. Good luck to you, Pete."

We shook hands and he walked away, never once looking back. Not at all the reaction I had anticipated. I had been prepared for a long verbal battle over my decision, expecting the hardest of hard sells from the CIA man. Perhaps I wasn't as important to their program as he had first indicated. Maybe he was sincere when he said if I wasn't a willing participant it would never work. His quick acquiescence disturbed me so much I actually felt guilty about pocketing the money.

******

I wandered around SeaTac airport trying to decide my next step. As promised, the CIA had spoken with Dharma and arranged a delay in my start date, which was still six weeks away. I figured I'd fly over to Bonn about two weeks ahead of time, to get settled in and reacquainted with Germany before starting my new job. That gave me a full month to kill. I didn't want to spend a month at my parents' house and had no place of my own. What few possessions I owned were still in storage at Fort Benning, waiting for me to tell the army where to ship them. With Jefferson's five grand in my pocket I could buy a plane ticket to anywhere I wanted, but I didn't know where I wanted to go.

Sometimes no decision is a choice in itself. Unable to decide where I wanted to go I took an airport shuttle to a downtown Seattle hotel and booked a room. I spent the afternoon walking around the city, mainly the waterfront. After a month in the Alaskan wilderness the city was disgusting to me: crowded, dirty and most of all incredibly noisy. I hated it.

I spent a very uncomfortable night in the hotel, waking frequently and never attaining REM sleep. Fortified with coffee the next morning I rented a car and drove north, with no particular destination in mind. Canada was only a couple of hours away but I really just wanted to get away from the big city.

I found myself crossing a bridge over Deception Pass to Whidbey Island. The view from the bridge was so spectacular I located a parking spot on one end and spent an hour just taking it in. Whidbey Island itself was nearly as beautiful, with small towns widely separated by large farms. It was hard to believe Seattle was just a few miles away. I had pretty much decided to spend a few days on Whidbey Island when a U.S. Navy jet roared overhead, so low I had to fight the urge to duck. For the next several hours the sky was filled with jets endlessly circling the island. A passerby told me it was just a fact of life on the island, which hosted a huge naval air station. He said the jets flew around the clock some days. "After a while you get used to it. Here on the island we call it the sound of freedom. It won't be long before you hardly notice them anymore."

I decided not to hang around and test his theory, taking a ferry across Puget Sound to Port Townsend, on the Olympic Peninsula. I drove aimlessly, enjoying the salt water and mountain views. Late in the afternoon I found a bed and breakfast in the tiny town of Sequim. The couple who owned the charming waterfront property assured me it was always quiet, with the possible exception of an occasional coyote howling.

Sitting in an old fashioned rocking chair on the covered porch digesting a huge home cooked dinner, I was too sleepy to appreciate the beautiful sunset. I dragged myself inside and collapsed into bed, falling asleep instantly.

In the early morning hours I looked down to see my sleeping form on the old four poster bed. It took me a few moments to realize I was out of body. Out of body, for the first time in eight years!

The intervening years seemed to slip away in moments and I quickly became comfortable in my astral state, so much so that I moved effortlessly through the ceiling and roof into the starry night above.

******

For the next two nights I explored the limits of my astral traveling ability. It seemed clear I had lost none of my former skills. I was able to pass through all physical barriers as if they didn't exist. I had complete control of my flying speed, height, hovering, etc. Best of all, I was able to *shift* to any point on earth, so long as I was sufficiently familiar with its location.

Speaking of earth, I even dared to try flying to the moon. In preparation for the trip I went to a local library and studied up on the moon's distance from earth, its relationship to other bodies in our solar system, and its orbit. To my great disappointment not only did I not *shift* there, I didn't move even a millimeter towards space. Either I needed a great deal more knowledge of celestial mechanics or I was simply incapable of astrally traveling into space.

Having failed to venture into space I decided to see if I was able to explore inside the earth. To my knowledge there was no substance I was unable to pass through when astral traveling, so I figured passing through earth or even solid rock should present no difficulties. As it turned out I was able to easily fly underground, but it was like swimming deep underwater at midnight. I could see nothing and immediately lost all sense of direction, including up from down. In moments I was so confused and scared I involuntarily *shifted* back to my bed in Sequim and woke up.

One good thing came out of my aborted attempt to explore inside the earth: I realized I was able to explore underwater. On my next OBE I *shifted* to the Caribbean island of Aruba where it was full daylight. I spent a thrilling twenty minutes "astral scuba diving." It was to become one of my favorite pastimes.

I called Jefferson to tell him I was having OBEs again. Mindful of his penchant for secrecy I spoke in oblique terms, but I'm certain he understood my meaning. Surprisingly, he didn't seem particularly interested and in short order ended the conversation. Just as in our meeting at the airport a niggling feeling of guilt pressed upon me. In some obscure way I felt I owed Jefferson something more. After all, if not for him I never would have astral traveled again.

During the days I continued to drive around the Olympic Peninsula. I loved the small towns - Port Townsend, Port Hadlock, Port Ludlow, Sequim. I particularly enjoyed visiting Fort Worden State Park and Fort Flagler State Park.

Both parks were old army posts, their usefulness as protectors of the shipping lanes in Puget Sound long ago faded into history. Many of the original coastal artillery batteries and army buildings had been preserved. As a former army armor officer I was fascinated by all of it.

Seeing the old army forts made me realize I now had an opportunity to astrally visit my hometown in daylight hours. I had been unable to do so as a kid since I almost never attained REM sleep during daylight hours. Now that I was on the west coast the three hour time difference worked in my favor. My eighty minute long REM interval would occur sometime after 5:00 AM, if I went to sleep around 10:00PM. That would be 8:00 AM on the east coast, full daylight.

Hovering over my empty bed in my parents' house was a unique experience for me. In my childhood astral travels when I returned home it was always to the sight of my sleeping form. It made me reflect upon all my travels since those years, in the real world. College, the army, the war. How far I had gone, both in distance and life experience. When I came out of my reverie I realized I was no longer alone in my room. Just as those many years ago, I sensed the presence of another astral traveler in the corner of the room, by the east window. Was it merely a coincidence or was it the hitchhiker, intentionally occupying the same spot to let me know it was her?

I moved ever so slowly towards the other presence. When I got within a few feet I stopped. I could see nothing, but my sense of the other person was much more acute, as the smell of an odorous object becomes stronger when closer. I still had no idea if it was the hitchhiker. I started to move closer, with the intent of making contact with the other presence. I felt sure if I was able to touch the other person I would know if it was her.

For every inch I moved forward the presence moved an inch back. Moments later we had passed through the walls of my house and were hovering over the yard. We danced like that a few more times, then I tired of it and lunged forward… into nothing. The other presence was gone.

******

The next day I called Jefferson. I was happy to have met the hitchhiker again, except I wasn't sure it was her. Plus, if it was her, did she just happen to find me or did Jefferson assign her to some kind of astral stake out? If it wasn't her, was it another of Jefferson's astral spies, a spy from another country, or just an innocent traveler? Did other countries even use astral travelers as our CIA does?

I knew there was no way to discuss any of this with Jefferson over the telephone, so I didn't even bother to try. "I have some questions and concerns I wanted to discuss with you. Is it possible to get together somewhere we could speak privately?"

"Sure. I'm at the company headquarters. I'll meet you at the front gate. What time can you get here?"

"Well, I'm on the west coast. I'll fly over tomorrow and meet you at 8:00 AM the day after tomorrow."

"Okay, see you then."

Why did I have the feeling Jefferson had been expecting my call?

Chapter Nine

At the CIA headquarters in Langley, Virginia Jefferson and I spoke in a small, windowless conference room. "This room is known as a SCIF. That stands for Sensitive Compartmented Intelligence Facility. Here we can openly discuss matters of the highest security classification. Don't think that just because we're at CIA headquarters we can talk freely anywhere. We can't, and if you do you'll quickly get yourself, and me, I might add, in some very hot water. Most floors in the building have at least one SCIF. If you are not sure where you are, please ask before discussing anything classified. In your case, Pete, everything having to do with you and the project are classified, so you need to be particularly careful."

"You never have told me the name of this project."

Jefferson chuckled. "Well, that's because it really doesn't have a name. Technically, it doesn't even exist. The army actually started the project many years ago. They call it Stargate. The CIA has always had agents working alongside the army on Stargate. Still do, in fact. They've had only very limited success so far so my boss started our own version of Stargate a few years ago. As you can imagine, doing so seriously irritated the army guys. We've gotten much better results than the army and now it's turned into a major bureaucratic turf war. In order to lessen the tension everyone pretends the CIA project doesn't exist. All of our special projects have names except this one, which everyone simply calls 'the project.'"

Jefferson quickly answered all of my questions. Yes, it was the hitchhiker in my old bedroom the other night. No, she was not assigned to watch for me, she did it on her own. Yes, we believe the Russians and Chinese both have projects similar to Stargate, but we don't know for certain. At present, both the army and CIA have astral travelers, but the exact number is classified. "What else is on your mind, Pete? Now's the time to ask. You came all the way across the country for this."

I had been asking myself the same question on the long airplane trip. Did I really come all the way from the west coast just to ask a few questions? Why was I really here? I took a deep breath and plunged ahead. "Since I'm here, I might as well ask - if I was to work for you what exactly would I be doing, and where would I be doing it?"

Jefferson's poker face showed no smugness at all, not the slightest hint of satisfaction. Inside, I'm certain he was doing mental high fives, because his big fish - me - was nibbling at the bait. "What you would be doing is easy to answer. You'd be spying on countries we're interested in. Right now that means the Russians, the Chinese and the North Koreans. Your inability to hear anything while astral traveling is unfortunate and will severely limit the type of intelligence you can gather, but we've still got plenty of assignments for you. Determining the number and type of weapons in an ammunition depot, for example, or the weapons load out of a warship or submarine.

"Finding and reading certain documents would be another type of assignment. You might not even need fluency in

Russian or Chinese. We'd teach you key words to look for and your eidetic memory would do the rest.

"We'd also want you to do some snooping on people. Just knowing a certain person is in a certain place is valuable. Who is sitting next to whom in a meeting of the Politburo, for example, tells us who's in favor and who's out. All you'd have to do is memorize faces, then look at photos to identify who you saw when you return. Photos. Basically, you'd be a human camera. I hope that doesn't offend you."

Jefferson paused to see if I was offended, or even still interested, I guess. I said nothing, giving him my best poker face in return. He continued, "As to where you would be; we'd probably start right here at Langley. Moscow is eight hours ahead of us. When it's 5:00 AM here, the start of your long REM sleep time, it's 1:00 PM there, so you'd be astral traveling there during daylight hours. Business hours.

"China and North Korea are thirteen hours ahead of us, so at 5:00 AM here it's 6:00 PM there. Still light most of the year, but outside of business hours. Certainly less than ideal. If we were to focus on China or North Korea we'd probably relocate you to one of our facilities in England or Germany."

Counting missiles. Memorizing documents. A human camera. Could anything possibly be more boring? I couldn't help but sigh. Noting it, Jefferson hurried on. "Pete, I know it sounds dull, but it's vitally important to the safety and security of our country." The CIA man saw his big fish losing interest so he wiggled the bait. "And you would be extremely well compensated."

It worked - I bit. "Okay, I'm listening. I've come this far, I might as well hear your offer. Dharma Pharma tells me I'll be making north of $100,000 a year after two years, with the company providing housing and stock options. Plus, I'd have a normal life."

Jefferson's eyes twinkled, not even trying to hide his delight in what he was about to say. "Working for us, you wouldn't be an official CIA employee. In fact, on paper you wouldn't be working for the U.S. government at all. Mulvaney & Proust will pay you $100,000 a year to start. That will be your official income. Plus, we would provide company housing for you. Off the books, we will pay you an additional one million dollars a year. We'll set up an offshore bank account for you so that money is tax-sheltered, or you can make your own arrangements if you prefer.

"We'd want a one year contract. After that, either party can opt out. Depending upon the results of your work we could renew for another year at the same or better salary, but not less. You would have to agree to relocate anywhere in the world, anytime, at our discretion, but as I mentioned earlier, the likeliest places are here, Germany or England. Prior to signing the contract we would insist on a successful demonstration of your ability to astral travel to a specific place of our choosing."

Holy cow, a million bucks a year, tax free, on top of the $100,000 official salary! It would take me ten years to make that at Dharma. The free housing in the Washington, D.C. area was probably worth at least another $20,000. For that much money I'd be willing to put up with a lot of tedium, but I wasn't about to let Jefferson know that. "Your wanting a demonstration of my flying ability prior to signing a contract is perfectly reasonable. I also have one condition I insist on before signing - I want to meet the hitchhiker face to face."

******

I thought Jefferson would clap his hands with glee at such an easy request. Instead, his expression changed like a dark cloud suddenly obscuring the sun. Even the temperature in the room seemed to drop. "What's wrong?" I said worriedly. "Has something happened to her?"

"No, no, she's the same as always. You just can't meet her. None of our operatives know each other, Pete. It's against policy. We're speaking in a SCIF. Remember what the 'C' stands for: compartmented. Everything we do is on a 'need to know' basis. It's standard procedure in highly classified operations. There is simply no reason for you to meet any of our other operatives. After all, we're not playing bean bag here. There are real bad guys out there who would love to get their hands on one of us. If any of us are captured the other side will surely use drugs or torture to extract every bit of information they can. The less any one person knows the safer we all are."

Jefferson wasn't telling me anything I didn't already know. I'd held a security clearance in the army and I was familiar with the ridiculously high levels of paranoia in the intelligence community, but something didn't smell right here. It didn't escape my notice that Jefferson had said the hitchhiker was "the same as always" instead of the usual "she's fine."

"Look, Thomas, I'm not asking about her personal background. Heck, I'm not even asking you to tell me her name. I just want to see her. I met her in the astral world and I want to put a face to the person I met. That's not too much to ask."

Exasperated, Jefferson changed tack. "It's more than just security, Pete. She doesn't like meeting people. She's extremely selective about who she interacts with. In fact, she insists I be the only person on our staff who speaks with her.

"We have a unique arrangement with her, not a contract. I guess you could say she's a volunteer. She works with us only when she wants to and I wouldn't want to jeopardize what is already a shaky relationship."

Hmmm. Jefferson was definitely hiding something from me, and now was the time to find out what it was, before I signed a contract. I couldn't truly say why meeting her was so important to me; I only knew that it was. "I'm sorry, Thomas, but this isn't negotiable. Either I meet her or I walk out the door. If you don't have the authority to make it happen then call your boss."

Jefferson startled me by laughing out loud, a bitter laugh without a trace of humor in it. "My boss? My boss is a politically appointed hack who doesn't even know what the project is about. I'm in charge of this project, Pete, and you've put me in a no-win situation. Of course I don't want you to walk away. I'm willing to violate protocol this one time to get you onboard but I can't force the hitchhiker to meet you. Are you hearing me? I can't make this happen if she doesn't want it."

In his frustration Jefferson couldn't sit still. He paced around the room, occasionally pausing to stare at the wall, as if a window were there. Finally, he turned to face me. "It happens she's in the building right now. The best I can do is to ask her. When she says no, as I'm sure she will, will you believe me, or will you walk?" Not waiting to hear my answer Jefferson stormed out of the room, slamming the door shut behind him.

******

I never really trusted Jefferson and I couldn't say why. Maybe it was the duplicitous way he had first approached me, misrepresenting himself and lying about having been present at the job fair. Maybe it was simply the fact that he was a CIA man. Perhaps I was frustrated at being unable to read his poker face. I liked him well enough, and to be fair, he had scrupulously kept his word regarding my Alaskan vacation. Still, I didn't trust him.

As I waited there in the windowless SCIF all kinds of crazy thoughts ran through my mind. I resisted the urge to see if the door was locked, knowing it didn't matter. I only had a visitor's badge and couldn't go anywhere in the building without an escort. All the doors opened only with electronic key card access, so even if I was able to leave this room I wouldn't get very far.

If he came back alone was I willing to throw away a million dollars? If he came back with some woman how would I know she was the hitchhiker and not a CIA agent pretending to be her? Our astral meeting had been life changing for me, but in this world how would I recognize her? Before I could fret further the door opened.

Propping the door open with his foot Jefferson pushed a wheelchair into the room. The woman seated in the chair was excruciatingly thin, almost emaciated, with long blond hair and an angelic face. By angelic I don't mean beautiful, for she was plain-looking. Rather, her face had the innocent look of a young child, even though she was probably close to forty years old. In addition to whatever physical condition caused her to be in a wheelchair she clearly was mentally challenged as well. Whatever preconceived image I may have had of the hitchhiker, this was definitely not it.

The door clicked loudly as it closed. Jefferson wordlessly stepped back to a far corner of the room, leaving me and the woman about fifteen feet apart, a conference table between us. I found myself staring at her. If she thought it was rude she gave no sign, staring right back. I saw no fear or challenge in her eyes, only curiosity. After an interminably long time, perhaps a full minute, she smiled and beckoned me closer. I stood. Three long paces brought me close enough that she had to look up to see my face, and I stopped, not wanting to invade her personal space. She held out both her hands, palms up, and extended them to me. I grasped her hands, swooned, and nearly fell to the floor as my knees buckled. For the second time in my life I experienced the indefinably intense feeling of oneness with another human being. After what may have been seconds or may have been hours I felt something akin to an electric shock and lost consciousness.

******

I came to, sitting in a chair in the SCIF. Jefferson slouched in a chair next to me, a bemused look on his face. The hitchhiker was gone. "What happened?" I asked. "Where is she? How long was I out?"

"She asked to leave after you went to sleep. You were out for over an hour. The hitchhiker assured me you were just sleeping but I had our staff doctor come in and check you out, just to be sure."

Still not fully awake, I said, "Wait a minute. Susan and I were holding hands and then…"

Jefferson bolted upright, astonishment etched on his face. He practically screamed, "How do you know her name?"

"What do you mean? She told me. We introduced ourselves… didn't we?" Suddenly I had a very weird feeling.

"Pete, you never spoke a word. Neither one of you. You held hands for a little while, maybe about two minutes, then you sat down, without letting go of her hands. Perhaps a minute later you put your head down on the conference table. Susan withdrew her hands and asked to leave. Do you realize what this means?"

Yes, of course I knew what it meant: Susan and I had communicated telepathically. As my grogginess fell away I realized I had somehow gone into REM sleep almost immediately after grasping her hands. We had communicated with each other while in the astral plane. That would mean she must also have been asleep, but the CIA man had said nothing about that.

Jefferson couldn't contain his excitement. "Pete, this is huge! Our scientists have been working on mental telepathy longer than astral traveling, with virtually nothing to show for it. This is a gigantic breakthrough!"

Something told me not to go there, and the lie came smoothly off my lips. "Sorry, Thomas, I hate to burst your bubble, but I have to. Something weird happened here, for sure, but it wasn't that. Susan introduced herself to me the old fashioned way - she spoke. She whispered her name to me, probably because you had warned her not to tell me, didn't you?"

That gave the CIA man pause. "Well, yes, I did. I told you, it's protocol, but I was standing right here, observing closely, and you two never spoke to each other."

I shook my head. "No, you were standing over there in the far corner. She had her back to you so you wouldn't have seen her lips move. Now I've gotten her in trouble, haven't I?"

"No, she's not in any trouble," he said, the disappointment plain on his face. "But you and I have a lot to talk about."

******

Jefferson was all business. It was obvious the strange interaction between me and the hitchhiker consumed him. "Pete, before we discuss this any further I want you to sign a non-disclosure agreement. You're not under contract with us yet and although your security clearance from the army is still valid you were never cleared for anything near this level. Let's get the NDA signed and then we can talk, okay?"

While I was reading and signing the document Jefferson made a pot of coffee. I needed those minutes to figure out exactly what I was and was not going to say. Once again, Jefferson had been straight with me. My first thought was he would say the hitchhiker simply refused to meet with me. My second guess was he would bring in a woman posing as the hitchhiker. Neither one of those happened. The woman in the wheelchair was the same person I met in the astral plane eight years previously. I can't tell you how I knew that but I knew it as surely as I know my own name. I also knew despite the fact Jefferson had always meticulously kept his word to me I still didn't trust him, and I couldn't say why.

"Alright, Pete, why don't you tell me what happened? Please try to be as precise as possible."

"I, uh, I'm not sure, honestly. I feel like somebody slipped me a mickey. You wheeled her into the room and we stared at each other for a minute or so. Her face looks so… I don't know… I guess 'vacant' is the word I'm searching for. My first impression was she had some type of mental disability, but then she focused her eyes on me and I changed my mind. It was almost hypnotic. I could feel her intensity, her intelligence.

"Then she told me to come over to her. No, that's not right. She didn't say anything, she waved me over with her hands. When I got close to her she smiled and whispered, 'I'm Susan.' No last name, just that. Her eyes were twinkling, as if she knew she was doing something naughty by telling me her name. Normally, of course, I'd have reciprocated, but as I said, she seemed to know she was breaking the rules, so I kept silent.

"We stared at each other again. I couldn't tell you for how long. I got lost in her eyes. When she extended her hands to me I naturally put my hands in hers. Thomas, I fell asleep! Right then. Standing up, no less. I don't know how or why it happened, but I'm telling you it did. Shortly before I woke up I went into REM sleep, so I must have been out a good while."

The CIA man stared hard at me, trying to read my face. I knew from years of poker playing he wouldn't find any clues there. "Pete, were you out of body? Were you and Susan astral traveling together?"

"No," I lied. "I wasn't even lucid dreaming. I wasn't asleep long enough. You asked if we were astral traveling together. Did Susan fall asleep too?"

Jefferson shook his head, clearly frustrated. "I don't know. She's a high functioning autistic. Sometimes she zones out for hours and I can't tell if she's awake or asleep. She held hands with you for about three and a half minutes total. I started timing it as soon as I realized something unusual was happening. You went out on your feet almost immediately after grasping hands. A few minutes later you managed to sit down. When she let go of your hands your whole body jerked and you seemed to wake up momentarily, then went right back to sleep. It's the strangest thing I've ever seen, and believe me, that's saying something."

I could only imagine what he'd say if he knew what really happened. Somehow Susan induced me into REM sleep and I immediately went into the astral plane, where I found her waiting for me. We didn't actually travel anywhere, just stayed right there and "talked," for lack of a better word. Communicated together while on the astral plane. Is that mental telepathy? Maybe. There are lots of ways of communicating without speaking - reading and writing, gestures, sign language, facial expressions; but to me, it felt like we talked. I'm not a scientist reporting the results of an experiment in clinical terms; I'm just telling you what it felt like to me.

If you're thinking we discussed the secrets of the universe you couldn't be more wrong. We were like two teenagers talking over the telephone - nothing but small talk and getting to know each other. I say "over the telephone" because I couldn't see her and I don't know if she could see me. We even said goodbye the way people do over the phone, but I wasn't about to tell Jefferson any of that.

Jefferson grilled me for another hour, then the doctor came back and gave me a quick once over, pronouncing me fit. Jefferson seemed to know I was holding things back, but he'd only press so far and then back off. Finally, he tired of it. "Pete, I've acceded to every request you've made. I'm certain you're not telling me everything but I'm willing to let it slide for now. My offer's on the table. Will you come to work for us?"

I took a few more sips of coffee as I pretended to ponder it, but the truth was he'd had me once he'd offered a million bucks a year - everything else had been a bluff.

Chapter Ten

I started working for the Central Intelligence Agency in August of 1992. Before I officially signed on I had to prove to Jefferson I could astral travel anywhere he wanted. There were numerous bunk rooms in the CIA headquarters, some of them well appointed suites. He escorted me to one of them and told me to make myself at home. The room had a refrigerator holding a selection of food and beverages. Dinner, in the form of restaurant takeout food, was available simply by picking up the house phone and asking the duty officer. Take out menus from half a dozen different restaurants lay on a side table. Except for the lack of windows I could have been in a decent hotel room.

Before leaving Jefferson explained my test assignment. I was to "fly" that night to the U.S. embassy in Nairobi, Kenya. Inside the secure communications room of the embassy I would find a framed document on one wall. I was to memorize the document and also report all the details of the room I could recall. A tape recorder and a pen and paper were available on my night table for me to record my observations.

I was familiar with the geography of Africa and knew I could *shift* to Nairobi. Jefferson produced a Nairobi street map with the location of the embassy marked on it and he described to me the location of the communications room within the embassy. When I told him I was all set he left.

That night I explored the CIA headquarters building during my shorter REM phases. Around 5:00 AM, during my long REM interval, I *shifted* to the U.S. embassy in Nairobi. I found myself in a conference room adjacent to the communications room and slipped through the wall to my target. Once inside I saw the lights were on and the space was unoccupied. I took it all in, hovering in the center of the room and slowing turning 360 degrees. There was only one framed document on any of the walls, obviously put there specifically for my test. It was a full page single spaced typewritten paper of gibberish in a mixture of English, French and German. No one with a normal memory could possibly recall it correctly. Jefferson was not only testing my astral ability but also my eidetic memory.

I spent forty minutes in the room according to the wall clock. Since it was midday there I used the remainder of my eighty minute REM period touring Nairobi before returning to Langley. Back in my room I woke up and dictated the contents of the framed document into the tape recorder, not bothering to record any of the other details, which seemed pointless to me.

I showered and shaved and was on my second cup of coffee when Jefferson knocked on the door. His eyebrows went up when he saw the blank writing pad. I pointed to the tape recorder and told him it was all there. He picked up the house phone and spoke briefly, then joined me in a cup of coffee. A few minutes later someone came and retrieved the tape recorder. Fifteen minutes after that the same person returned, handed Jefferson a paper, and left.

"Congratulations, Pete. Your transcription of the Nairobi document was perfect. Welcome aboard." We clinked our coffee cups together in a mock toast, and that was it - I was officially an astral spy for the CIA.

******

I lived at the CIA headquarters for the next two weeks while undergoing an array of psychological and physical examinations, including several electroencephalograms. I filled out and signed reams of paperwork, among them an official employment contract with Mulvaney & Proust. To my surprise I learned Mulvaney & Proust actually existed and had a building in nearby Arlington, Virginia, where I would be given my own office.

I spent several days with psychologists exhaustively exploring my childhood astral traveling and lucid dreaming experiences. I was completely open and honest with them, except for one thing: I never told them about Miss Grant, the woman who was largely responsible for my astral ability. I had this nightmare vision of the CIA descending upon my former sixth grade teacher and putting her on the payroll, teaching legions of spies how to remember their dreams and perhaps one day become astral travelers. Instead, I told the shrinks I started lucid dreaming at age six and had my first out of body experience at age ten. I knew from Jefferson that fit the standard profile of most astral travelers and they accepted my version without question.

After each day with the head doctors my nights were my own, with one exception. Near the end of my second week at CIA headquarters Jefferson took me to a large room on the fourth floor. Inside the room were a series of upright barriers, perhaps one foot high by one foot wide. There were dozens of them, arranged like dominos, about two feet apart. Jefferson explained, "We've always wondered if there is any material through which an astral traveler cannot pass. These blocks run the gamut - paper, glass, various types of wood, metal and rock. Some are quite exotic, such as diamond, titanium, kevlar, even some materials from NASA.

"We've also wondered if an astral entity can be detected by any means. To that end, we've installed in this room cameras and other instruments to detect changes across every known spectrum we can measure.

"Your assignment tonight Pete is to fly to this room and attempt to pass through each and every one of these blocks. Our scientists don't expect any of the materials to actually block you, but they are hoping to detect you as you pass through some of the more unusual materials. An astral footprint, if you will. You've told our researchers there is nothing you haven't been able to pass through but we're fairly certain you've never encountered some of these substances. If you are impeded in even the slightest way please be sure to note it."

Of course there was one thing I was not able to pass through while in the astral plane - another astral traveler. I had related my first experience with the hitchhiker to the shrinks and we spent hours talking about it, so Jefferson surely knew of it. I wanted to spend more time with her so I brought it up. "You must know I bumped into Susan in the astral plane years ago. Bumped, as in, did not pass through.

Why not have her in the test room with me and let us bump into each other a few times while the cameras and whatnot are rolling?"

Jefferson frowned. "A wonderful idea, Pete, and one I'd love to arrange, but unfortunately it isn't on the agenda. Susan absolutely refuses to take part in any laboratory testing, and we don't currently have any other astral travelers capable of choosing their destination."

That night I flew to the test room during my first ten minute REM phase and again later in the night. I passed effortlessly through every test block and Jefferson told me later the instruments had failed to detect any anomalies. With Susan on my mind, I searched every room in the building, looking for her earthly body or even a wheelchair. I found neither.

I got my first paycheck from Mulvaney & Proust and also my first deposit to my offshore bank account. Not willing to trust the CIA with my money I put my business degree to use and set up my own account in the Cayman Islands. The $83,000 wire transfers would occur once a month for the first year.

When all the administrative requirements were finally out of the way Jefferson took me to my new residence in McLean, Virginia, a short drive from both CIA headquarters and Mulvaney & Proust. "This is where you'll live when you're working for us, Pete. It's a CIA safe house with elaborate security protection. On paper it's owned by Mulvaney & Proust so it works with your cover story. You'll go to 'work' Monday through Friday at

Mulvaney's office building but your real work will be done here when you're sleeping. I'll give you your remote viewing assignments either in person, by courier, or over secure telephone. You'll dictate your observations into a tape recorder and also brief me as warranted. Nothing difficult about it. In fact, your biggest battle will be fighting against boredom."

****

My first year of employment with Mulvaney & Proust was uneventful. I moved into my employer-provided house in McLean and commuted to work Monday through Friday to my office in Arlington. Each location had encrypted telephones and I generally received my remote viewing targets over them. Every morning after a mission I dictated what I had seen into a tape recorder and locked the recorder into a wall safe in my den. Each evening when I came home the tape had been removed and replaced with a fresh one. Occasionally Jefferson would phone me at Mulvaney and ask for clarification on something I had recorded, but weeks often passed with no contact between us.

Although it was not specified in my contract, I usually worked as a remote viewer five nights per week, Monday through Friday. In keeping with my cover story, or legend, as the CIA referred to it, I had weekends off to do as I pleased. Jefferson insisted I conduct astral missions only from a secure CIA facility, of which there were many all up and down the east coast of America. I always carried a pager. If an urgent assignment came up on a weekend while I was away from home Jefferson would page me and direct me to return home or spend the night at one the many CIA facilities scattered throughout the northeast.

I was earning $8300 a month and had no rent, mortgage or utility bills to pay, so it didn't take long to pump up my Virginia bank account. That first year I didn't even think about my Cayman Islands account, I just dumped the $83,000 there every month.

In November of 1992 Jefferson gave me permission to go to my parents' house in Connecticut for the long Thanksgiving weekend. I drove up from Virginia, stopping in Atlantic City, New Jersey to play some poker at the casinos. While waiting for a spot at a poker table to open up I decided to try my hand at blackjack, which turned out to be a life changing experience for me. Blackjack is another card game all about odds and probabilities, but unlike poker, bluffing is not part of the game, making winning at blackjack a breeze for someone with my memory. My first night at Caesar's Atlantic City casino I not only cleared $7500 but the management gave me dinner and my room free for the night. The toughest thing about casino gambling was resisting the urge to consume the free alcoholic drinks they kept offering me.

I cut my time at home short so I could spend another night in Atlantic City. I stayed at a different casino but had the same results, returning to McLean with $15,000 more in my bank account. After that, I made weekend trips to Atlantic City a couple of times each month. My casino gambling at first caused Jefferson some major heartburn but when I explained to him it was virtually impossible for me to lose due to my eidetic memory he dropped his objections.

The more frequently I played and won the more I came under scrutiny from the casino security people. I was counting cards, which is not cheating, but casinos have the legal right to ban anyone for any reason, and they always ban card counters. I made rounds to all the casinos and was careful never to overstay my welcome, even losing on purpose or breaking even some weekends so as not to poison the well. On my one year anniversary at Mulvaney & Proust I had earned $100,000 from them and twice that much from Atlantic City. Oh yeah, and the tax free million in the Caymans. Life was good.

******

In August of 1993 I signed on for another one year contract with the CIA. Apparently my "work" at Mulvaney & Proust was satisfactory because my second year salary there was raised to $150,000 per year. Better yet, my secret salary with the CIA was also bumped up fifty percent, to $1.5 million per year. $125,000 each month was now going into my Cayman Islands account.

I invested my money rather conservatively at first, taking many of the recommendations of the bank vice-president managing my account. My investments made twelve percent overall that first year, which is a bit above average for a reasonable investor.

In mid-September of 1993 Jefferson phoned me on the secure telephone. He told me to pack a bag and report to him at CIA headquarters. He said I would be working seven days a week for a while and sleeping in one of the headquarters suites. My first thought was Jefferson was going to screw me now that I had signed another one year contract, but I was wrong. Something big was happening.

The CIA learned through their sources that Russia was on the brink of a constitutional crisis, perhaps even a coup or revolution. All their assets, including me, were being focused on figuring out what was happening there. A military coup even in some backwater third world country was of interest to the CIA, but a military coup in Russia, with their thousands of nuclear weapons, could pose an existential threat to the United States. In the covert world of spies, this was as serious as it gets.

I had been spending my eighty minute REM interval counting warheads and doing other important but mundane tasks. Now Jefferson wanted me to fly to Russia every REM period, every night, and monitor people, not weapons. I memorized the faces of dozens of Russian politicians and senior military officers. I *shifted* several times each night to the Kremlin and key military bases, reporting back on who was meeting with whom, and their demeanor. Were the meetings casual or tense, friendly or adversarial? Were there obvious factions, groups of people siding with each other against others in the room? I spent night after night following Boris Yeltsin, then the president of Russia, everywhere he went, taking careful note of whom he met with and for how long. Jefferson would swear a blue streak when one of my reports stated Yeltsin spent every minute of my viewing time on the phone, meeting in person with no one. I could report Yeltsin was gesturing wildly and yelling, talking calmly, or whatever, but as to the content of his conversation and to whom he was speaking, I was clueless. It drove Jefferson crazy. Occasionally I was able to give Jefferson one or more phone numbers Yeltsin had dialed. I have no idea if it mattered.

It was certainly more interesting than counting bullets, but I wondered how much good I was doing. On September 21, 1993 Yeltsin ordered the Russian parliament disbanded. They responded by ignoring the order and impeaching him. Street fighting broke out between police and anti-Yeltsin protestors. The whole world was on edge and at CIA headquarters it was an insane asylum. Our own strategic military forces had quietly gone to a heightened state of alert. Things came to a head on October 4th when Yeltsin ordered the parliament building flattened, with the members of parliament meeting inside. Scenes of Russian tanks shelling the parliament were featured on television screens throughout the world. When the smoke cleared Yeltsin and his backers retained control and the crisis eased. Finally, about ten days before Christmas Jefferson told me I could move back to my McLean home and return to a five day work schedule.

Jefferson was effusive in his praise of my work during the crisis. He claimed my remote viewing was a major factor in guiding United States policy. Personally, I didn't see it, but then, I didn't know what Jefferson knew. That whole "compartmented intelligence" thing was in play. I was merely a cog in the machine. I was able to report conclusively on one thing, though - body count. When it was all over the official Russian media had the total number of dead at about two hundred. That was complete nonsense. Two hundred per day every day for two weeks is more like it. I saw truckloads of dead protestors gathered off the street and dumped in mass graves. If nothing else, the CIA learned Boris Yeltsin was a brutal, ruthless man, not one to be trifled with.

Hoping to take advantage of Jefferson's post-crisis good mood I asked for vacation time until after the New Year holiday, and he granted my request. Not only that, he okayed my going to the Caribbean. All CIA personnel with high security clearances have to receive permission before leaving the country on personal business.

I went first to see my banker in the Caymans, whom I had never met in person. Then I flew to the Bahamas, because casino gambling is illegal in the Cayman Islands while the Bahamas has many casinos. I had no concern there about winning too much money since I didn't plan on returning anytime soon. In a week there I bet big, won big, and lived the high life, sending almost a million dollars to my Caymans Islands account when I was through. I now had just over two million dollars in overseas banks.

Chapter Eleven

When I returned to work in January 1994 Jefferson came over to Mulvaney & Proust to speak with me in person, which was very unusual. He started by again telling me how valuable my reporting on the Russian crisis had been, but… isn't there always a but? I might have been far more valuable, in his opinion, if I was able to read Russian. If I could, I might have spotted important documents, which I could then have memorized and reported on. To that end, from now on, rather than sitting in my office at Mulvaney twiddling my thumbs all day long I was going to learn the Russian language.

I thought I'd be a student at the Defense Language Institute in Monterey, California, and was looking forward to spending some time in California, but Jefferson had other plans. California was three time zones farther away from Moscow and I couldn't spend months there. Instead, he was bringing a Defense Language Institute tutor to me. "Besides, Pete, with your eidetic memory you'll pick up Russian much faster than regular students. And once you become fluent in Russian we'll bring in another tutor to teach you a new skill - lip reading."

******

From January to July of 1994 I spent my days learning to read and speak Russian and spent my nights in Russia. Some nights I would be tasked with weapons counting but more often now I was observing people and memorizing documents. I became fluent in both speaking and reading Russian but was a total failure at lip reading in any language. Despite that, Jefferson was magnanimous and congratulated me on having mastered my fourth language.

In August of 1994 Jefferson and I concluded our contract negotiations and I signed on for a third one year term. This time, instead of waiting for Jefferson's offer I told him I wanted two hundred thousand as my official salary with Mulvaney & Proust and two million dollars for my offshore accounts. It was my opening bid in the negotiations and I fully expected the CIA man to laugh in my face. Instead, he agreed so quickly I kicked myself for not asking for much more. Seeing the chagrin on my face Jefferson magnanimously gave me a long weekend as a "signing bonus" and suggested I use it to attend my ten year high school reunion back in Connecticut. I had been debating whether to go or not and had previously discussed it with him. I decided to attend. My parents would be happy to see me and I had an ulterior motive for going to the reunion, of course - I wanted to see Melissa.

Yes, I was over her, it wasn't about that. I admit it took me all of my college years to get past our break up. Then I was in the army, most of those years overseas. I dated some and I certainly wasn't a monk, but I never had a serious love interest. Never really wanted one. Once I went to work for the CIA my life seemed a little bit too weird for a relationship. All of a sudden I looked up and ten years had passed! Where did they go?

Our class reunion was held in a decent hotel and was typical of most reunions. It kicked off at 2:00 PM with an unstructured social mixer. People drifted in all afternoon and there was a big surge of alumni just before dinner at 6:00 PM. Dancing was scheduled from 8:00 PM - 11:00 PM.

I arrived about 3:15 PM. I recognized a bunch of my classmates but honestly, I had very few friends in high school and it felt awkward being there. A few of my former classmates came up to me and we chatted for a bit. To my surprise, several people asked about my time in the army. Apparently the army public affairs office had sent a notice of my ROTC graduation to my hometown newspaper.

I scanned the room carefully for Melissa but did not see her. Finally, I spotted my friend Josh. He had dropped the punk rock look he favored in high school and looked presentable, but he had a bit of a goth look about him now. We spoke for quite some time and I was comfortable enough with him to ask about Melissa. He said he had lost track of her right after high school graduation.

About 5:30 PM a strikingly beautiful red haired woman came up to me and addressed me by name. I was mystified and hugely embarrassed, because I had no idea who she was. After some good natured teasing she identified herself as Jill Armstrong, which absolutely floored me. Jill had been a classic plain Jane in high school, with mousey brown hair and flat as a board. The woman standing next to me could have been a Playboy centerfold.

"I know, I'm not the same girl I was back then. I blossomed my sophomore year in college. My mother always told she had been a late bloomer and I would be, too. Back then I thought she was just saying that to buck up my spirits, but she was right. The red hair is fairly new, though. I change the color every now and then.

"You, on the other hand, Pete, are still the same handsome guy you were in high school. Is your wife here with you?"

"Wife? Oh, no, I've never been married. Never even got close. How about you? You must be married. Children? You sure don't look like you've had any kids."

Jill smiled, lighting up her whole face and revealing flawless teeth. "Are you flirting with me, Pete? Oh, to answer your question, no kids. I got married when I was in graduate school and divorced when I started my doctoral work."

"Divorced already? Forgive me for saying so, but you must have married a moron."

Jill beamed again. "You are flirting with me!"

I didn't even pretend to hide it. I was smitten with her. "Yes, I sure am. I still can't believe you're Jill Armstrong. Or do you go by your married name now?"

"No, I went back to Armstrong with the divorce. So, tell me about your life since you left. I know you ended up at San Diego State and went into the army."

We got caught up on the basic stuff fairly quickly and sat together for dinner. Jill had earned a PhD in economics at the University of New Hampshire, then went to work on the New Hampshire governor's staff. She was currently living in Concord, the state capitol.

After dinner we continued our conversation. Dozens of our male classmates came over to introduce themselves to Jill. Those who had not seen her in years were as shocked as I was at the dramatic change in her appearance. Not surprisingly, all the women in the room stayed away from her - she was that pretty.

As we sipped our drinks, she caught me looking around. "You're looking for Melissa, aren't you? I don't think she's here."

Embarrassed again, I could only nod. "I apologize, Jill. As gorgeous as you are I'm finding it hard not to stare at you, but yes, I confess I was hoping Melissa would be here. I got over her many years ago, but still, I was just curious."

"I get it, Pete. You guys were together for almost three years back then. It must have been tough breaking up."

"Yeah, I was out of my mind for her, with visions of marriage, kids, a house with a white picket fence, the whole shebang. Fortunately for me, someone was looking out for my best interest and clued me in to what was really going on. Say, it was you who called me, wasn't it?"

Now it was Jill's turn to be embarrassed. Her face turned the color of her hair. "You recognized my voice? I thought you didn't even know I existed."

Chagrined, I meekly plead guilty. "I only had eyes for Melissa back then. Blinders is a better word for it. And I was wearing beer goggles a lot in those days, too. I gave up drinking after I left the army." I lifted my glass of Seven Up as proof.

Jill and I discovered we had a great deal in common. Classic movies and books when indoors, but we both much preferred to be outdoors enjoying nature's beauty. Jill ruefully told me, "I fell in love with scuba diving on a graduation vacation to the Bahamas, but I never go anymore. The waters in northern New England are not very clear and way too cold, even in summer."

I could hardly believe my good fortune. "I love the Bahamas! I was there last year and every minute I wasn't at the blackjack tables I was underwater." With my fingers crossed, knowing I was pushing my luck, I said, "Wouldn't it be great to go back there together?"

Amazingly, she didn't shoot me down altogether. "Maybe someday, Pete. We'd have to get to know each other better first, and with you living in Virginia and me in New Hampshire that doesn't seem likely."

"Well, I'm willing to give it a shot," I replied. "I usually come up here to Connecticut to spend the holidays with my folks. New Hampshire's just a few more hours up the road. And they have these things called airplanes, too. It's only an hour and a half flight from Virginia to New Hampshire."

We were both staying in the hotel that was hosting our reunion and agreed to discuss it further over dinner the next night. I was elated. Jill got commandeered by some old girl friends and I found myself briefly alone until my old pal

Wayne came up to me. I recognized his face but his body was another thing altogether. The muscular high school athlete that I knew had been replaced with a red faced fat man. He must have put on eighty pounds. The goofy mutton chop sideburns he wore only served to make him look even fatter. I mentally attributed his red face to high blood pressure but when he spoke to me I realized he was quite intoxicated.

He nearly crushed the life out of me with his bear hug greeting. He might have looked fat, but underneath all that was an incredibly strong man. We gave each other the quick and dirty synopses of our lives, something I had done two dozen times already that evening.

Wayne had suffered a football career ending knee injury in his junior year at Boston College. He stayed on to complete his degree in physical education and was now teaching phys ed at our old high school. And of course he was the school football coach there as well.

I was trying to think of a good segue into asking him about Melissa when he brought her up himself. "You might not know it, Pete, but Melissa and I dated for a while in college. Not steady or anything, just on an occasional weekend. She spoke of you quite often."

"Well, I hope she had a few good things to say about me. I was hopelessly in love with her back then."

Wayne laughed way too loudly, as drunks are wont to do. "Duh! Everyone in school knew you two were together. It's just that Melissa had a different idea of what 'together' meant." Realizing he might have gone too far he quickly added, "Sorry, pal, I don't mean to tick you off."

I waved my hand dismissively. "Nah, I'm way past that. In fact, it looks like Jill Armstrong and I might be getting reacquainted."

Surprised, Wayne said, "Was that Jill you've been talking with all night? Holy cow, where was she hiding in high school?"

"Yep, I had the same reaction. She called herself a late bloomer."

Wayne boomed out his drunken laugh again, drawing stares from several people around us. "Man, better late than never, for sure. She's a knockout."

I took his elbow and steered him away from everyone. In a low voice, hoping he'd get the message, I said, "Wayne, any idea where Melissa is these days?"

He scowled. "Yeah, maybe. As brainy as that girl was she made some pretty dumb decisions. She just loved to party and got in with the doper crowd at Radcliffe. All those hoity-toity girls there, drinking tea with their pinkies pointed in the afternoons and smoking dope in the evenings. Melissa was real popular because she supplied them with anything they wanted, using some of her old connections from high school.

"Near the end of her junior year she got busted by the campus police in a drug sting. The university didn't want the bad publicity so she wasn't prosecuted, but she had to leave school. Last I knew she was living in Chicago. Nobody's heard from her in years."

******

Jill and I met for dinner in the hotel the next night. We both had rental cars but couldn't think of anyplace better to eat. Jill wanted to know more about my work. "You told me you're an international business consultant, Pete. What exactly does that mean?"

I gave her my standard cover story. "Well, to be candid, it's a fancy title and not much more. In a nutshell, I'm an interpreter. I learned to speak German and French while stationed in Europe with the army. My employer does a great deal of business there. With my business degree I have a good understanding of how companies work - manufacturing, marketing, research and development, stock valuations, that kind of thing. I'm one of the company's front men. I set up deals, get the ball rolling, then turn it over to the experts and our company lawyers who do the nitty-gritty detail work. When they're done I come in on the back end, making sure our clients understand everything we've done for them."

Jill asked, "I thought English was the language of international business. And don't the European companies have their own interpreters?"

"It is, and they do. Mulvaney & Proust might be a relatively small firm, but we do big business with big companies. Most of the firms we deal with have lots of English speakers; especially at their senior levels of management, but it's a mark of respect to speak to clients in their native language. Also, when tens or hundreds of millions of dollars are at stake no one is willing to trust conversational English or the other guy's interpreter."

"Do you travel much?"

"Some. Mostly I'm on the phone in my office in Arlington. When I do travel it's often on short notice, to handle some perceived crisis (at least that was true!). For the money they pay me I surely have nothing to complain about.

"Enough about my work. Tell me about yours. Congratulations on getting your PhD, by the way. Quite an achievement, Doctor."

Jill smiled, acknowledging my compliment unabashedly. "Thank you. My doctorate is still new enough for me to vividly recall in horrifying detail all the hours I put in to get it. It paid off, though. Most economists end up teaching, but I've got a great job, actually working in my field, and I feel very fortunate. I'm not yet in Governor Merrill's inner circle, but I might be in his next term. He's up for reelection this year and if the polls are accurate he's a shoo-in."

"So you'll be in Concord for the next four years at least, then."

"Maybe. New Hampshire governors serve only a two year term for some odd reason. The office has no term limits, although historically no governor has ever served more than three terms and it's become the norm to step down after six years. This will be his second term if he wins."

"So, if tradition holds we're still looking at possibly four more years. Would it be selfish of me to hope the polls are wrong and he loses in a few months?"

Jill laughed, a beautiful sound, and playfully slapped me on the arm. "Yes, it would be selfish! I may not make the money you do but I like my job and want to keep it."

I considered the implications of her statement for our relationship, if we ended up having one. Not wanting to go down that road yet I said, "I know it's generally considered impolite to discuss politics over dinner, but since it's your job, can we make an exception?"

When she nodded her assent I asked, "Merrill's a Republican, isn't he? I assume that means you are, too?"

"Yes, of course I am. Couldn't have gotten the job otherwise. How about you?"

"Well, I've always voted Republican, but I don't wear it on my sleeve. If I really thought hard about it I might actually be closer to Libertarian. Basically, I just want the government to keep its hands out of my pockets. Most elections that means Republicans get my vote."

Jill nodded, thoughtful. "Mulvaney really must be paying you well if you're worried about paying too much in taxes. Good for you."

"Yes, they are, and I'm only just starting my third year with them. Plus, I've made some very good investments. I'm not wealthy yet, but I aspire to be, and sooner rather than later. I hope I don't sound like I'm bragging, but it's important to me that you know I've made something of myself, Jill, especially since…" I couldn't find the words to explain myself and just mumbled something into my food.

"You don't have to prove anything to me, Pete. I've always liked you, and I still do."

Jill sensed my shame and I was sure she knew what I meant, but this was too important to leave to assumptions. I took a deep breath and plunged ahead. "Look, I made a total fool of myself for three years in high school, mooning over Melissa while she never felt the same way about me. I was an idiot, and everyone in high school knew it except me. When I finally woke up I was so ashamed I gave up Harvard University and ran as far away as I could get, all the way to California.

"Even worse, I completely ignored someone who actually cared about me - you. I'm not that stupid kid anymore, Jill. I've gotten over it, and I've grown up, but it took years, and maybe in one respect I haven't changed all that much. I've never been one to date a bunch of girls, but when I fall for one, I fall hard, and I can feel myself already falling for you. I don't expect any commitments from you now; it's too early for that. But if we start seeing each other and do eventually reach that point, I need to know you'll be honest with me and not string me along. I couldn't take that again." There. It was out in the open.

Jill sipped her wine while she collected her thoughts. She looked like she was about to speak, then reached for her wineglass again. Finally, she was ready. "Pete, I know how badly Melissa hurt you. Believe me, I know because I lived through it myself. My husband started stepping out on me practically before our leftover wedding cake got stale. I saw the signs and refused to believe it, but eventually I couldn't ignore them anymore. Thank God we decided to put off having children until I was out of school. When I finally wised up I didn't even offer him a second chance. Once was more than enough for me. Trust me; I am totally a one guy and one guy only girl."

After dinner we walked around town, holding hands like the high school lovers we never were, talking for hours. We agreed to stay in touch by phone and exchanged both work and home phone numbers. We made tentative plans for me to fly up to Concord. She suggested a month from then. I countered with two weeks and we settled on three. When we said goodnight and goodbye Jill kissed me full on the lips. I felt like a school boy again.

Chapter Twelve

The autumn of 1994 was an idyllic time for me. I was making more money than I ever dreamed possible (how's that for a pun?). Since my face to face meeting the previous January with my personal banker in the Cayman Islands my stock portfolio value had grown by nearly twenty percent in only seven months. After winning big in the Bahamas I returned to the Caymans long enough to tell my money manager to change my portfolio from conservative investments to high risk ones. I figured even if my stocks tanked I could win the money back playing blackjack. He sold off my blue chip stocks and dumped all the money into tech stocks such as Microsoft, Dell, Oracle, Cisco Systems, Qualcomm, and many other lesser known companies.

I flew up to New Hampshire for weekends with Jill in September and October, and in between we spoke regularly on the telephone. Once a week or so I'd surprise her with a delivery of flowers or chocolates to her desk at work. I thought perhaps I was overdoing it but I later learned it is not possible to overdo flowers and chocolates. She told me her coworkers ended up eating most of the candy because she always worried about her figure, but she loved the idea of getting chocolates and never asked me to stop sending them.

In November of that year her boss, Governor Steve Merrill, easily won reelection to his second term. He was so popular the election was more or less a formality and it caused none of the usual stress and angst amongst his staff.

We both went home to our parents' houses in Connecticut for Thanksgiving. Although we spent Thanksgiving Day itself apart, over the long holiday weekend we got together several times and met each other's families. Meeting the families made our relationship start to feel serious, at least to me.

Before leaving Connecticut Jill and I agreed to go to the Bahamas together, a big step for both of us, for a week over the Christmas holiday period. Jill stubbornly insisted on paying her own way until I told her how much Mulvaney & Proust was (officially) paying me. I don't know what she thought I was making up to then but after that she stopped arguing about splitting the cost.

Immediately upon returning to Virginia I formally asked Jefferson for permission to go to the Bahamas over Christmas, and he consented. Jill had no such issues with her vacation, of course, and we quickly worked out the details. Since we would both be home in Connecticut for Christmas with our families we would fly together from Bradley Field to Miami, Florida, then make the short hop to Nassau in the Bahamas. I was counting the days.

******

Things began to get a little screwy in Russia a few days later. The long simmering tensions between the Muslims in Chechnya and the government in Moscow were starting to boil over. Jefferson had me bird dogging the Russian President Yeltsin, some of his military leaders, and even some of the Chechens.

On December 1st the Russians started a major aerial bombing campaign in Chechnya. I thought Jefferson would have me sleeping in the headquarters building as he had in the previous crisis, but he said it wasn't necessary. All the analysts predicted the Chechens would quickly fold under the onslaught, and if it came to an actual ground war everyone agreed the Russians would crush them in a matter of days. Everyone was wrong.

The Chechens shrugged off the aerial bombardment and on December 11th the Russians rolled a massive army towards Chechnya. Halfway there a remarkable thing happened: the Russian general leading the army stopped the advance and resigned in protest, saying it was wrong to use the Russian army inside Russia. Many senior military officers followed his example. The CIA was caught completely flatfooted and went into full panic mode. All Christmas vacations were cancelled and I was ordered to sleep in the headquarters building. I argued heatedly with Jefferson about losing my vacation, telling him how important it was to me and Jill. I already had airline tickets, hotel reservations, tours arranged, etc. He kept his cool, as always. He apologized profusely but said it was just a part of life in the spy business, and referred me to my employment contract. I didn't have a leg to stand on.

I delayed breaking the news to Jill in the faint hope the crisis would end abruptly and my vacation would be saved. However, that very night when I *shifted* to Russia I observed Russian troops sabotaging their own gear, disabling armored vehicles and personnel carriers by the dozens in order not to continue on to Chechnya. Such acts could mean death by firing squad. The troops would never dare such a thing unless ordered to do so by their commanders. A military revolt was underway and the uprising in Chechnya was going to last a long time. The Russian government might even be toppled in a military coup. My vacation plans were toast. I briefly entertained the idea of not telling Jefferson what I had seen, but in the end, my sense of duty won out and I resigned myself to a miserable Christmas.

Jefferson helped me work out a cover story to explain to Jill my sudden cancellation of our Christmas plans. A critical business situation had arisen in Germany. Tens of millions of dollars in contracts were at risk and Mulvaney & Proust was pulling out all the stops to keep the contracts from going to a competitor. I was their point man and would be in Europe for several weeks, perhaps even a month or more. It sounded pretty lame to me, but when I told Jill over the phone she said that although she was disappointed, she understood. Many months later she told me she didn't believe it for a second. She thought I had gotten cold feet and was rethinking our relationship. It hurt her badly and nearly wrecked our budding romance.

******

Near the end of January 1995 the First Chechen War, as it came to be known, had ground to a stalemate. After several failed attempts, the Russian army, led by a new commander, had finally taken Grozny, the Chechen capital city. However, the Chechens continued to fight on in bloody guerilla warfare. Once it became apparent the army would remain loyal to President Yeltsin the CIA stood down from crisis mode and things got back to normal for me. I still flew to Chechnya most nights, but I was back to sleeping in my own bed and "working" in my office at Mulvaney. I had seen so much carnage on the battlefield I was becoming immune to it. In the years that followed I would see much more in various places around the world. You either find a way to shrug it off or lose your mind.

The last weekend of January I flew to New Hampshire to see Jill after six weeks of very limited communications. We met for dinner at her favorite restaurant. I could tell right away she was troubled. "How was Germany?" she asked.

"Okay, I guess. I was extremely busy and had very little time off. Compared to being in the Bahamas with you it was the pits. I am so, so sorry about having to cancel our vacation plans, Jill. Can you ever forgive me?"

"Well, the regular deliveries of bouquets and chocolates helped, but let's face it, my desk in Concord doesn't compare to a beach in Nassau."

"I'll make it up to you, Jill. We'll get to the Bahamas, and anywhere else you want to go. Just tell me when you can go and I'll make all the arrangements. After messing up my Christmas vacation my boss owes me."

"What companies were you working with in Germany? As an economist I'm quite interested to hear the details. Don't worry, you won't bore me."

Even though she was smiling I could tell Jill wasn't just making polite dinner conversation. She didn't quite believe my story and was interrogating me. Jefferson had warned me this might happen and I was prepared for it. "I'd love to discuss it all with you, but unfortunately I'm bound by a non-disclosure agreement. The principals can publicly announce whatever they want whenever they choose, but my company, as consultants, has to stay in the background. I'm sorry."

A long, uncomfortable silence followed as we both picked at our food, pretending to eat. Finally, Jill blurted out, "Pete, were you really in Germany or did you just have second thoughts about our relationship? Wait! Never mind, don't answer that. I want this to work, Pete, I want us to work. I really, truly do. I care about you very much and hope you feel the same way about me."

She paused to sip some water, holding up her hand to indicate she wasn't finished speaking yet. When she had gathered herself she said, "Just tell me this - look me in the eyes and tell me there's no other woman involved - I need to hear you say that." Her voice cracked at the end and her eyes brimmed with tears.

My heart broke to see this amazing woman so torn up, and knowing it was all my fault. I took her face in both my hands and brought us close together. "Jill, there is no other woman, only you. I'm falling in love with you. Maybe I'm already in love with you and just too scared to say it out loud or admit it to myself. My work kept me from going to the Bahamas, and I swear to God that's all there is to it."

We kissed across the table and it felt right, and good, but suddenly I thought of the hitchhiker, and that unique feeling of oneness we had shared. Was I lying to Jill, and to myself? Was there another woman in my life?

Chapter Thirteen

I often think, sitting here in my prison cell, in addition to this book I could write another entitled "The Real History of the World," or "The History of the World through the eyes of a CIA Spy." I found myself present at some of the most important events of recent times, and much of what is widely believed to be true and accurate is either wrong or woefully incomplete. I realize, however, you are reading this primarily due to your interest in astral projection and my life as a remote viewer for the CIA, so I will endeavor to stay on topic and avoid delving into historical minutia unless it had a major impact upon my life.

I worked very hard in the first half of 1995 to restore Jill's faith in me. I flew to Concord two or three weekends a month so we could spend time together. I offered to pay for her to fly down to Virginia anytime she wanted but she always demurred. I could tell she still didn't fully trust me. Perhaps she imagined if she came to Virginia she would discover my secret wife. I so badly wanted to tell her my "secret wife" was the CIA. I argued endlessly with Jefferson about it but, as always, he cited national security and reminded me of the contract I had signed forbidding disclosure of my real employment status.

On a Sunday evening in July 1995 Jill phoned to tell me she would be coming to Washington, D.C. the next morning to attend an economics conference at Georgetown University. The conference was a Monday to Friday thing but her evenings would be free and she asked if we could spend them together. It struck me as extremely unlikely Jill had just been informed of the conference. She probably had her travel plans in place at least a week previously, yet she waited until the last minute to inform me. I realized this was a test and attributed it to her lingering doubts about my monogamy. I did not remark on the short notice and simply told her I was thrilled we would be spending more time together. Jefferson was not so enthusiastic.

As usual, major world events of interest to the CIA were happening and I was right in the middle of them every night. The war in Bosnia was in full swing. A horrific massacre of thousands of civilians had just occurred in Srebrenica. I was traveling there every night trying to obtain an accurate accounting of the number of dead and attempting to identify the perpetrators for later prosecution for war crimes. A Bosnian Serb military unit known as the Scorpions had committed the atrocity. Each night I would *shift* there and memorize the faces of as many Bosnian military officers I could find, then match the faces to photos from the CIA files. In a few instances I sat down with a CIA sketch artist if no matching photo was found.

Jefferson was concerned I would disrupt my sleep patterns if I stayed up late in the evenings with Jill. I promised him we'd be in bed by midnight every night. It took him a second, but when he got my meaning he wasn't pleased. "You can't be up all night screwing your girlfriend when you're supposed to be in Bosnia!"

Without going into the nitty-gritty details, I grudgingly admitted to my boss I was incapable of having sex all night and would get plenty of sleep. I was mentally preparing my arguments about why Jill should spend the nights in my CIA-provided house when he floored me by saying, "Don't even think about staying overnight in her hotel room. If you're going to spend the night together it has to be in your house." Well, okay then, you're the boss.

Jill's visit was a significant turning point in our relationship. We spent our evenings hitting many of my favorite haunts and slept every night at my house. She arranged to fly back to Concord on Sunday evening so we had the weekend together after the conference ended as well. I gave her the grand tour of all the famous Washington, D.C. landmarks. With my boss's permission I also showed her around Mulvaney & Proust, introducing her to many of my colleagues there, including Jefferson himself. And yes, I flew to Bosnia every night and did my job.

It was like a great weight had been lifted from Jill's shoulders. Her secret fears of me having a wife or another girlfriend were vanquished. I sensed her ebullient mood and before she left on Sunday we discussed marriage for the first time.

******

August rolled around and it was contract renewal time again. Jefferson pressed hard for me to sign a multi-year agreement, but I refused. In fact, I had little interest in continuing my work with the CIA. The constant exposure to war and all its ugliness was beating me down. Counting nuclear warheads on a submarine was boring but counting horribly mangled dead bodies every night was killing my soul.

Jefferson promised to find other assignments for me and to send me to war zones less often. He reminded me of the CIA's host of on-call psychiatrists and psychologists who were standing by to treat or counsel me as desired. He offered to double my salary, both official and unofficial.

By way of explaining my disinterest in continued employment I told him, "Jill and I are probably going to get married next year."

"Congratulations, Pete! I think that's wonderful. She seems like a fine young woman."

"Thomas, don't you get it? I can't go on lying to her about what I do. I'm not going to lie to my wife - it goes against everything I believe in. You won't let me tell her the truth and I can't lie to her, so the solution seems simple - I'll find another line of work."

Jefferson gave it some thought, or at least he pretended to do so. Looking back on it, I'm sure he had been expecting this for some time and had long ago prepared his answer. "Pete, the majority of CIA personnel are married. Their spouses know who they work for. When you feel the time is right you can tell Jill you work for the CIA. What you can never tell her is exactly what you do for us. That's not negotiable.

"I suggest you tell her you are an analyst. Be vague about specifics. She works in politics, she knows about security clearances and keeping secrets. Bring her down here one of these days and I'll personally escort her through headquarters, give her the whole dog and pony show the VIPs get, because as your wife she will be a VIP. She'll love it, the spouses always do. Then we'll swear her to secrecy and remind her that to the rest of the world you're only an executive with Mulvaney & Proust. How's that sound?"

"It sounds like you want me to lie to my wife. I told you, Thomas, I'm not going to lie to her anymore. How am I going to explain my absence the next time you order me to sleep every night in CIA headquarters? What happens when you send me to Europe or elsewhere for some crisis? An analyst wouldn't need to leave his desk. For that matter, an analyst wouldn't need the Mulvaney & Proust legend."

Jefferson smiled. "Actually, Pete, some of our analysts travel quite often, but let her figure things out for herself, it's better that way. Trust me on this, I've been in the business a long time. If she pushes you on what you really do and you feel you must tell her something, then tell her you're a field operative, and that's true in a way, but that's as far as you can go. You can never, under any circumstances, talk about the project. The non-disclosure agreements you have already signed are valid for life, and beyond."

I laughed out loud. "Beyond life? Kind of melodramatic, isn't it?"

Jefferson was not amused. "Not at all. 'Beyond life' simply means you cannot arrange to have anything published about the project after your death. It's the legal phrase in your agreement. Is your eidetic memory failing you?"

"No, I recall it. I just don't like the idea of lying to Jill. It nearly destroyed us once already. You could have saved us a lot of heartburn by telling me this months ago."

"Months ago I wouldn't have given you permission to tell her. Girlfriends and boyfriends come and go. We can't have our people shooting their mouths off to every pretty face they meet. Now that you've told me you're thinking of marriage it changes things."

"I'm still not comfortable with the idea of not leveling with her. A lie by omission is still a lie."

"There are degrees of truth, Pete, and sometimes omissions are necessary. It's not just here at the CIA. Do you think our senior political leaders tell their spouses everything? How about our military officers? If they did we'd soon have no secrets at all, and no national security. Once she knows you work for the CIA she'll understand. Many of our spouses get a kick out of living their part of the cover story. It's part of life in the fast lane."

Jefferson seemed to love this cloak and dagger stuff, but I hated it, and decided to tweak him a bit. "So that's it? I just tell her I work for the CIA? What if she's a Russian spy?"

The CIA man didn't laugh, and his answer chilled me to the bone. "She's not, Pete. After your first couple of dates we did a thorough background check on her. It's standard operating procedure. She's a true blue American girl."

In August of 1995 I signed on for another year. True to his word, Jefferson had doubled my salary to $400,000 a year from Mulvaney and four million a year tax free to my offshore accounts. I'm sure I could have easily gotten double or even triple that much. Four million dollars wasn't even pocket change to the federal government, it was more like a tiny bit of lint in one of their seemingly bottomless pockets filled with everyone else's money.

Chapter Fourteen

I loved Jill, of that I had no doubt. At the same time, my feelings for Susan, the hitchhiker, haunted me. I barely knew her, yet I felt closer to her than any other person in my life, even my family. Was it love? If it was, then what were my feelings for Jill? I had to know the answers before I committed to marriage.

I had been trying for months to find Susan on my own. I hadn't seen her in the real world or the astral world since our meeting three years previously. Jefferson told me she came to headquarters fairly often. Each night when I first went out of body I spent a few minutes searching CIA headquarters for her, but I never saw her. In frustration I finally asked Jefferson to tell her to contact me.

"Pete, you know I can't do that. It's against policy."

"You said the same thing three years ago, Thomas, right before you arranged for me to meet her. You make the policy here, you told me that yourself. This is a mental health thing. I'm going crazy, and I need to talk with her about a few things only another astral traveler would understand. If I have a mental breakdown a few months down the road how is that going to fit into your precious policy?"

Jefferson knew when he was beaten. "Okay, Pete, I guess I knew this was coming. Actually, I'm surprised it took this long. I'll tell her you want to see her. If she decides to see you you'll have to meet in one of our SCIFs, of course.

******

I met with Susan three days later, in one of the CIA's special compartmented intelligence facilities, as Jefferson had mandated. She looked thinner than the last time we met, if that was possible. Even her hair seemed thinner. It was like she was melting away.

Jefferson pushed her wheelchair into the room and, unlike the last time, he left and closed the door behind himself, leaving us alone. "Susan! I'm so glad you decided to see me. I…"

She raised a skeletal hand and stopped me in mid-sentence. She wheeled herself close to my chair, removed a small afghan from her legs and surprised me by draping it over both our heads. When we were covered up she leaned in close and whispered in my ear. "I don't trust Jefferson. I'll come to you in the night, in the other world. Stay here for a while, as if we talked." With that, she leaned back in her wheelchair and relaxed. Just speaking those few words seemed to take a lot out of her. In moments her eyes glazed over and I knew I was alone in the room. I waited for another fifteen minutes but she did not stir. I gently removed the lapghan from our heads and replaced it on her lap, then left the room.

******

Jefferson was beside himself, but I was adamant. "Thomas, what Susan and I talked about is none of your concern. All you need to know is I feel much better than I did before and I'm ready to continue my work."

None of that was true, of course, since Susan and I had not really talked at all. She obviously suspected Jefferson had video surveillance in place for our meeting and used her lapghan and whispering to foil it. Based upon the degree of Jefferson's ire I had no doubt she was correct. I could only hope Susan kept her word and came to me in the astral plane.

Two nights later, she did. I was in my third REM interval, the forty minute one, and had just gone out of body. I sensed her presence in my bedroom immediately, but as before, I did not know for certain it was her. Only after she allowed me to touch her did I know. Again, that indescribable feeling of oneness enveloped me. I was euphoric. I meant to say hello and thank her for coming to me, but instead I mentally blurted out, "I love you!"

She gently replied, "No, Pete, this is not love. It's a wonderful, special feeling, but not love. Whatever it is, I believe it's something we can never experience on earth, only here, in the astral plane. Perhaps we'll find this feeling again in heaven, if such a thing as heaven exists.

"Every time I meet anyone in the astral plane this is the feeling we share. Others have told me the same thing. Eventually you will meet someone else here and feel it again with them, complete strangers. But strangers is the wrong word. There are no strangers here, only friends you haven't met yet.

"I know you are questioning your feelings for Jill and comparing them to what you're feeling right now. Yes, I've been watching you on occasion over the past few years. I live a very physically limited and boring life in the real world. Here in the other world I can fly!

"I care about you, Pete. I care about you very much, but you and Jill are lovers. You and I are friends. Special friends to be sure, but friendship is not love. Be content with that, Pete, as I am, as we must be."

We "spoke" for my whole forty minute REM phase and I learned much from her, and about her. Susan is undoubtedly the most remarkable person I have ever met in my life. In order to protect her privacy I am not going to share most of the conversation with you. I will tell you she gave me a stern warning: "Beware of Jefferson."

******

Not long after meeting with Susan I flew to Concord to be with Jill. I had every intention of telling her I worked for the CIA and asking her to marry me but I just couldn't seem to find the right moment. All too soon the weekend was over and I had to return to Virginia. I convinced her to fly down to see me for our next get together.

In October 1995 Jill came to Mulvaney & Proust for the second time. By prearrangement, Jefferson met us there. After a great deal of introspection I had realized I was terrified of telling Jill I worked for the CIA. To me, telling her I worked for the CIA was tantamount to admitting I had been lying to her for the past year. I was so ashamed I just couldn't bring myself to do it. To my great surprise Jefferson bailed me out. "Bring her down here, Pete, and I'll tell her. We'll put it all on me - that way I'll be the bad guy, not you. If she gets ticked off it'll be at me and not you. After all, I'm the one who wouldn't let you tell her."

Jefferson was smooth; I have to give him that. After a few minutes small talk at Mulvaney he told Jill it was time she got a tour of our other work space, as he put it. We stepped out of Mulvaney's front door and into a limousine Jefferson had somehow conjured out of thin air. During the short drive to CIA headquarters Jefferson talked about everything except where we were going. It wasn't until we got out of the limo in front of the main building that Jill realized where we were. She spoke four words, "Is this a joke?" then lapsed into a stunned silence. Ten minutes into the tour of CIA headquarters Jill laughed at some clever pun Jefferson made and I knew everything was going to be okay. That evening, in a romantic spot overlooking Chesapeake Bay I asked Jill to marry me. For some strange reason this gorgeous, intelligent, highly educated and accomplished woman said yes.

******

We set a wedding date for May 1996 in our home town in Connecticut. Neither one of us was particularly interested in having a big wedding. Jill had been previously married and I was not the type of person who had dozens of close friends and loved to socialize at parties. Still, we were made to understand it meant a lot to our families, so we acquiesced. Thankfully, both our mothers had enthusiastically volunteered to handle all the wedding planning details.

As we had the year before, Jill and I planned on spending a lot of time together in Connecticut over the Thanksgiving holiday period. Unfortunately, for the second time in less than a year I was forced to cancel my vacation plans and remain on duty in Virginia. Radovan Karadzic, the head of the Bosnian Serb army, and Ratko Mladic, his chief of staff, had been declared war criminals by the United Nations. They immediately went into hiding. With the details of the Srebrenica massacre now squarely in the public eye President Clinton was pressing our military and CIA hard to find and arrest them. Even though I was missing Thanksgiving with Jill and my family I felt good about spearheading the effort to find these butchers. I had witnessed their gruesome handiwork firsthand and badly wanted them brought to justice. Regrettably, I and all the others looking for these mass murderers were unsuccessful and they remained free for years to come.

Now that Jill knew I worked for the CIA I didn't have to lie to her about why I would miss Thanksgiving. Ironically, to explain my absence she told everyone back home the same cover story about a German business deal that I had told her the previous Christmas. She later told me it was kind of fun and exciting covering for me. Jefferson's comments about "life in the fast lane" came back to me and I had to concede, once again, he had been right on the money.

Chapter Fifteen

Jill and I were hoping to make it to the Bahamas the day after Christmas this year, but even though we both had approved vacations, based upon my track record she wasn't overly excited. In the end, everything worked out for us and we spent a fabulous, sun-soaked week in paradise, much of it underwater.

Lying together on a beach blanket under the stars one balmy night, Jill suddenly sat up straight. "Pete, let's get married tomorrow. I don't want to wait anymore."

"What about our big wedding back home in May? Everyone's looking forward to it, and our mothers would never forgive us."

Jill snuggled next to me on the blanket and looked into my eyes. "I know you're more than just an analyst for the CIA, Pete. The story Jefferson told me never really rang true to me and you having to miss Thanksgiving confirmed it. I'm laying here loving you and loving this place but I worry any minute that fancy cell phone of yours will ring and you'll have to go back to work. If it wasn't possible you wouldn't be carrying the darn thing."

Plaintively, she went on, "Sure, I know our families are looking forward to our big wedding. Honestly, I wasn't too keen about it at first but the idea's been growing on me. The idea of the wedding being postponed at the last minute for some national security crisis has also been growing on me. I don't want to worry about it anymore. Let's get married tomorrow and be done with it. We can still plan on a big wedding reception back home next May. It wouldn't be such a big deal if the reception was postponed because of your work. Please say yes."

I kept a straight face but inwardly chuckled at Jill feeling like she had to give me the hard sell. Of course I said yes. She didn't know it, but she had me at "Let's get married tomorrow."

******

Jill and I welcomed in the new year of 1996 still in the Bahamas, our idyllic vacation uninterrupted by anything other than a short thunderstorm late one afternoon. We flew back to our jobs the next day, tanned, exhausted, and, oh yes, married.

Being married with your spouse living and working 500 miles away is not the ideal situation, but we both knew it was only temporary. Under our original plan we would have been married in May and I would have quit my job in August. That sounds a lot better, doesn't it? Now we would just have to deal with the geographic separation a little while longer.

It was a twelve hour drive from my house in Mclean, Virginia to Jill's apartment in Concord, New Hampshire, but only a ninety minute flight. Double that for airport wait times and getting to and from the airport and it was still only three short hours.

We were young, newly married, and madly in love with each other. And I was rich. A lot wealthier than Jill knew.

You know the old saying about money not buying happiness? That may be true, but if you're already happy money can most definitely make life much easier and even happier for you. Often we would meet at a country inn or bed and breakfast in upstate New York, Pennsylvania or Connecticut. Atlantic City, with its casinos, was another destination, as was the Foxwoods Resort Casino in Connecticut. All these places were more or less halfway between us so the drives were relatively short. With one exception, I always insisted Jill pick the location for our weekends together. I felt it might help mitigate the fact we couldn't be together every day like a normal married couple. Every weekend was like another honeymoon.

February 19th that year was President's Day, a federal holiday, giving everyone a three day weekend. Jill and I both had it off. I decided to surprise her and told her I would pick our meeting place. I chose Key West, Florida and her airline tickets were waiting for her at the airport. We had a wonderful time.

Jefferson had forbidden me to tell Jill my actual job at the CIA, but he made no such prohibition about another of my secrets - my eidetic memory. Jill knew I was smart, after all, we had been in many of the same honors classes together in high school, but she had no idea I had a photographic memory.

I told her about it during our Bahamas vacation and proved it to her at the blackjack tables. I won more than enough to pay for our entire vacation several times over. Upon leaving one of the casinos, however, I was politely but firmly told never to return.

Prior to Jill learning of my eidetic memory every time we discussed marriage she agonized over where we would live once married. She loved what she was doing and really wanted to remain as part of Governor Merrill's staff. She was one of his inner circle advisors in his second term and she greatly enjoyed the game of politics. He was immensely popular and had no credible challenger for reelection to his third term. Historically, no New Hampshire governor had ever served more than three two year terms, so Jill was looking at staying in New Hampshire until January of 1999. After that, with six years' experience on a state governor's staff, she could easily find a political job in Washington, D.C. The problem, as she explained it to me, was she loved me so much she wasn't willing to live apart for all that time. She loved her job, but she loved me more. I was making $400,000 a year with the CIA (she didn't know about the secret four million going offshore) while she was making $39,000 a year as the New Hampshire governor's economic advisor. Jill held a doctorate in economics, but she didn't need her PhD. to figure this one out. It made no sense economically for me, making ten times her salary, to quit my job and move to New Hampshire. She thought the only way for us to be together every day was to quit her job. My eidetic memory changed the equation for her. I assured her I had quite a large nest egg already and with my photographic memory I could always make a very good living gambling. I was tired of working for the CIA anyway and ready for a change. We agreed when my contract expired in August I would move up to New Hampshire.

Chapter Sixteen

On April Fool's Day Governor Merrill gathered his inner circle of advisors and solemnly informed them he had decided not to run for reelection to a third term. Everyone thought he was joking. Some still didn't believe it until he publicly announced it to the shocked citizens of his state a few days later. He simply had had enough of politics and wanted to spend more time with his family.

It left Jill and the rest of his staff scrambling for jobs. The governor recommended her to several Republican congressmen but nothing panned out. 1996 was a presidential election year and all the national politicians were intensely focused on that. No one seemed to have the time for anything else.

I commiserated with her and told her I would happily live with her anywhere she found a job, in politics or not. She shotgunned her resume to all the republican governors but found no takers. Pete Wilson, the governor of California and a friend of Merrill, sent her a nice handwritten letter. He was sorry he did not have a position on his staff for her but he happened to know an assistant professor of economics position was opening up at the University of California, San Diego. Wilson had been the mayor of San Diego for many years. He wrote he would be happy to recommend her for the job if she was interested. As governor, and with his San Diego connections, it virtually guaranteed her the post. If hired, she would start teaching in the fall, at the beginning of the new school year. Both

Governor Wilson and Governor Merrill told her a few years in academia would burnish her credentials and make it easier for her to return to politics if she desired.

Jill had never been particularly interested in teaching and she was not overly excited about the UCSD job. I, on the other hand, had fond memories of San Diego from my four years there in college and would be happy to return. San Diego has the best weather in America. Miles of beaches, with Mexico, mountains and the desert all just a short drive away. That was all good, but it was the prospect of scuba diving year round that sold her on living there.

Jill applied for the position and in very short order, no doubt thanks to Governor Wilson, she had the job. With our future plans now settled I told Jefferson I would definitely not be renewing my contract. He was displeased, to put it mildly, and spent many hours over the next month or so futilely trying to talk me into staying. Eventually he came to the realization no amount of money, perks, or other inducements would change my mind, and he gave up.

******

In May, without my having asked, Jefferson gave me the Friday before and the Monday after our Saturday wedding reception off. I think it was his way of showing me he held no grudge about me leaving the CIA. Whatever his reasons, I wasn't about to say no.

The wedding celebration, as Jill liked to call it, went off without a hitch. Get it? We had already gotten "hitched" back in the Bahamas. If you're not laughing, it's only because you're not sitting in prison like I am, where I search desperately for humor in my dreary little world.

Our mothers were glowing and crowing about the whole thing; congratulating each other on what a fine job they did organizing the event. Being mothers, they also took the opportunity to scold us for our unnecessary Bahamas elopement. Never a big fan of large social gatherings, I trudged through all the obligatory handshaking, hugs and small talk with long ago friends and some barely known relatives, most of whom were quickly becoming intoxicated on all the free beer and liquor.

My brother Stan, still living the bachelor life and loving it, introduced me to Linda, a girl he had recently met. She and I hit it off immediately when I learned she had also served in the army in Operation Desert Storm. Once I completed my required rounds with everyone else, I circled back to Stan and Linda to continue our conversation. It turned out Linda had enlisted in the army to honor the memory of her father, much as I had chosen to be an armor officer to honor mine. Her father, a career soldier, had gone back to Vietnam for his third tour in 1970 and never came home.

"He was shot down in a helicopter along with eleven other men in Cambodia," she told me. "The bodies of my father and one other man were never found. They were listed as Missing in Action for several years. They never showed up on any of the lists of American POWs and were not among the men released by the Vietnamese in 1973. In 1979 my dad was officially declared dead. I'm sure they're right, especially after all this time.

"For a while my mom and I were involved with the League of Families and other POW/MIA organizations. Some of those folks make a very convincing argument that a few of the missing men are still alive, being held somewhere. I don't really believe that, it's just been too many years, but there's a tiny part of me that will never be sure. Did you know at the end of the Vietnam War over 2,500 men were listed as Missing in Action? Every one of them left behind family and friends who can only wonder, even if just a little bit, as I do."

Linda and I went on to talk of happier things and shared a bunch of funny anecdotes about our time in the army, but it was the story of her missing father that stuck with me. I realized I was in a unique position to settle the lingering doubts of her and thousands like her.

Chapter Seventeen

In the nine months since signing my last one year contract things had settled into a routine for me at work. True to his word, Jefferson sent me to Chechnya far less often, though I still went once a week on average.

I was spending far more time in the Middle East. Saddam Hussein was daily violating the United Nations sanctions that had been imposed on him after Desert Storm. I was searching every possible hiding place looking for his hidden weapons of mass destruction. The Iranians were always up to something. The Israelis constantly needed information from U.S. intelligence on something or someone. I *shifted* to the Middle East three or four nights every week.

Jefferson told me one day if he had a dozen more people with my abilities it still wouldn't be enough to fulfill all the intelligence requests he received. It was his subtle way of letting me know he was watching my back and keeping his word not to burn me out. I think he was exaggerating, but nonetheless, it was clear he was using me for less psychologically taxing assignments. I appreciated it very much, but it didn't stop me from asking him for something more.

"Thomas, I have a favor to ask. I've been reading up on the POW/MIA issue and it has me intrigued. Lots of credible, serious people believe there may be U.S. POWs still alive in captivity somewhere, especially those from the Vietnam

War. It occurred to me I am uniquely qualified to find the truth.

"I know you just told me how incredibly busy we are but please, hear me out. I want to search for U.S. POWs. I've given it a lot of thought and it'll be easier than you think. You give me a list of all the prisons in Southeast Asia that might possibly be holding U.S. POWs. It should only take an analyst a couple of days to produce an updated list. Surely one already exists. Once I have the list, on my own time I'll familiarize myself with the exact location of each prison, enabling me to *shift* there instantly. I could search a prison in a matter of minutes, then *shift* directly to the next one, and the next."

Seeing the frown on Jefferson's face I pressed on before he could object. "How hard could it be? Combat operations in Vietnam ended twenty two years ago. Military personnel, the actual warfighters, are between the ages of 18-45, with the vast majority in their 20s and 30s. All I have to do is look for any non-Asian prisoners in their 40s to 60s. I'm sure there are Americans in prison in Asia for criminal offenses, but they'll be in regular prisons. POWs would be hidden in military prisons. If I find any likely prospects I'll look at photo arrays, as I did with the Bosnian Serbs to make a positive identification."

Jefferson was shaking his head side to side, the way my father used to do when as a kid I ran some cockamamie idea past him. He stopped to look at me and asked, "Are you finished?"

When I nodded he said, "I won't bother giving you the hundred reasons why your half-baked idea won't work. No, I'll just give you one - we can't spare the time. I should be working you seven days a week 365. There'll never be time for optional tasking. And don't tell me you'll only do it on your days off. You're with your wife every minute of every weekend. You'd need access to detailed maps and other CIA data that could only be accessed in a secure facility."

I had anticipated this objection and was ready for it. "I'll do my prep work on weekdays after normal working hours, on my own time, here in this building. And yes, I'll only look for POWs on weekends. I give you my word on that."

Jefferson was back to the head shaking. "Pete, have you really thought this through? We're not just talking about looking in Vietnam. There's also Cambodia, Laos, and Burma. All those countries were and are far friendlier with Vietnam than they are with us. Both China and Russia have military ties with Vietnam, then and now. They're gigantic countries, each with hundreds of military facilities. And since China is a player, then North Korea must also be considered. All those countries hated us then and still hate us now. The list of military prisons would be in the hundreds, maybe even a couple of thousand. And if the prisoners are kept somewhere other than a known military prison where does that leave you? It's an impossible task."

"Thomas, everything you've said makes sense. One big thing you haven't said is 'You're barking up the wrong tree. There are no live POWs.'"

The CIA man paused, weighing his words carefully. "I don't know that any U.S. POWs are alive today. There was a time, shortly after that war ended, when many of the people here were certain we left hundreds behind. I was working as a field agent back then, in Europe, so I had no firsthand knowledge. Even over there, though, we heard the scuttlebutt. But there was never anything solid, what we call 'actionable intelligence.'"

He sighed deeply. "We have a list of military prisons for every country on the planet. How up to date they are is another matter. How many prisons do you think you could search in a weekend?"

"I'm not sure. It would depend upon how big each one is, how many rooms, whether the rooms were lighted or dark. Ten, at least. Maybe twenty."

"Pete, you're leaving the firm in ten weeks. That's 200 prisons, tops, out of a thousand. Four out of every five will go unsearched."

"Maybe so, but I'd still like to try. It's important to me, Thomas."

Jefferson put his hands over his face and kneaded his forehead. Finally, he looked up at me. "Okay, Pete, I'll set it up."

******

When presenting my argument to search for POWs I had arrogantly asked Jefferson, "How hard could it be?" I now knew the answer: pretty damn hard. I started with

Vietnamese military prisons. The "updated" list of fifty six locations was a joke. The first prison I searched held thousands of prisoners - chickens. The location of the second prison was either incorrect or the prison building had been demolished. I flew an expanding circle search at about 1000 feet above the ground but the thick jungle quickly defeated me. Next I tried actually flying through the trees, but I could only see a few feet in any direction. I never found it. The third prison location was in an urban area. The building I *shifted* into was not a prison but rather an administrative complex. I quickly searched fourteen nearby buildings before finding the prison, which was empty and disused. One of the prisons I searched actually held small numbers of Asian men. In one of them the basement floor was completely blacked out and so dark I couldn't see a thing. The thought of American POWs being held all these years was horrifying. The idea they might be held in total darkness was too disturbing to contemplate, but I had to be sure. I made a mental note to keep checking it until I found it lighted.

I had memorized the locations of twenty five Vietnamese military prisons, hoping to check them all the first weekend. The estimate I had given Jefferson of 10-20 turned out to be a little off - I found and searched seven.

Chapter Eighteen

Tuesday afternoon, June 25th, 1996, Jefferson phoned me at my desk at Mulvaney and brusquely ordered me to report to him immediately at his office in headquarters. Upon arrival I could sense the tension, and quickly found out why. Terrorists had just bombed the Khobar Towers building in Dhahran, Saudi Arabia, where U.S. Air Force personnel were housed. The eight story high rise building was nearly completely destroyed by a massive truck bomb, and about one third of it had collapsed into rubble. Jefferson told me I would be sleeping in the headquarters building. My mission that night was to thoroughly search the rubble for survivors. Specially trained search dogs would be sent, but the attack had caught everyone flatfooted and it would take time to get the dogs and handlers there.

That night, due to the urgency of the situation, I *shifted* to Dhahran during my first REM interval even though it only lasts about ten minutes. It was 11:30 PM my time, 6:30 AM in Saudi Arabia. I only had enough time to see it was still chaotic there. Large groups of people were searching the rubble. Armed military personnel from the U.S. and other nations were guarding the perimeter. At least a dozen filled body bags were laid out in a parking lot. Ambulances were arriving and leaving regularly. Walking wounded were everywhere. It looked eerily similar to the Oklahoma City bombing of a year earlier. My time was up and I *shifted* back to my bed.

Ninety minutes later I returned to REM sleep and Dhahran. This time I plunged right into the debris pile and began searching. I quickly located a human leg but was unable to find the rest of the body. I popped up out of the rubble to note the location, then went back in. With just a few minutes left on my second REM period I found a survivor, a young black man in a tattered working uniform. He was trapped, bleeding from many different places, and appeared to be severely injured. I flew straight up out of the debris and was memorizing my exact position when I felt myself *shift* back to my bed, my second REM interval over. I woke myself up and wrote down my best estimate of the location of the survivor and the leg, using triangulation from obvious landmarks such as the corners of buildings or parking lots. Then I phoned the duty officer and told him I had time critical information to be delivered to Jefferson. Less than thirty seconds later a young woman entered my room after knocking softly at the door. I handed her the paper and she left without a word.

I desperately wanted to return to Dhahran, but I was too jazzed up to go right back to sleep. I lay in my bed, using the sleep-inducing self-hypnosis techniques the shrinks had taught me. After twenty minutes that seemed like hours I drifted off to sleep. Ninety minutes later I was in REM and back in Dhahran.

Normally, my third REM phase would last about forty minutes, but waking up had disrupted my sleep pattern. I had no idea how long this REM interval would last. Upon arrival at the scene I first returned to the survivor I had found. Most of the debris above him had been removed and a concentrated effort was underway to carefully lift him clear. Jefferson had wasted no time getting my info to the scene.

I resumed my grid pattern search and discovered another survivor, a very young man, probably still only a teenager. Both his legs were crushed flat, his torso laying at an impossible backward angle to them. It was hard to believe he was still alive, but his eyes were open and he turned his head to look at me. Huh?

I saw his lips moving and I heard him say, "Are you an angel?"

Flabbergasted, it took me a moment to realize I hadn't actually heard him speak. He had communicated to me mentally the same way Susan and I "talked" in the astral plane, yet he was conscious. And he was dying.

I wanted to comfort him, lie to him and tell him he was going to be okay, but I didn't know if lying was even possible in the astral plane. "I… uh, I'm a friend." Susan's words came back to me. "We're all friends here; you don't have anything to worry about."

"You're so beautiful. Will you hold me? I'm cold."

I moved closer, until I was in contact with his chest. That inexpressible feeling of oneness with another person enveloped me. The dying airman's eyes filled with wonder and joy. "You *are* an angel," the young man said. There was the tiniest sound, that of an iridescently beautiful soap bubble shining in the sun, suddenly winking out of existence. The feeling of oneness, and the airman, were gone.

******

Four hours later Jefferson knocked on my door and entered with two cups of steaming hot coffee. "I knew you were awake," he said, pointing to a corner of the room where a pinhead camera resided.

In fact, I had lain awake for hours before getting out of bed and performing my usual morning routine. I gratefully took the coffee he offered.

"You did good last night, Pete. You saved a life. If it wasn't for your eff…" he saw I was crying and stopped. He stood up and looked at the wall, as if there were a window there, so as not to embarrass me by staring. After a bit, without looking at me, he said, "Do you feel like talking about it?"

For hours while lying awake in bed I had debated with myself how much I should tell Thomas. All it took was his simple, caring question. I told him everything. I had to tell someone about that young airman dying in my astral arms or I'd go insane. Jefferson listened intently to every word, never interrupting. I cried through quite a bit of it. Once, when I glanced at Thomas, I thought I saw tears in his eyes as well.

Chapter Nineteen

Jill and I spent the long 4th of July weekend in San Diego, scouting neighborhoods where we might want to live. We'd decided to rent rather than buy since Jill viewed the UCSD job as only temporary until she could return to politics. We quickly settled on the Point Loma area and spent the remainder of our time in San Diego sightseeing.

We had been sitting in lawn chairs atop the cliffs at Torrey Pines for hours, watching the parasailers above us and the boats and surfers far below us, just soaking up the ambiance. Neither of us had spoken for quite some time when Jill shattered the tranquility. "Pete, are we okay?"

Her out of the blue question stumped me. "Huh? What do you mean?"

"I mean us. Our relationship."

"Oh, babe, of course we're okay. I love you more than ever. Surely you know that."

She smiled, but only for a moment. "Yes, I do, but it's obvious something is bothering you. It's your work, isn't it?"

My silence only confirmed it for her. "Are you having second thoughts about leaving the company?"

"No. Yes. No." A huge sigh escaped my lips. "It's complicated. A lot of stuff has happened lately. I just need time to work through it in my head. I'm sorry."

"I've never asked you what you really do for the CIA…" she said softly, her voice trailing off to nothing, her eyes pleading with me to tell her. Once again, my silence was her answer.

******

A week after we had returned from California Jill phoned me at my desk at Mulvaney & Proust, something she rarely did. "Pete, can you talk? It's important."

"Of course, honey, go ahead."

"I just got off the phone with the UCSD provost. They've withdrawn their offer of employment. The position has been given to another candidate."

"What! How is that possible? I thought you signed a contract?"

"I did, but it was conditional, upon approval of the faculty senate, which I was assured was just a formality. Obviously it wasn't."

"I don't get it. The faculty senate rejected you? Why? How? They don't even know you."

"Apparently they wanted a minority candidate. That's the official reason, according to the provost. But he also said some of the senate members claimed there was undue political influence on my behalf. I guess Governor Wilson isn't too popular amongst some of the professors there."

"Oh, Jill, I'm so sorry. Don't worry; something will turn up for you."

"Honestly, I'm not really upset about it. I was never too keen on teaching, and most college campuses have little tolerance for republicans anyway. This faculty senate vote proves it. I probably would have been miserable there.

"Meanwhile," she went on, "I'm still out of here at the end of July. I guess I'll be shopping my resume around Washington, D.C. in person, knocking on doors until you leave Mulvaney."

Upon hearing no response from me she said, "Pete? Are you there?"

"Yeah, sorry. I was just thinking - perhaps I might know someone who can open a few of those doors for you."

Chapter Twenty

Jefferson and I sat down in his office two days later and I filled him in on Jill's situation. I was hoping he'd take my strong hints, but no, he was going to make me say the words. I cleared my throat, sucked up my pride, and said them. "I need a big favor, Thomas. Jill's desperate to find a job here in Washington, and I can't stand the fact my wife's desperate about anything. This has nothing to do with money; I've got plenty of it. It's all about Jill being happy, and she won't be happy until she's working again as an economist."

"Well, Pete, we have a number of economists on staff here. I have no idea if we need any more, but I can find out. And of course I'll put in a good word for Jill." Jefferson was pretending not to get it, or he was just obtuse this morning. It was early, perhaps he needed more coffee. I just couldn't tell, and it drove me crazy that I still hadn't learned to read his poker face.

"No, that's not what I mean and you know it. She wants to work in politics, and here we are at the political center of America, if not the entire world. Surely you must know some politicians, or have some political connections. Jill's a PhD. with three years' experience on a state governor's staff. She'd be an asset to anyone."

Thomas replied, "I know very little about politics and I don't know any politicians personally. My job has always kept me out of the limelight. Can I assume Governor

Merrill has already tried to pull some strings for her and struck out?"

"Exactly. Merrill told her everyone in D.C. is focused on the elections to the exclusion of everything else."

Jefferson scoffed at that. "Granted, this is a presidential election year, but that doesn't mean the rest of the business of Washington comes to a halt. In fact, I'd argue it's just the opposite. Can I be blunt, Pete? New Hampshire is a tiny state, and outside of his state nobody ever heard of Merrill. He probably carries very little weight in this town."

"I'm sure you're right. I hadn't considered that aspect. But that's actually good news. It means if somebody who does carry some weight recommended her she might get a fair shot."

"I told you, Pete, I'm not that guy. I may as well be the invisible man."

"How about your boss? He's a political appointee. You're always ranting about what a political animal he is."

Jefferson looked at me, his eyes giving away nothing. "Pete, you've asked me for favors in the past, and I was happy to help when I could. I've given you extra time off, authorized a lot of out-of-country travel. I went way out on a limb for your POW project. Those were favors, things within my purview I could choose to grant or not. If I have to ask my boss to do something for you then I'll owe him a big favor, and you know I can't stand the man. You're asking for something far more than just a favor."

"What would you call it then?" I asked him.

"Contract negotiations."

******

Contract negotiations. There it was. Jefferson didn't need any more coffee. He had been playing poker with me the whole time, and he just showed his hand. He looked pretty confident about his cards, too. He didn't realize I had an ace up my sleeve - I would happily lose the contract game if it meant Jill getting a Washington, D.C. political job.

"Okay, Thomas, deal me in. You get your boss to find Jill a political job here in D.C. and I'll sign on for another year."

Jefferson laughed out loud, a rarity for him. "You can't be serious, Pete. Look at this from my point of view. You want me to go to my boss, whom I detest, and admit I am unable to retain my most valuable asset without his assistance. There are only three possible outcomes: One, he refuses to help. I lose face with my boss and I lose you. A poor result for me. Two, he tries to help but can't find a job for Jill. I lose face with my boss, I owe him a huge favor just for trying, and I still lose you. An even worse outcome for me. Three, he finds a job for Jill and you sign on for one more year. I lose face with my boss, I owe him a big favor, and I spend the next twelve months wondering what you're going to ask for next time. That's a whole lot of downside and not much potential upside for me. You've got to make it worth my while."

Thomas eventually conceded he was certain he could convince his boss to ask around on Jill's behalf. "It's only a question of how much I have to grovel," he said sourly. Still, he could not guarantee anyone would actually hire her. In the end, I agreed to sign on for one year if Jefferson's boss made inquiries even if Jill failed to find employment. Two years if Jill landed a job. Jefferson pushed hard for a three year commitment. Reluctantly, I agreed to sign on for a three year contract if Jefferson made a serious effort to update the list of military prisons and allowed me to do preparatory work on my POW project during business hours. If Jill and I were going to be living together in the Washington area I didn't want to spend my off hours away from her. I would still do the actual POW searching on my weekends.

******

In late August of 1996 I signed a three year contract with the CIA as a special projects consultant. My official salary with Mulvaney & Proust would be $500,000 for the first year and increase by $100,000 each year thereafter. My secret offshore salary would go to $5 million per year and be capped at that figure.

Jill went to work for Alfonse D'Amato, the republican senator from New York, at his Washington, D.C. office. D'Amato was the chairman of the powerful Senate Banking Committee. Virtually every bit of business conducted by the committee dealt with either micro or macroeconomics. Jefferson's boss had come through big time. Jill was in seventh heaven. I wondered if I'd made a deal with the devil.

Chapter Twenty One

Jill and I spent Christmas vacation of 1996 in the Cayman Islands. I was no longer welcome at any of the Bahamas casinos and the scuba diving is fabulous in the Caymans. Plus, of course, my personal wealth manager was there. Before leaving the states I told Jill I would have to check in with Jefferson at least once during our vacation, using the secure facilities at the U.S. Consular Agency in Georgetown on Grand Cayman. That was a white lie. A couple of days into our vacation she was headed for a morning at the hotel spa and I left for the consulate. At least that's what I told her. Instead, I met with my banker.

Jill knew I had money in offshore accounts, but she thought it was the proceeds from gambling. She had no idea the CIA was paying me a secret fortune. If I told her that I'd have to tell her why, and I was prohibited from doing so.

I instructed my banker on what he could and could not tell Jill. For example, the regularity of the deposits did not comport with gambling winnings, and I'm sure the amount amassed was quite a bit more than she thought. In fact, it was quite a bit more than I figured - nearly twelve million dollars. Half of that was from the CIA and my gambling winnings, but the rest was the result of shrewd investing, primarily in tech stocks.

I decided to move half of the money, six million dollars, to other offshore accounts. This would serve two purposes - I would only have to explain half the money to Jill and the rest would be distributed to other tax havens, making it even more secure.

The next day we returned to visit my banker together. Jill was astonished at how much money I had, and I was glad I had moved half of it the day before. She grilled my banker with a long series of pointed questions about our arrangements and the investments he was making on my behalf. My wife, the economist.

******

1997 was an unremarkable year, if such a thing is possible for a CIA astral spy. I was spending more and more time in the Middle East and North Africa on missions related to Islamic terrorism. The Taliban in Afghanistan were becoming more prominent on the world stage, as was Osama bin Laden. Algeria suffered dozens of terrorist attacks and was a particular focus for me.

Jill and I settled into domestic life together. She absolutely loved her job on the Senate Banking Committee staff and quickly became a valued member of their team. Most weekends I was able to continue my search for American prisoners of war. Per our contract agreement, Jefferson had assigned more manpower to updating the list of military prisons in countries where Vietnam War prisoners might possibly be held. That turned out to be both good and bad. Good, in that most of the buildings I searched actually turned out to be current or former prisons. Bad, in that the number of buildings had more than doubled to over two thousand. Worst of all, a little historical research showed it was common practice to periodically move military prisoners from one facility to another. A prison I had searched and found empty yesterday might be full of prisoners tomorrow, a macabre version of whack-a-mole.

Sixteen months of searching yielded no trace of any American POWs. I had worked my way through all the Southeast Asian countries and was ready to start on Russia, China or North Korea. Although Russia had the largest number of military prisons the analysts' information on them was the best of any of the countries. China had nearly as many military prisons as Russia. The info on North Korea was the worst, by far. To say it was sketchy would be a serious understatement.

My initial fervor for the POW project had cooled considerably over the last few months and I had no desire to waste my weekends searching North Korean chicken coops. With only two weeks left in the year and our Caymans vacation looming I decided to take a couple of weekends off, then start refreshed in Russia after the new year.

Chapter Twenty Two

1998 was not a presidential election year but it was a year of great turmoil for Washington, D.C. political insiders. The Bill Clinton-Monica Lewinsky scandal tore the city apart along party lines. Politicians on both sides who were normally quite congenial became bitter enemies. Jill's boss, Senator Alfonse D'Amato, tried to straddle the divide and got caught in the middle. He would not be reelected.

Washington, D.C. was embroiled in the politics of impeachment for all of 1998. By the end of the year the democratic president would be impeached. The republican speaker of the house would resign and his replacement would also resign even before officially assuming the post. For Jill, it was a rude awakening. Her time in New Hampshire state politics was the rookie league compared to Washington, D.C. Her first year and a half in D.C. was wonderful - invigorating, educational, challenging, and fun. She was like a Hollywood movie fan with a backstage pass at the Oscars. Now she saw politics for what it really is - blood sport. She tried to stay on the sidelines and simply do her job, but by May of 1998 she was so fed up she was talking about leaving politics.

None of the political drama had any effect on me or my job. Politicians come and go in Washington as regularly as the tides, but the CIA carries on regardless. In May I was reassigned from tracking terrorists to counting nuclear weapons, the same thing I did when first hired. Only this time I was counting nuclear weapons in India and Pakistan.

Both countries had recently conducted nuclear weapons tests and Pakistan officially joined the elite club of nuclear armed nations. I spent every night in the region for several weeks until tensions eased between the two countries.

In August I was once again called upon to search through rubble for survivors of terrorist truck bombs. The American embassies in Kenya and Tanzania had been simultaneously bombed by Islamic terrorists. Hundreds of people were killed and thousands injured. Jefferson credited me with saving several lives.

As the year went on Jill liked working in Washington less and less and I enjoyed my job more and more. To me, there is nothing more loathsome than a terrorist - an indiscriminate killer of innocent men, women and children. In fact, women and children are frequently their main targets. I am proud to say I was personally responsible for the capture or death of many terrorists. How many people in the world can say that? I saw up close and firsthand what they did and hated them for it. And I loved tracking them down.

In November Jill's boss lost his bid for reelection. She assumed she would also lose her job and wasn't at all upset about it, but Senator Phil Gramm of Texas, the incoming chairman of the Senate Banking Committee, personally asked her to stay on and work for him. Gramm was a hard line fiscal conservative who held a doctorate in economics. He and Jill were kindred spirits. She agreed to stay.

Chapter Twenty Three

I look back fondly on the last years of the twentieth century. Yes, 1998 was rough for Jill, but she weathered the storm and came to enjoy working in politics again. Bill Clinton was impeached but not convicted, and things in Washington slowly returned to normal.

During those years I was mainly employed as a terrorist hunter and made many millions of dollars doing so. I would happily have done it for free. When my three year contract expired in August of 1999 I signed on for another three years with Jill's enthusiastic support. I had made enough money officially and through gambling that I now felt comfortable living a more ostentatious life style. We traded in our Toyotas for new cars. Jill got a high end SUV and I bought a vintage Corvette. We bought a large house on forty acres near Clifton, Virginia, with a few horses and farm animals, just because.

In addition to an elaborate security system, Jefferson had CIA technicians install encrypted phone, video and computer links so I could get my assignments and make my daily reports without having to leave home. We picked up a beautiful sailboat, a Morgan Out Island 51, and kept it in the Cayman Islands. It was a big tub, a floating Winnebago that would never win any races, but it was perfect for scuba diving and island hopping. We would just fly over, hop aboard, spend a week or weekend gunkholing, then fly back.

I continued my search for POWs, but it had reached the point of being only a hobby for me, rather than a calling. I came up empty in Russia and was about halfway through China. The analysts convinced me to periodically recheck the most promising prisons in the various countries, on the chance POWs may have been moved to them after my initial search. I realized I could be doing this for years to come.

By the year 2000 I had close to seventy million dollars in offshore banks. My guy in the Caymans was either a genius or incredibly lucky. Either way, he made me a fortune in tech stocks and dumped them right before the dot-com bubble burst, locking in my profits. My Qualcomm stock alone, bought for $250,000 back in 1994, netted me $14 million.

Jill was now a true Washington insider. She had plenty of experience and a network of contacts on both sides of the aisle. She felt certain if she were to take a year or two off when she was ready she could return to any number of political staff jobs. Why was she thinking of taking a year or two off? She was pregnant.

******

In January 2001 we were blessed with a beautiful baby girl. Mother and daughter were both healthy and happy, so naturally I was happy too. Jill loved motherhood. Since I was still working and she was not, she insisted on tending to baby Adilyn when necessary during the night so I could get more sleep. Even so, the presence of a newborn baby in our house frequently disrupted my sleep and my REM periods. Jefferson was concerned about it but I assured him it was minor and rarely affected my work. I was lying, but there was no way for him to know it.

On April 1st, 2001 a U.S. Navy airplane on an intelligence collection mission collided in mid-air with a Chinese warplane. The damaged American plane was forced to make an emergency landing on Hainan Island, which is part of communist China. The twenty four crewmembers were taken prisoner. It was an early test for our new president, George W. Bush.

Jefferson ordered me in to sleep in the headquarters building until the crisis passed. Jill was accustomed to this as it happened once or twice every year. Each night I was able to observe the American prisoners were not being tortured and generally treated well. On April 11th they were released and I was allowed to return home. Jefferson told me my reporting was a major factor in defusing what could have been an extremely ugly international incident.

I was rather pleased with myself. I had a wonderful, lovely wife and a beautiful baby girl. My work was important and rewarding, and the pay was phenomenal. I reached a pinnacle in my life when in late April of 2001 I found a group of American POWs in North Korea. The problem with being on a pinnacle is there's nowhere to go except down.

******

I had finally finished searching the Chinese military prisons and started on North Korea, the last country on the list. I left North Korea for last because according to the analysts it was the least likely place for our POWs to be.

Searching the Southeast Asian countries first made sense because that was where the POWs had originally been captured and held. Russia had been the principal ally of Vietnam during the war, so that country was also a good bet. China and Vietnam had a very complicated relationship. They were more often enemies than friends. China was only a minor player in the Vietnam War and in the years after the war ended China's and Vietnam's armed forces actually engaged each other in combat several times. In the opinion of the analysts it was highly unlikely any POWs were being held in China and even less likely they would be in North Korea. North Korea played virtually no role in the Vietnam War. If American POWs ended up there they would have been moved from Vietnam to China and then through China to North Korea. Our analysts found that scenario extremely unlikely. They were wrong.

North Korea is a client state of China and relies heavily on the Chinese for life-sustaining staples such as food and fuel. With that kind of leverage the North Koreans have no choice but to acquiesce to virtually all Chinese demands.

Some intelligence analysts long argued that Vietnam had failed to repatriate hundreds of American prisoners when the war ended. The Vietnamese almost immediately reneged on every promise they made in the peace agreement. If the United States responded to those breaches by restarting an aerial bombing campaign, there was little the Vietnamese could do about it. A group of American POWs would be a huge bargaining chip.

As it turned out, the U.S. had no stomach for any more fighting and Vietnam's post-war transgressions were ignored. The American prisoners went from being an ace in the hole to an unwanted liability. They couldn't be released because it would reveal Vietnam's duplicity and enrage the USA. Likewise, if the prisoners were killed and word got out severe American reprisals were guaranteed.

Now that I had found the prisoners the sequence of events seemed obvious. Vietnam was in turmoil for years after the war ended. The odds were good that the American POWs would be found or word of their presence leaked out. To prevent that, the Vietnamese secretly transferred them to China. Like the Vietnamese, the Chinese had no desire to be caught holding American prisoners of war, so they forced their North Korean puppets to take them. North Korea is so secretive it is known as the Hermit Kingdom. It is an intensely insular society with a massive police state. The western intelligence agencies probably know less about North Korea than any other country on earth. It was the perfect place to stash the POWs.

******

I met with Jefferson in his office. Something this important had to be discussed face to face. The CIA man was incredulous when I told him of the prisoners. I had counted ninety seven men. Eighty two white men, nine blacks and six men who appeared to be Hispanic. All seemed undernourished and most of them appeared to be in their seventies, a good ten to fifteen years older than expected. Thirty years in captivity could easily account for the men looking much older than their true ages.

After peppering me with questions for over an hour Jefferson finally ran down and seemed to deflate, like a balloon with a slow leak. He looked like a man who has just been told he has a terminal disease. "This is the worst possible news, Pete. Horrible."

Huh? I had expected the exact opposite reaction. "Thomas, what in the world are you talking about? Ninety seven men we wrote off as dead are alive. We should be dancing in the streets in celebration."

He shook his head; sadness etched in his face, his voice hoarse with emotion. "I never really thought any of them were still alive. I can't believe you found them. It's dreadful, terrible news. Don't you see? We'll never get them out. Those poor devils, suffering all these years. Officially, they've all been dead for decades. Are we going to invade North Korea to free them? Risk a nuclear war with China? It's hopeless."

I have to admit I hadn't thought it through. Still, there had to be something we could do. "How about a surgical rescue mission? I can pinpoint their precise location, detail all the North Korean defenses. We send in the special ops guys. They helo in, grab the prisoners and helo out."

"Pete, I did a few snatch and grabs back in the day. For one man, maybe two. Not a hundred. It's impossible. You'd need a fleet of helicopters just for troop and prisoner transport. We used eight CH-53s in Iran in 1979, and that was for only sixty prisoners. And we failed.

"Don't forget helicopter gunships to cover the troop carriers. Fixed wing aircraft overhead or at least loitering nearby in case it all goes bad. All that to try to sneak in and sneak out against some of the most heavily defended airspace in the world. It'll never happen."

"Why can't we apply diplomatic pressure on them? Tell the world about the prisoners and embarrass the North Koreans into releasing them."

Jefferson looked alarmed. "No! We'd be signing their death warrants. The North Koreans are already pariahs. They couldn't care less about world opinion. The moment they know we're aware of the prisoners they'll kill them all and dispose of the bodies. Now, if we had hard evidence to show the world, photos or videotape, that might change the equation, but getting proof of the prisoners is going to be darn near impossible. We'd have to put agents on the ground."

Jefferson thought for few minutes. "This is an awful tough nut to crack, Pete. I need to brief my boss, and he'll brief the director, who'll tell the president. This is huge. In the meantime, we'll get the brain trust working on a solution. And you need to identify as many of the men as possible. It'll take me a few days to get all the MIA photos together. You don't have to worry about doing this on your weekends anymore. It just became an official mission."

Chapter Twenty Four

Every night after finding the POWs I went back to North Korea. Some nights I'd spend all my REM time there studying faces. Other nights, when I was busy hunting terrorists, I'd *shift* to North Korea only long enough to confirm the prisoners hadn't been moved.

Two weeks after I'd found the POWs the CIA had photos of only 500 of the 2,500 missing in action servicemen. Amazingly, photos of the MIAs were not readily available but had to be assembled from government archives.

Working with the 500 photos I had yet to identify a single person. The pictures were at least thirty years old and all showed vibrant, youthful service members. The faces I had memorized were of pathetic, cadaverous old men.

Jefferson assigned someone to scan all the photos into a computer. Using a computer aging program, all the photos would be aged to present day. I was hoping it would make identification a lot easier.

Impatient with the infuriatingly slow process of gathering, scanning and aging the photos I tried a new tack. I focused on eight POWs in North Korea who had prominent or unusual facial features: very large noses, dimpled chins, facial moles. One of the prisoners had a large port wine stain birthmark on his face.

I went back through the hardcopy photos of the first 500 and found a match! Finally, confirmation that at least one of the prisoners was an American serviceman who had gone missing in action in Vietnam. If one was, surely they all were.

Over the next six weeks, with all the photos received, scanned and aged, I pored over them for hours. I had identified sixty two of the ninety seven prisoners. There were ten others I was fairly certain of, but I was unwilling to say for sure. At my next meeting with Jefferson I unloaded on him.

"Thomas, when are you going to stop jerking me around with the photos?"

"I have no idea what…"

"Stop, please. Lying about it will only tick me off even more. I see the same core group of photos every time. But I also see some new photos each time, and photos from previous sessions are missing. What kind of game are you playing?"

"Pete, your memory is phenomenal, but it isn't infallible. You've looked at thousands of photos. Some of them are variations on the aging process. You may be seeing two or three differently aged photos of the same man."

"Yeah, I get that. That's not what I'm talking about. You're intentionally throwing in ringers, aren't you? You're testing me."

Jefferson sighed, and nodded his head. "I told them it wouldn't work, but they insisted."

Rather than respond I simply stared at him until he continued. "Look, before this POW thing only the director and one of his deputies knew exactly what we do here and how successful you've been. Even my boss was not fully apprised. Your discovery of the POWs led to six more people, my boss included, being briefed into the program. Four of the six were highly skeptical of your abilities and demanded proof you weren't somehow just scamming us about the POWs. If all you were shown were photos of MIAs, then you couldn't pick a wrong guy. Along with the real MIAs I was ordered to show you pictures of servicemen who were not MIA from Vietnam or never even served there. If you identified a number of people incorrectly the doubters would have their proof you were conning us. If you ignored the ringers and only ID'd real MIAs as being in North Korea that would prove you were on the level. It's the same thing cops do when they show a witness a photo lineup - only one of the photos is the real bad guy.

"I'm sorry, Pete. I know it caused you a lot of extra work and wasted valuable time. I fought against it, but I lost. For the record, you haven't picked a ringer yet."

"What's the plan, Thomas? It's been two months since I found those guys."

"It's out of my hands, Pete. A joint military/CIA ad hoc committee was formed last week. We're waiting on the committee's recommendations."

"Last week! What have they been doing for the last two months?"

"The wheels of government grind exceedingly slowly, when they move at all. It took them a month just to agree on the number of committee members, what rank they would be, and who would be the chair. Then at the last minute the Air Force insisted on bringing in a general instead of a colonel. Naturally, the Navy had to counter with an admiral. Most of the MIAs are aviators who were shot down, so they felt entitled. My boss is only the civilian equivalent of a colonel, so the director felt it necessary to replace him with a deputy director. It's insane. I'm amazed we can actually fight and win wars."

"How long until the ad hoc committee comes up with recommendations?"

Jefferson shrugged. "Who can say? And once they do, then it has to be run through the political people, including the state department. Once those bozos get involved all bets are off. Now you know why I never get involved in politics."

******

The more time that passed the more frustrated I became. Some of those men had been held in captivity for thirty five years and we were arguing over nonsense instead of finalizing a plan to free them. No one seemed to have any sense of urgency about rescuing our men.

I found myself thinking of my brother's girlfriend's father and wondered if he was among the men in North Korea. After all, she was the one who got me started on the whole thing. I never learned her last name, so I called Stan to ask him. After some small talk I eased into it.

"Say, Stan, are you still in contact with Linda, the girl you brought to my wedding reception? I really liked that gal, her being an army vet and all."

"Nah, we only saw each other a couple of times. She was just in town visiting a friend. She lives in New York City."

"Oh. I was hoping to learn more about her father. She told me he was shot down in Vietnam. What was her last name? And do you still have her phone number? I'd like to get in touch with her."

"Yeah, bro, so would I. You know those Italian girls can get pretty wild. Unfortunately the number she gave me is disconnected. I tried calling her once after your reception. Anyway, her last name is Marchetti."

******

Every MIA photo had the man's full name, service number and date of birth attached. I shuffled the photos of Army Sergeant First Class Joseph Alonzo Marchetti like a hustler playing three-card Monte: the two slightly different computer aged ones and the picture of him from his service jacket, taken when he was thirty two years old and newly promoted. I normally looked at photos on a computer but had printed these out, as I sometimes did in ambiguous cases. I quickly determined Marchetti was not among the POWs in North Korea, but kept staring at the photos anyway. Something was bothering me and I couldn't put my finger on it. Finally, it struck me - Joseph Marchetti bore no resemblance whatsoever to his daughter Linda. I remembered Linda's face clearly. Not only because of my eidetic memory but also because she was a very beautiful woman. Joseph had a dark olive complexion, as is common among the descendants of southern Italians. Linda's skin was as white as a snowbank. Moreover, I could not detect the faintest vestige of the father in my mental picture of his daughter. There could have been a dozen simple explanations for it, but my subconscious mind was screaming at me that something was wrong. I just couldn't let it go.

After dinner that evening I told Jill I had to make a couple of business phone calls and went into my home office. I found the phone number of an army buddy of mine who had remained on active duty after I mustered out. Once we got caught up on old times I told him why I called.

"I need a favor, Jon. I'm trying to track down information on a Vietnam MIA. A while back I got interested in the POW/MIA thing and now it's kind of a hobby of mine. I've got the man's full name, DOB and service number but nothing else. I was hoping to find some information about his family members so I could interview them. Could you possibly get that info for me from army records?"

"Well, I suppose so, if you don't mind waiting forever. All those records are collecting dust in St. Louis. I'd have to make some phone calls and see if I could get some civilian clerk out of his chair. And I'd have to make up an official reason for the request.

"You know, there's an easier way, Pete. Just get on the internet and go to one of those people finding sites. You might get lucky and get the info in five minutes for free. At worst, you'd have to pay a small fee. That's how I'd do it."

And it was as easy as that. It took me longer to register and arrange payment than it did to get the information. I learned Joseph Marchetti and his wife had two children, a son named Alonzo and a daughter named Linda. I was given addresses and phone numbers for all of them. His wife had remarried and was living in Mesa, Arizona. Alonzo had an address in northern California. Linda's address and phone number were in Tacoma, Washington. I had just wasted twenty dollars on out of date information, since I knew from Stan she lived in New York City now. Still, there was a small chance the Tacoma number was a cell phone and she still used it. I dialed the number.

******

"Hello?"

"Hi, I've probably got the wrong number. I'm trying to reach Linda Marchetti."

"Yes, this is Linda. Who's calling?"

Her voice didn't sound familiar to me but it had been a few years and my eidetic memory was always more visually oriented. "This is Pete Ludvick. We met at my wedding reception in Connecticut five years ago. My brother Stan brought you."

The woman laughed. "Sorry, wasn't me. You do have the wrong number. Goodbye."

"Wait! Please, I know this is weird, but you did say your name is Linda Marchetti. Was your father named Joseph? A soldier?"

The silence went on so long I thought she had hung up. Finally, she said, "Who is this again?"

"My name is Peter Ludvick. The Linda Marchetti I'm looking for is the daughter of Joseph Alonzo Marchetti, an army sergeant lost in Vietnam."

"Yes, my father was killed in Vietnam in 1970. I was three years old. What is this about?"

"Actually, he was listed as missing in action initially. I met a Linda Marchetti at my wedding reception in May, 1996. You, uh, I mean she, came to the reception with my brother. We talked about your father being listed as MIA. It was of particular interest to me because I'm a former army officer. In fact, the woman at my wedding reception said she had also served in the army. Did you?"

"No."

"And you never attended a wedding reception in Manchester, Connecticut?"

"Connecticut! Mister Ludvick, I never heard of you or your brother and I'd certainly remember attending a wedding reception all the way on the other side of the country, even if it was five years ago. I think you probably had way too much to drink at your reception. Now please, don't bother me again."

Chapter Twenty Five

What to do? A lot of people believe intuition is a kind of second sight, like ESP or some other nonsense. I know better. Intuition is simply your subconscious mind putting together the pieces of a puzzle you didn't even know you were working on. Your mind receives all kinds of input all day long and files it away. If things match up, when facts learned over time all mesh and make sense, life goes on. When they don't match up, when some pieces don't fit your subconscious template, it nags and eats at you until you finally get a flash of understanding - that's intuition.

I hadn't trusted Jefferson from the git go and could never really say why. Then Susan explicitly warned me about him. Then there was the thing with the bogus MIA photos - was it really some CIA bigwigs who didn't trust me or was it Jefferson trying to delay my identifying the men? Either way, he had lied to me. Now I discover this - a woman posing as Linda Marchetti got me interested in Vietnam MIAs just at the time I was getting ready to leave the CIA. Why? Because I couldn't search for MIAs unless I continued to work for the CIA. Only the CIA could provide me with a list of all the military prisons I needed to search.

 Wait a minute. If Jill had gotten the UCSD position I would have left the CIA regardless of my interest in MIAs. She had the job, then suddenly she didn't have the job. Did Jefferson somehow cause UCSD to rescind their offer? Then Jefferson conveniently got his boss to find Jill a Washington, D.C. political position. Not just any position, but a plum most political economists would drool over. And I was so grateful I signed on for three more years.

When Senator D'Amato lost his bid for reelection in 1998 Jill was out of a job. She was fed up with politics and ready to leave. Was it just luck that Senator Gramm asked her to stay on? With Jill still working in D.C. politics I signed on for another three years in 1999.

For that matter, what was the real story with New Hampshire Governor Merrill suddenly resigning when he was immensely popular and faced virtually no opposition for reelection? Maybe that was the start of it. I had been poised to quit the CIA and move to New Hampshire. Suddenly Jill was looking for work. The California teaching position came up, then it was gone. Everything that would have taken Jill and me away from Virginia and the CIA fell apart and everything that kept Jill and me in the Washington, D.C. area fell into place. Every time.

What to do?

******

Had nine years working for the CIA made me a raving paranoid? Or was I right to suspect everything that had happened over the past five years had been manipulated by Jefferson to coerce me into staying at the CIA? I proved the Linda Marchetti I met was an imposter, but everything else was mere speculation at this point. I needed more proof.

Back to the internet. I found a corporate security firm with offices on both coasts. I knew from my years with Mulvaney & Proust that corporate security firms are employed by most major corporations and they do much more than just security - they also conduct discreet investigations of people and companies.

I met with a representative of the firm in early July of 2001 and laid out my concerns. I wanted to know two things: What were the circumstances surrounding Jill being denied the UCSD position? Was it just bad luck and political correctness, or something more? And what was the real reason behind Governor Merrill's shocking resignation?

The security rep assured me her company had the resources necessary to undertake the jobs. She suggested two months should be sufficient to complete the investigations. We agreed on bi-weekly progress reports, to be given over the phone unless significant findings were made, then it would be done in person. The price tag was outrageously high, but I shrugged it off - I was a very wealthy man.

******

On September 8th, a Saturday, I told Jill I had to go into the office for a few hours. Instead, I met with the security rep to receive her final report. She wasted no time on idle chatter.

"Let's talk about Governor Merrill first. No one we spoke with believes his official reason of wanting to spend more time with his family. Back when it happened the media went crazy trying to find the real reason. Some reporters spent a full year on the story and still came up empty. Our investigators also found nothing to contradict his publically stated reason. Whatever was behind his resignation may never be known. We're flogging a dead horse in New Hampshire and would just be wasting your money to keep after it.

"The UCSD situation is an entirely different matter. A minority rights organization known as the Coalition for Social Justice, or CSJ for short, made a big stink about your wife getting the job. CSJ appealed directly and forcefully to the most influential members of the faculty senate, using real hardball tactics. Publically they claimed Jill had received the job offer only because of Governor Wilson's influence, and equally qualified minority candidates had been denied a fair shot. To bolster their claim they distributed a copy of Governor Wilson's letter to your wife. The governor admitted writing the letter and recommending Jill but denied pressuring anyone to hire her.

"Privately, CSJ threatened to picket the faculty members' homes and offices. We confirmed two cases of threatened blackmail and one case of a bribe being offered. Their intense pressure worked. Several highly respected faculty members convinced enough of the others to reject your wife. A Hispanic man was hired in her place.

"On its face this may seem to be a case of a highly organized liberal rights organization successfully lobbying a like-minded group of faculty members, a rather common occurrence. However, we believe otherwise.

"Our investigators found no record of the Coalition for Social Justice existing prior to their protest of your wife's hiring. Even more damning, CSJ disappeared after this single event. Typically, when a newly formed rights organization has initial success they use it as leverage to grow their membership and fund raise. None of that happened. Instead, the CSJ just vanished. Also, we determined four different people claimed to be members of the organization and interacted with various faculty members. We were unable to track down any of them or even learn their names. Finally, there is the matter of Governor Wilson's letter to your wife. This was a personal letter he hand wrote. There were no copies, only the original received in New Hampshire by your wife. How did the CSJ, a small, heretofore unknown group in San Diego manage to obtain a copy of a letter in New Hampshire? How did they even know of its existence?

"Based upon the facts we uncovered we concluded the following: There was a concerted, well-financed effort to deny your wife the position at the University of California San Diego. The Coalition for Social Justice was a false front created solely as a vehicle to pressure the faculty senate. We were unable to determine who was behind the organization or what motivated them to put forth such an effort to deny your wife the position."

I didn't need her to tell me that. I already knew the answer.

Chapter Twenty Six

For the next few days I brooded over what to do about Jefferson's Machiavellian machinations. Thankfully, I was able to work from home that week. If I had come face to face with the lying scumbag right then it would have turned ugly fast.

Tuesday morning I was having coffee in my home office while poring over the POW photos on my computer. I had identified all but twelve of the men. Of those, I had narrowed down the possibilities to fifty MIAs. The computer geeks had given me five differently aged computer enhancements of each, for a total of 250 photos. If I couldn't positively ID them the next step would be to sit down with a sketch artist.

Jefferson told me the ad hoc committee considering options to free the POWs had concluded a military incursion to rescue them was not feasible. The focus shifted to diplomatic means, which made the state department the primary player. That was bad news, as no one at the CIA had any respect for the state department or its negotiating abilities.

The state department people had immediately said that without hard evidence of the POWs existence no diplomatic effort could succeed. To that end, the CIA had arranged for two North Koreans to attempt to bribe one of the prison guards to take photographs of the POWs. How the CIA had persuaded the two North Koreans was not disclosed to me. I put little faith in the effort.

On the plus side, a large majority of the CIA, military, and political people involved were now convinced the POWs were alive and being held in North Korea. Only a tiny portion of them had been briefed on me and my abilities. The rest were simply told a human intelligence asset, or "humint" in CIA jargon, was the source of the information.

Jefferson said the president himself had been advised on the POWs and it was only his awareness of the situation that forced the ad hoc committee to finally make recommendations and spurred the CIA bigwigs into taking action.

All my knowledge of this came from Jefferson, of course. I had never dealt with anyone else during my time with the CIA. Now that I knew he had been lying to me and manipulating me for years I had to wonder if anything he told me was true. Maybe it was all another elaborate scam to keep me happy. Maybe the president hadn't been told anything. Maybe there was no ad hoc committee. Maybe I was losing my mind.

Jill knocked softly on my office door. We had an understanding she would never enter my home office without permission due to the nature of my work. "Pete?" she said through the closed door. "Honey, you need to come out and look at the TV news. Right now."

We sat in front of the television trying to make sense out of the smoke billowing from the upper floors of the north tower of the World Trade Center in New York City. An airliner had crashed into it. Not a small private plane, but a gigantic airliner, piloted by professionals. How could that happen? A few minutes later we stared in horrified disbelief as a second huge airplane plowed into the south tower. I ran upstairs and grabbed my always packed "go bag." I kissed Jill and Adilyn goodbye and was headed to the garage when my office phone, our house phone and my cell phone all started ringing.

******

Stuck in traffic on the drive to CIA headquarters I listened to an all-news radio station. I switched stations frequently hoping to learn something new, but all the reports were the same - nobody really knew anything at that point.

When I was still ten minutes from headquarters I saw a large fireball and smoke plume erupt several miles away. Moments later I learned from the radio the pentagon had just been hit. I wanted to scream in frustration and rage.

CIA headquarters was abuzz with activity, of course, but when I got to my office I found myself alone. It was another thirty minutes before Jefferson arrived. Ironically, in my office inside CIA headquarters I was cut off from radio, TV and the internet and had no idea what more might be happening. When my boss arrived he quickly filled me in.

"These attacks are the work of Osama bin Laden and the Islamic terrorist group Al-Qaeda, the same bastards you've been chasing for years. Only now it won't just be you and a handful of CIA agents and military special operators. This is going to turn into a major shooting war, Pete. Osama bin Laden just went from being one terrorist amongst many to the most wanted man in the world. Your mission will be to find him. With the resources we'll be throwing at this and your help it shouldn't take more than a couple of days, a week at the most."

I barely heard a word the man said. All I could think about was how he had manipulated and lied to me and Jill for years. How could he stand there and speak to me like a friend and colleague after stabbing me in the back again and again?

We were in the early minutes of one of the biggest events in modern American history and my boss just told me I would be a key player in it. I was as angry as I had ever been in my life. I just wasn't sure who I was more enraged at, Osama bin Laden or my boss, Thomas Jefferson.

Chapter Twenty Seven

As anticipated, Jefferson told me I'd be sleeping in the headquarters building for the next few nights. I didn't need to study any pictures of Osama bin Laden - I had located him twice previously, but back then the powers that be decided he wasn't worth the trouble and I was moved to higher priority assignments. Jefferson told me he would prepare a photo gallery of bin Laden's lieutenants for me to study and the analysts would determine the best locations to start searching.

I checked in with the duty officer and got my bunkroom assignment. As I was settling in to the room I turned on the television to get caught up on the terrorist attacks. Shockingly, both of the twin towers had completely collapsed. A fourth airliner had also been hijacked, but the passengers had fought back and the plane crashed into a field in Pennsylvania. All civilian air traffic throughout the country had been grounded.

My thoughts immediately turned to the collapsed towers. I had found survivors in the Khobar Towers rubble, then again in the ruins of the U.S. embassies in Kenya and Tanzania. I might be able to save a few lives at the World Trade Center.

******

Jefferson knocked on the bunkroom door two hours later, a portfolio with photos under one arm. He handed me the folder and started to speak. I stopped him with a raised hand, like a traffic cop.

"Thomas, bin Laden and the rest can wait one more night. I want to search the twin towers for survivors."

"You can't Pete. It's illegal. Our charter only allows us to operate outside the United States. That's why we didn't use you in the Oklahoma City bombing."

"I'm ashamed to say searching for survivors in Oklahoma City never occurred to me. Back then I was so focused on courting Jill I had blinders on. But I don't give a hoot about the law, Thomas. No one will ever know I was there. If I locate survivors just get the word to the rescue teams and let a search dog take the credit, like you did in Saudi Arabia and Africa."

"I can't do it, Pete. As much as I'd like to, I just can't do it. Congress would crucify us if they ever found out. It's out of the question."

"I'm doing it, Thomas, with or without your permission. Assign me to find bin Laden and I'll salute and carry on. In the morning I'll say I didn't find him. In the meantime, the rescue teams will be getting some precise directions to locate survivors."

Jefferson dropped his usual poker face and sneered at that. "From whom? Some kook who says he saw them in a dream? Get real, Pete. Do you have any idea how many nutcases and self-proclaimed psychics come out of the woodwork when something like this happens? If it doesn't come from a credible source no one is going to give it a second thought."

"I can save lives, Thomas, the lives of innocent Americans. Are you just going to ignore them until they die, like the POWs?"

That stung him. "That's unfair, and you know it! I let you run with the POW search. I dedicated CIA resources to your effort for five years. I could have said no. At least give me credit for that."

"Oh, I'll give you credit for more than that. I credit you with putting the whole idea in my head, via 'Linda Marchetti.' Or should I say the woman posing as Linda Marchetti?"

My words hung in the air like a cloud of poison gas. Even I was surprised. I'm not sure I meant to say them out loud, but there was no going back now, so I plunged ahead. "I know the woman I met at my wedding reception was just playing a role - planted by you to put the POW search idea in my head. I spoke with the real Linda Marchetti and confirmed it.

"I also know you arranged for UCSD to rescind Jill's job offer. Do I need to add in all the other levers you've pulled to keep me working for you here at the CIA? You've been playing me like a Stradivarius for years. Somebody else can find bin Laden. I'll never work for you again. I quit."

******

Jefferson took some time to compose himself by making a pot of coffee at the side table. I noticed he used decaf, so if I drank some it would not affect my normal sleep pattern. Even now, the man was scheming. He silently and patiently waited for the coffee to finish brewing before pouring himself a cup and sitting down in one of the chairs.

Still he did not speak. The television was looping between live shots of the World Trade Center rubble and video tape of the planes flying into the towers and the towers collapsing. It was making me sick to my stomach so I grabbed the remote and shut it off. Finally, Jefferson spoke. "I'll say one thing for you, Pete - your timing really sucks."

If that was an attempt at humor it fell flat. I didn't rise to the bait and remained silent. The ball was in Jefferson's court and I was content to let him squirm. He finished his coffee and got a second cup before starting again. He made no attempt to deny anything. I have to give him credit for that, if nothing else.

"What I did I did for our country. Prior to your arrival our remote viewing program was a joke, always teetering on the edge of being permanently shut down for lack of results. The two other travelers we had who were capable of directing their travel did not possess your accuracy or reliability, nor did either one have a photographic memory. You are, by an order of magnitude, the best and most effective astral traveler we've ever had. Once your astounding capabilities became apparent it was a game changer for us. My boss and the director made it abundantly clear I was to do whatever was necessary to retain you. I'm not trying to pass off what I did as simply following orders. I agreed one hundred percent with their sentiments, and I still do.

"There was a time in the mid-1940s when the United States was the only country in the world to possess nuclear weapons. It's the only situation I can think of that compares to your status with us today. You give our country a decisive edge over every other nation on the planet. We weren't about to let you just walk out the door."

Now it was my turn to get a cup of coffee while I pondered what I had just heard. How would you respond to someone who said you were the most important national security asset in the world?

"You could have been up front with me. Did anyone even consider honesty as a bargaining tactic?"

"No. We're paying you five million dollars a year off the books. If you knew how valuable you really are, how badly we wanted to keep you, would five million have been enough, or fifty million, even five hundred million? An aircraft carrier costs that much, and we've got a dozen of them. We only have one of you."

I shook my head in disgust. "In the end, it always comes down to money, doesn't it?"

"It isn't only the money, Pete. The CIA has a very large black ops budget, but even we couldn't hide that kind of expenditure from congress. They would demand to know what we were spending it on, and of course we couldn't tell them. Rather than tell congress about our secrets we might just as well send an email to the New York Times and cut out the middlemen.

"And even if we came to an agreement on money what other demands might you make? Our psychologists told us no one would be able to handle that kind of power, knowing you are invaluable and irreplaceable. It's human nature."

I sneered at the self-righteous jerk. "Human nature? You never thought of me as a human being. Right from the beginning you thought of me as a tool, even referred to me that way. Now I learn I'm more than a tool. I'm a weapon, better than an aircraft carrier. There hasn't been a weapon like me since the atomic bomb was invented. Do you even listen to yourself?"

The CIA man tried a different tack. "It's been an exceptionally bad day for America, for all of us. Thousands of our citizens are dead. We'll be at war within days, and it's going to be a long, hard slog. Both of us are stunned, angry, and not thinking clearly. How about we agree to shelve this discussion 'til another day?"

"No, I don't think so. This boil has been festering for a long time. I need to lance it right now."

Jefferson nodded, his face grim. "All right, Pete, let's get it over with then. I admit I manipulated certain events to steer you toward staying with us. Is that what you've been waiting to hear?"

He went on. "Jill never wanted a teaching position. We both know that. I know it because she told me so herself.

And you told me she was desperate to find a political job here in Washington. My boss got your wife her dream job with Senator D'Amato. When he lost his bid for reelection my boss arranged for Senator Gramm to keep her on. And when Jill is ready to return to work her job will be waiting for her, I guarantee it. Is that such a bad thing?

"The person you met at your wedding reception was an undercover operative with another agency, not Linda Marchetti. We knew from your psychological profile you would be intensely interested in the POW/MIA issue and want to search for them. All we did was dangle the possibility in front of you, and you did the rest on your own. I never imagined you would actually find live POWs after all these years. I still can't get over it. If any of those men ever make it out they'll owe it all to you and your special ability. You did phenomenally good work on that, Pete. Those men were lost for thirty years and you found them. Regardless of what you think of how that assignment got started the end result is miraculous. By the way, we're hoping to have the proof we need, photos of the prisoners, smuggled out of North Korea any day now."

I waited for him to continue on with his mea culpa, but apparently he wasn't going to admit to anything else, so I prodded him. "So tell me, how did you force Governor Merrill to resign? Blackmail? Bribery? A honey trap? He was the first domino to fall."

"What? Oh no, we had nothing to do with his resignation. I admit it was quite fortuitous, though."

"Give me a break, Thomas. If Merrill had stood for reelection Jill would have stayed in New Hampshire another two years and I would have left the CIA. You had to engineer it."

"Nope. It was just plain luck. Sometimes stuff happens. However, since I'm baring my soul to you, I will say that had Merrill been reelected we would have reached out to Senator D'Amato or someone else to offer Jill a golden opportunity in D.C."

I didn't believe him for an instant. He had spent nearly forty years in the CIA and lying was a way of life to him. I was sick to death of it and told him so. "Nothing you've said changes anything, Thomas. I know my contract still has another year left. Too bad. Sue me. I'm done with you and the CIA."

"Pete, I know you feel betrayed. Maybe you hate me. I understand that. You do have almost a year left on your contract and I expect you to honor it. Speaking of honor, don't do it for me or the CIA or the money. Do it for your country. You already fought in one war. As of today we're in another one. I know you're a patriot. You *are* unique. You *are* irreplaceable. Your country needs you now more than ever."

"You bastard, playing that card on me today, of all days. I'll honor my contract and give you one last year. Then I'm gone."

Chapter Twenty Eight

Thousands of people lay dead beneath the rubble of the World Trade Center. I couldn't do anything about that, but I was hoping to help find the trapped survivors. There are always survivors. Some last for minutes, some for hours. A rare few hang on a day or more. Jefferson had specifically forbidden me to search for them, but to hell with him, I was going to do it anyway. How could I not? If I found survivors I'd find a way to get them rescued, even if I had to go to New York City and do it myself.

That night I lay in bed waiting for sleep to overtake me so I could start searching for survivors. Every minute I lay awake reduced the chances of me finding someone alive, yet I couldn't get to sleep. I went through all the self-hypnosis and calming techniques the shrinks had taught me, to no avail. I just could not get Jefferson's duplicity out of my mind. I had proved "Linda Marchetti" was a phony. The investigators I hired had proved Jill's UCSD job had been maliciously ripped from her grasp. But that didn't hold a candle to Jefferson admitting to my face he had arranged both events, and he was proud of it! It angered me to no end.

I couldn't stop thinking about the letter. Jefferson had paid some scumbag to break into Jill's apartment in New Hampshire and make a copy of Governor Wilson's letter. What if she had unexpectedly come home and something went horribly wrong? It enraged me. Even now the lying weasel refused to admit he had forced Governor Merrill to resign. If he had simply told me the truth, that my country needed me, none of it would have been necessary. I hated him for it.

After hours of tossing and turning I finally drifted off to a light, fitful sleep. I never achieved REM sleep so I could not go out of body to search for survivors. It made me hate Jefferson more than ever.

******

The next night I fell asleep later than usual but managed to enter REM sleep. By the time I was able to search the World Trade Center rubble it was early morning on September 13th. Although it would not be daylight for hours the rubble was lit up like high noon with dozens of high powered emergency lights. I searched every minute of each REM interval, using my standard grid pattern and flying right through the rubble. I found no one. Only twelve people made it out of the debris alive. The last survivor was rescued half a day before I got there.

Jefferson never knew I was searching the debris pile, of course. He thought I was *shifting* to Afghanistan each night. Afghanistan is a large country and the CIA wasn't even sure bin Laden was there. I spent the next five nights sleeping in the headquarters building. When it became obvious the intel guys had no idea where bin Laden might be Jefferson put me back on normal routine and sent me home.

In the past, I'd come home from an extended stay at headquarters and Jill would try to figure out what I'd been working on. She knew I couldn't tell her but that didn't stop her from trying. She'd scan the television and newspapers and scour the internet, then throw a news item my way. "Was it the North Korean missile tests? How about the attacks in the Gaza strip?"

Sometimes, just to mess with her, I'd give her some kind of ambiguous sign, like an arched eyebrow or a frown. She could interpret it either as an affirmation or denial, whichever made her feel better. It was a little game we played.

When I came home this time there was no need to play games. She knew why I had been called into work. When she put Adilyn down for a nap we sat together to talk. America would never be the same again. My work for the CIA would never be the same either, not because of 9/11 but because of my boss's treachery. Jefferson had broken faith with me so I felt justified in breaking faith with him. He had involved Jill by ordering a burglary of her apartment and manipulating her employment opportunities. She was my wife, the mother of my child, the love of my life. She deserved to know what was really going on. I told her everything, right from the beginning.

******

Jill had a few questions, as you might imagine. A few hundred. Before she had a chance to ask them Adilyn awoke, demanding to be fed. She retrieved our daughter from her crib and sat back down on the couch with me, Adilyn already contentedly at her breast. The sight of them so filled me with love I knew I'd made the right decision by telling her.

I patiently answered all of her questions, then answered some more. Adilyn was on the floor in front of us, busy trying to eat one of her toys. Toys, toes, it didn't matter. Everything went into her mouth. That was her thing lately - she was teething.

Eventually Jill stopped asking questions and lapsed into a period of silent reflection. As for me, I felt better than I had in years. It was like the weight of the earth had been lifted from my shoulders.

******

Jill was in complete agreement with my decision to quit the CIA the following year. She was appalled and shaken by Jefferson's underhanded tactics. She was particularly upset about his forcing Governor Merrill, her former boss and political mentor, to resign. I told her Jefferson claimed to have had nothing to do with that, but Jill didn't buy it, and neither did I. It underscored why I could no longer work for the man - how could I work for someone I didn't trust?

The next morning I awoke and was going through my morning bathroom routine when Jill appeared beside me, rubbing sleep from her eyes. "Where did you go last night?" she asked.

"Afghanistan. Still looking for bin Laden. The intel folks have no idea where he's hiding."

"I watched you in your sleep when I got up to feed Adilyn. You never moved. No twitching, no tossing and turning, no mumbling, nothing. Just peacefully sleeping, like any other person. It's so hard to believe you were in Afghanistan last night."

"Actually, I was there this morning, only minutes ago. I normally wake up after my last and longest REM phase. Today was no different."

"Pete, I believe you. I know everything you told me yesterday was the truth. I could see it in your eyes; hear it in your voice. But intellectually it's so hard to grasp. There's a part of me that says it just can't be, and I hate it that at some level I'm doubting you, even just a tiny bit."

"Well, I had to pass a test to convince Jefferson. I can prove it to you the same way. Change the combination on our safe so only you know it. Write me a note and place it in the safe, along with a lighted flashlight. I can't see in the dark. Tonight I'll fly into the safe, read the note, and tell you what it said in the morning."

The following morning Jill came down to breakfast with Adilyn in her arms. I watched over the rim of my coffee cup as she placed her in her high chair and commenced feeding her some foul-looking greenish gray goop. Adilyn actually seemed to enjoy the stuff. Not long afterward I did my fatherly duty by changing her diaper.

Once Jill was settled in with her coffee I said, "Honey, don't you want me to tell you what your note said?"

"Well, yes, of course, but I didn't want to seem overly anxious. I already believe you, Pete. You don't have to tell me anything, you know. This whole note thing was your idea, not mine."

I had been planning to jokingly tell her she inadvertently left the note face down and I was unable to read it. Seeing her level of anxiety I decided to play it straight.

"'The best and most beautiful things in this world cannot be seen or even heard, but must be felt with the heart.' Helen Keller said that, but you wrote it down and put it in the safe. Very appropriate. You also wrote 'My heart never doubted you, Pete. I love you even more for proving it to my brain.'"

Chapter Twenty Nine

For the remainder of September and the first half of October I *shifted* to Afghanistan every night. I also checked on the POWs in North Korea each night. One of the men had been missing for over a week and I could only assume he had died.

Although I had not found bin Laden I found several arms caches, fortified bunkers and even vehicles stashed in caves. We had so few forces in the country then the locations were passed along but not attacked.

I was still getting weekends off to spend with my family, which kind of surprised me. Also, Jefferson had emailed me to say our weekly meetings at his office were cancelled until further notice. I hadn't seen or spoken with him in a month. I think he recognized how incredibly angry I was and he was giving me time to cool off.

In the latter part of October Jefferson emailed me to inform me our weekly meetings were back on. At our meeting, the atmosphere was frosty but professional. He briefed me on the deployment of our troops to Afghanistan. We still had only a few special operations teams in country, not counting the CIA/spec ops team devoted exclusively to hunting bin Laden. Diplomatic entreaties to the Taliban, the governing force in Afghanistan then, to hand over bin Laden and several other named terrorists fell on deaf ears. As a result the United States would be fighting the Taliban within days.

Our discussion of Afghanistan over, Jefferson hesitated. After a moment he said, "Pete, there's another item of discussion. I've got news on our POWs."

Jefferson knew how much the POWs meant to me. I wasn't going to give him the satisfaction of asking him. I was so sick of his manipulations. He gave me a questioning look. I waited in silence.

"Our North Korean operative has gone missing. The one who was going to bribe one of the prison guards to take pictures of the prisoners. He's more than two weeks overdue to report in. Either he was caught trying to bribe a guard or more likely he absconded with the bribe money we gave him. It's a major setback. It will take us months to get another asset in place to try again. And if the first operative was actually caught at the prison the North Koreans will be waiting for us to try again."

"Those men are dying, Thomas. One of them is already gone. The longer we hesitate the more we'll lose. There's got to be a military option."

"There was. The ad hoc committee recommended against it but even so, Delta Force was training intensively for a rescue, as a last resort. That's no longer an option. Delta's deploying to Afghanistan tomorrow, to start hitting the Taliban. I'm sorry, Pete."

******

On December 5th Jefferson phoned me at home and told me to report to CIA headquarters for an operation expected to last as long as a week. I had been dreading this. It meant I would be forced to interact with Jefferson on a daily basis.

When I arrived he briefed me on the operation. "Humint sources in Pakistan tell us Osama bin Laden is in a cave complex in Tora Bora, a mountainous region of Afghanistan on the Pakistan border. We're getting this from two different sources, one of whom has provided reliable information previously.

"Your job will be to find bin Laden and track him. We already know there's a good sized enemy force in the area, most likely there to provide security for bin Laden. Once we engage them he'll know we're coming for him and may bug out. The area is vast and rugged, far from any villages. It's winter and there are only a small number of mountain passes accessible. He can't go anywhere fast. Once you find him you should be able to keep tabs on him each night fairly easily."

Things didn't quite work out the way the CIA figured. In fact, they didn't work out at all. I never found bin Laden because he was never there. I saw hundreds of Taliban and Al-Qaeda fighters. I drew detailed maps of the various caves and the weapons, supplies and men in each of them.

Jefferson says he passed on all my information to the Afghanistan section in headquarters. I assume they passed it on to the CIA team we had at Tora Bora, and they in turn shared it with the military special operators. That's a lot of assumptions. I mention it because I knew for a certainty bin Laden was not at Tora Bora, but the battle to capture him went on as if he were. Our military air assets rained bombs on those mountains for three days around the clock, in the hope of collapsing the caves. Each night I would *shift* there and find the caves intact, the materiel and men inside unaffected. Every night I would diligently search each cave, every nook and cranny, but I never saw bin Laden.

I ended up sleeping at headquarters for two weeks straight, the longest stretch yet for me. Afterwards, Jefferson told me the onsite commanders chose to disregard my information regarding bin Laden's absence. As far as they knew I was just another "humint" source. Two others were saying bin Laden was there and that was good enough for them.

By the end of 2001 the Taliban government had been toppled and one friendlier to the United States had taken its place. Thousands of American troops were in Afghanistan and thousands more would follow in the months ahead. The United States had seen this all before in Vietnam and those in the military and the CIA settled in for the long, bloody haul ahead.

Chapter Thirty

Things had gotten into a routine so quickly in Afghanistan Jefferson gave me my usual Christmas/New Year vacation. For the first time in five years we would not be going to the Caribbean. With Adilyn still not yet a year old we celebrated the holidays at home.

During the vacation period Jill and I had many long talks about our future. I had over 75 million dollars in overseas banks and five million more in American banks and brokerage firms. We would never need to work again, but Jill felt she still had a lot to contribute to society. She talked about being on the boards of various charitable organizations, working for a think tank, or both. Knowing she had gotten her Washington D.C. political positions only because of Jefferson's intervention soured her on any future work in politics.

As for me, I was counting the days until I left the CIA. The 9/11 attacks and the subsequent war in Afghanistan were consuming all the oxygen at the CIA. The POWs in North Korea were put on a back burner and given little more than lip service. Our military forces had been so reduced in size and capability over the years since the Soviet Union fell apart we were no longer capable of fighting two simultaneous wars in different parts of the world. If a POW rescue attempt turned into a war with North Korea and possibly China we couldn't win it. Faced with that stark reality our government chose to let sleeping dogs lie, and let our forgotten POWs die of old age in captivity. As much as I despised him, Jefferson had been proven right once again. He said from the beginning we would never get the POWs home.

After the CIA I pictured myself as a carefree jet-setting gambler, flying around the world with Jill and Adilyn to exotic gambling meccas such as Monte Carlo, Macau and Puerto Rico. Not to mention Las Vegas and Reno, Nevada, and the hundreds of Indian casinos springing up all across America. We'd buy our own private jet. Perhaps I'd take flying lessons and eventually pilot it myself.

My vision of the future wasn't just about me, though. I'd keep traveling astrally. Anytime there was a natural disaster I'd *shift* there and search for survivors. I'd figure out a way to get the word to the authorities. Money buys access, and I had plenty of it. I'd keep an astral eye on the POWs and find a way to get them freed. If the United States government wasn't interested in them I'd get the word to other intelligence services, or the media, or some receptive politicians. I had the money and they were rapidly running out of time.

I'd even keep looking for Osama bin Laden. I had studied countless maps of Afghanistan and Pakistan and they were all still there in my eidetic memory. If I found him it would only take one phone call to Jefferson. As much as I hated that man I hated bin Laden even more.

******

The first half of 2002 passed quickly. Adilyn learned to walk in March. By June she was talking a lot but not actually making sense yet. Of course, the same could be said of many adults. Jill was learning everything she could about the charities that interested her. I was *shifting* to Afghanistan and Pakistan most nights, with an occasional jaunt to Moscow or Iraq. Moscow to count nuclear weapons and Iraq to look for them, or evidence of other weapons of mass destruction. Our POWs remained in North Korea, their number now down to ninety three.

I kept waiting for Jefferson to call me in to give me his big pitch for my continued service with the CIA. He knew how much I despised him, so I was betting his boss or even the director himself would personally issue the job offer. In mid-July, when the call finally came, I was kind of disappointed it would only be Jefferson. I had been looking forward to telling his bosses where to stick their offer.

******

When I walked into Jefferson's office two days later I was surprised to see the director of the CIA sitting in Jefferson's chair, with no one else in the room. When he stood and introduced himself to me I reluctantly shook his offered hand. It would have been too awkward not to.

He started off by apologizing for Jefferson's past transgressions, but did not dwell on them. "Jefferson is retiring. If you stay on with us you'll be working with someone new."

Next he appealed to my patriotism and sense of duty to country. Finally, he got around to salary and benefits. "Fifty million dollars, Pete. Annual salary, no more contracts. Anytime you feel like it you could resign and walk out the door. The president himself has approved the amount and will help us hide it from congress. You're still a young man. If you stayed with us another twenty years you'd make a billion dollars, that's billion with a B. Assuming normal investment returns you'd be one of the richest men on the planet by the time you retired. We're talking about generational wealth, Pete, passed on to your children, and your children's children."

I was about to politely decline when he held up one hand. "I don't want your answer now. Take a few days off. Go home and discuss it with Jill. That's right, you heard me. This is too important to keep to yourself. You have my permission to tell her what you really do and why you'd be getting paid so much money. The non-disclosure agreements Jill has already signed will cover it."

Chapter Thirty One

The two unexpected days off gave us a four day weekend. We decided to charter a small private plane and fly up to Bar Harbor, Maine to escape the July heat in Virginia and discuss the director's offer. The recently established Transportation Security Administration (TSA) had made commercial airline travel a nightmare worthy of a Stephen King novel.

Jill and I were both dumbstruck by the director's offer. No more Jefferson. Fabulously wealthy. Quit anytime. It was too good to dismiss out of hand. We had to seriously consider it. We sat alone together under a beach umbrella in a secluded cove, the private property of the bed and breakfast where we were staying. Adilyn lay between us swathed in blankets in her car seat, marveling at the world.

"The war in Afghanistan is only going to get bigger. We'll be there for years to come. We'll also be going into Iraq pretty soon, too. No one's said anything official yet but I can see it coming. I like the idea of being in the fight when our country's at war."

Jill took another sip of her drink and then nodded. "I know how much you hate the terrorists, honey. You'll be happier tracking them down then running around the world gambling. What kind of life would that be for our child, anyway?"

We spent quite a while discussing all the positives before turning to the negative. There really was only one. "I'm inclined to take the offer, but I still don't trust them. Every time I think about what they did my blood boils."

"The director told you Jefferson is retiring. More likely he's forcing him to retire in order to retain you. It's a doubly sweet victory for you, honey."

"But I still don't trust them. It's not just Jefferson, he's only a cog in the machine. I don't trust the CIA. They sent a strange man to break into your apartment just to get leverage on me. You could have been killed. I'll never forget or forgive that. It will eat at me every day. How can I work for them under those conditions?"

"Sweetie, I think you're exaggerating the danger a bit. I'm not nearly as upset about it as you are. And all that is in the past. The director told you so."

We sat there, each lost in our own thoughts, no longer really enjoying the magnificent view in front of us. The hypnotic susurration of the surf had nearly lulled me to sleep when Jill said, "Pete, I think I've got the answer. A test, just like Jefferson and I tested you to remove our lingering doubts."

That got my attention and I snapped out of my languor. "What sort of test?"

"You don't trust the CIA because of what Jefferson did to you, to us. But with him out of the picture maybe your distrust is unwarranted. The director apologized to you for what Jefferson did, so maybe Jefferson did it all on his own. Your problem is the 'maybe.' You need to know for sure.

"I think I know how to erase your doubts. The director asked you to call him on Monday to accept or decline his offer. Tell him you're declining it. If it was solely Jefferson, out of control and way off the reservation, the director will wish you good luck and move on. If not, well, if not they'll do something to try to trick you or force you to keep working for them. After you tell the director you're not interested give it a week. If nobody twists your arm to stay then you know the director was sincere in his offer and all the crazy stuff in the past was Jefferson acting on his own. Tell them you changed your mind and decided to accept the offer."

I waited for more but no more was offered. "And?"

"And what?"

"And what if somebody does twist my arm? What if they twist my arm completely off and beat me over the head with the bloody thing? Do I really want to poke that hornet's nest?"

"Well dear, you're the one who said you couldn't work with hornets. Better to find out now than later."

Chapter Thirty Two

On Monday morning I called the director from the secure telephone in my home office. I didn't bother with small talk as I'm sure he is one of the busiest people on earth. "Sir, after talking it over with my wife I've decided to decline your offer."

"I'm disappointed to hear that, Pete. I'm afraid I can't offer you anything more."

"Your offer was quite generous, Director. We just felt it was time to move on to something else. I'm sorry."

"So am I. Please report to Jefferson at his office tomorrow for out briefing. If you ever change your mind just give me a call. Goodbye."

I clicked off the speaker phone and turned to Jill. "Now what?"

She playfully slapped me on the arm. "You heard the man, Pete. If you ever change your mind just give him a call. Wait a few days. When all your doubts about any possible double dealing have passed call him back and say you changed your mind."

******

I met with Jefferson in his office the next day, as ordered. As always, he wore his poker face. "I was sorry to hear you turned down the director's offer, Pete. I think you're making a mistake."

"I really don't care what you think anymore, Thomas. I only hope my leaving doesn't allow you to weasel out of retiring."

Not even a twitch from the man. He could have made a fortune playing poker. "Pete, there're two sides to every equation. Light and dark. Good and evil. Yin and yang. Alpha and omega."

"I'm fluent in four languages, Jefferson, but I have no idea what the hell you're talking about."

"I'm talking about the director's offer. He only showed you the carrot."

"Ahhh, I see. And you're about to show me the stick."

"Yes I am. Since you refused the carrot I have no choice. We're at war and our country needs you. It's that simple. If you refuse the director's offer we will have you involuntarily recalled to active duty in the United States Army. The military services have already put out a call for Arabic speaking veterans and other critical specialists to voluntarily return to active duty. If they don't get enough volunteers they will start involuntarily recalling them. They can do that in time of war, officially declared or not.

"Your case is even easier, since you were a commissioned officer. Go home and reread the oath of office that you swore to and signed. It says you were appointed by the President of the United States and serve at his pleasure. The wording is archaic but the meaning is clearly defined legally - you can be recalled to active duty at any time, for any reason, for the rest of your life.

"Once you're back in active service the army will order you to report to us for duty. You'll be paid the wages and benefits appropriate to your rank of first lieutenant, about $50,000 per year, versus the $50 million the director offered you. As an active duty officer you will be subject to all military laws and regulations. If you refuse to carry out your orders you will be court-martialed and imprisoned. The penalties for dereliction of duty are particularly harsh in wartime. If you think I'm just making all this up call an attorney and get a legal opinion."

I couldn't believe I was hearing this. "I gave the army four years. I gave the CIA ten more. I've given enough, done far more than my share. All I want is a normal life with my family."

"You're not a normal person, Pete, and you'll never have a normal life. That's just something you're going to have to come to grips with. Go home and talk it over with your wife. Her stake in this is just as big as yours. When we talk again tomorrow you have to decide: accept the director's offer or be recalled to active duty in the army. You have no other options."

******

After I got home I briefed Jill on my conversation with Jefferson. She was skeptical of Jefferson's claim about the legality of recalling me to active duty. There was no need to call a lawyer to confirm or refute it, however. She confirmed it in less than five minutes on the internet.

"I told you I didn't want to poke that hornet's nest, but now I'm glad I did. I'll go to prison before I work for those scumbags. Let 'em try to recall me to active duty. I'll hire a dozen lawyers to fight it."

"Oh Pete, he's got to be bluffing. They'd never really do that to you. We're at war and they're playing hardball, that's all it is. Call his bluff. Then when he folds his hand make sure you call the director and let him know the crazy stunt that maniac tried to pull on you. Maybe they won't let him retire. Maybe they'll fire him instead."

******

I walked into Jefferson's office only half believing he had been serious the day before. He cleared up any ambiguity by handing me two pieces of paper. "This is a copy of the presidential order returning you to active duty in the United States Army. And this is a copy of the army order assigning you to the CIA. The easy way or the hard way. $50 million or $50,000. What did you decide?"

I crumpled up the papers and tossed them into the trash can. "I decided you can go to hell. Let the army come get me. They'll have to get through my lawyers first."

I turned my back to him, opened the office door and came face to face with two military policemen in uniform. "Lieutenant Ludvick," the smaller one said as the larger one put his hand on his baton. "Sir, we're here to escort you to Fort McNair to see General Pendergast."

"I mustered out of the army ten years ago, sergeant. You have no authority over civilians."

"You are Ludvick, Peter E.? You match the photo we have."

"Yes, I am. But I'm not in the army, I'm a civilian."

"Our orders are clear, Lieutenant. We're authorized to use force if you refuse to cooperate."

"This is ridiculous. I'm going to call an attorney. I…" I realized Jefferson was sitting ten feet behind me, enjoying the show. I wasn't about to give him the satisfaction of seeing me squirm. "All right, soldier, let's go."

******

During the twenty five minute drive to Fort McNair the MPs said not a word to me or to each other. Before getting into their sedan they searched me and took my cell phone. At least I wasn't in handcuffs.

The military policemen drove me to an administrative building on post and escorted me to an office inside, where the general was waiting. He dismissed the MPs, then walked around the desk and shook my hand warmly. "Good to see you again, Pete, although the circumstances are a bit strange, even for the CIA."

"It's good to see you too, Sir. You look well. And you're wearing stars now. Congratulations." General Pendergast had been my commanding officer during the Gulf War. He was a lieutenant colonel back then. "Fort McNair is an awfully small post for a two star general, isn't it?"

He smiled at that. "I'm a pencil pusher at the pentagon, Pete. A CIA bigwig asked me to meet you here to explain the situation you're in. I guess they figured since you and I had some history you might listen to me."

"You were a fair man and a good CO. I'll listen, but you're not going to change my mind."

We sat down in the small office. "Pete, I'll tell you what they told me. You're a ten year CIA operative with a special skill set they desperately need right now, but you're quitting the company. To prevent you from walking away they've pulled some strings, got you recalled to active duty, then seconded back to the CIA. Is that about right?"

"Close enough."

"I don't work for them Pete. Truth be told, I don't care much for spooks, never have, and I think what they're doing to you really stinks. Here it is in a nutshell: you're screwed. If you don't play ball with them you'll be court-martialed and end up behind bars in Fort Leavenworth. I know they already told you this but they figured if you heard it from me you might actually believe it. Please, believe it. These jerks will push it all the way, and you'll lose."

"How much time would I do if convicted?"

"It's hard to say. I'm not a lawyer, but it seems to me they have a slam dunk case against you for dereliction of duty. That's a maximum of two years in prison."

"I'll take my chances, General."

"I was also told they may charge you with misbehavior before the enemy. That's a lot more serious, Pete."

"What's the penalty for that, Sir?"

"The maximum penalty is death."

I'd be lying if I said that didn't give me pause, but then I realized it could never be proven. While I had spent countless nights in enemy territory over the years my physical body had never left Virginia. Let them try to convince a military judge otherwise. "They've got no case for that, General. I'm looking forward to my day in court."

"Good for you! I hope you beat the conniving slime." He took a deep breath, then frowned. "Let's get it over with. Lieutenant Ludvick, your orders are to report for duty at CIA headquarters. Are you refusing to obey them?"

"I am."

"Very well. You're under arrest for dereliction of duty. You are confined to the limits of this post until ordered differently. You'll be billeted at the officers' quarters. A JAG officer will be assigned as your defense counsel or if you wish you may hire a civilian attorney at your own expense. Do you understand your new orders?"

"Yessir. May I have my cell phone back?"

Chapter Thirty Three

Jill found a great lawyer for me, a retired army JAG colonel who now worked in private practice. He and Jill visited me in my quarters at Fort McNair. The lawyer let Jill see me alone first.

Jill had been a rock over the phone - furious at the CIA and all business. When she saw me in person she broke down in tears. "Oh, Pete, this is so wrong, and it's all my fault. I pushed you into this with my stupid test."

"No, baby, no. I'm glad we tested them. Sooner or later something like this was bound to happen. Now we know the director's talk of me quitting anytime I wanted was pure baloney. As long as I have my unique abilities they'll never leave me alone. They'd work me until I died. Better to deal with this now."

We talked for nearly an hour. I realized the lawyer must be steaming mad, but I had to tell her one more thing. "Jill, don't forget I can still fly. I can visit you and Adilyn every night. If I end up in prison at least I'll have that." I thought the idea might comfort her, but instead it provoked a fresh torrent of tears.

****

The attorney introduced himself as Luis Hernandez. I immediately liked him because he was not your usual stuffed shirt lawyer. "I grew up in El Paso, Texas. Enlisted in the army to escape the street gangs. Got a battlefield commission in Vietnam. The army sent me to college, then law school. I retired in 1999 as a bird colonel. Not bad for a Tex-Mex kid from the wrong side of the tracks.

"Pete, even though I'm your lawyer you can't tell me about your work. I've asked for the proper security clearance but the CIA refuses to discuss it at this point. If we go to trial and you think it's critical that I know, we'll revisit it then. For now, I think we're okay. Honestly, they don't have much of a case. I'm surprised they've pushed it this far."

"My old CO said the case was a slam dunk."

"Oh, you're guilty all right. The army gave you an order and you disobeyed it. That's cut and dried. I was a trial judge my last six years of service. Under these circumstances I can't imagine any judge giving you more than a dishonorable discharge, and I know most of them personally. Maybe sixty days in the stockade if you get one of the real hardcase judges."

"There was talk of charging me with misbehavior before the enemy."

Hernandez laughed out loud. "The CIA boys were a little confused. Whatever you did or didn't do as a CIA operative cannot be adjudicated in a military court because you weren't in the army then. Disobeying an order to report to work in Virginia hardly constitutes misbehavior before the enemy. The only charge is dereliction of duty. I'm confident we can strike a plea bargain and avoid trial."

Jill and I looked at each other. It couldn't possibly be this easy. "Sixty days in jail and a dishonorable discharge? This is the CIA's big stick?"

The lawyer said, "A dishonorable discharge is actually a pretty big deal. You'll be a convicted felon. It will be awfully hard to find a decent job."

Now it was my turn to laugh. "Luis, I probably shouldn't tell my lawyer this, but I'm a multi-millionaire. I never have to work another day in my life. Sixty days in jail is a joke. We have to be missing something here."

"No, as I said, it's cut and dried. If the CIA was trying to hammer you they blew it."

******

Five weeks later, due to a plea bargain, I left the army for the second time, this time as a convicted felon with a dishonorable discharge. It galled me not to fight the CIA over this, but Luis convinced me a trial would take months longer and the result would be the same or worse. I couldn't bear the thought of spending months away from my daughter during this critical stage of her life, so I took the plea bargain.

At home I played with Adilyn until she fell asleep in my arms. Once she was tucked into her crib Jill and I made love like newlyweds - it had been a long five weeks, and we had been through hell.

Afterwards, talking in our living room, I did something I hadn't done in more than ten years - I drank a beer. Then another, and many more. I only stopped when I fell asleep, drunk.

The next morning I woke up with a hangover the size of Cleveland. Jill was sympathetic and did her best to ease my pain by cooking me a nice breakfast and keeping my coffee cup filled. Adilyn, just by being her adorable self, probably did more than anything else to improve my mood.

Near noon our doorbell rang. The closed circuit camera showed two men in suits. I knew right away it could only be bad news, but I never imagined how bad. I briefly considered not opening the door, which was made of reinforced steel, but whatever new turmoil was about to enter my life would only be delayed, not thwarted. I opened the door.

"Peter Ludvick, we're United States Marshals. We have a warrant for your arrest."

The fact that I wasn't the least bit surprised speaks volumes about how much I hated and distrusted Jefferson and the CIA. "On what charge?"

"Tax evasion. You'll have to come with us." The marshals were kind enough to let me hug and kiss Jill and Adilyn before they handcuffed me.

Chapter Thirty Four

The marshals actually seemed like decent guys. Both were military veterans, though neither had been in the army. If they were aware of my newly minted dishonorable discharge it didn't seem to bother them. They chatted freely with me on the drive to the Washington, D.C. jail. Since the District of Columbia is a federal enclave they are able to house federal prisoners awaiting trial.

The guys who arrested me were old hands and knew I wouldn't resist them. Tax evasion is a "white collar" crime generally committed by wealthy people who are otherwise law abiding citizens, so an arrest is usually without drama. Of course, hard core criminals such as Al Capone and mafia chieftains also evade taxes, but even they willingly submit to arrest and rely on their lawyers to free them. I was no exception.

Jill was phoning our lawyer even before I was out of our driveway. Luis Hernandez saw me at the D.C. jail three hours later. "The CIA must be seriously peeved at you, Pete. It's got to be them behind the curtain on this. They struck out with their army stunt. Now they're back up to bat with this."

"Walk me through this, Luis. How long am I going to be in jail? Can I post bail? What happens next, and when?"

"Well, you'll have to spend the night here. You'll have an initial appearance before a federal magistrate tomorrow, where there will be a formal reading of the charges and bail will be discussed. The federal prosecutor and I will argue over bail and the judge will decide.

"The judge will set a date for a preliminary hearing, which has to be within fourteen days of the initial appearance if you are in custody, twenty one days if you're free on bond. At the prelim we'll have a chance to see a good portion of the government's case against you. They have to convince the judge there is sufficient evidence to bind you over for trial, otherwise the charges are dismissed.

"We'll also have an opportunity at the prelim to argue again for bail or reduced bail, as the case may be. Then there is discovery, pretrial motions, possibly evidentiary hearings. Eventually we get to the trial itself, which could last for days or weeks, depending upon the complexity of the case. Cases like this are often quite complicated and take time to present.

"After the trial, if you are found guilty, there are post-trial motions and finally sentencing. If the defendant is in custody the whole time the judge will make every effort to speed things along. If the defendant is out on bond these things can drag on for a year or even two."

I sat there silently, trying to get my head around everything. Luis jumped into the void. "There's more, Pete, and it's not good news. The government is also charging you with money laundering in addition to tax evasion."

"Money laundering? I don't get it."

Luis explained, "Tax evasion can be charged for your willful failure to pay taxes on your earnings, regardless of the source of the income, criminal or legitimate. In other words, the income could be entirely legitimate but if you attempt to hide some or all of it from the government that's tax evasion.

"Money laundering is charged only when money obtained through a criminal enterprise is routed, or 'washed' through a series of other banks or businesses so as to appear to come from a legitimate source. Money laundering is a more serious crime than tax evasion."

I started to interrupt him but he stopped me. "Wait, there's even more. You're also being charged with violation of Title 18 of the United States Code, section 793 - unauthorized disclosure of classified information."

That was quite a hornet's nest I had poked.

******

After my lawyer left I had plenty of time to think over what he had told me. The tax evasion charge carried a maximum ten year penalty. The charge of money laundering had a twenty year maximum sentence. The charge of unauthorized disclosure of classified information carried a ten year maximum sentence *for each violation*. We didn't know yet how many violations they would be alleging.

The money laundering charge was completely bogus. I had done nothing criminal to make money so I couldn't be guilty of laundering. I may or may not have been guilty of tax evasion. My accountants and financial advisors assured me everything they did, setting up all those offshore accounts, was legal, albeit right on the edge of legality. I had a sinking feeling their idea of legal didn't quite square with Uncle Sam's version.

The last charge, unauthorized disclosure of classified information, really bothered me. The only person I had ever talked to about my work was Jill. I told her everything when I came home enraged shortly after 9/11. After that, we talked about my work on a daily basis, just as a normal husband and wife would do. I didn't see how the CIA could know about those conversations. Did it even matter? In July of the following year the director himself gave me permission to tell her everything. I was cautiously optimistic.

******

I had been idiotically optimistic. At the arraignment the next day that became crystal clear. One count of tax evasion. One count of money laundering. One hundred ninety eight counts of unauthorized disclosure of classified information. If found guilty of every count and given the maximum sentence I was looking at over two thousand years in prison.

The U.S. attorney asked for no bail. My lawyer asked the judge to set a reasonable bond. Here's what the federal prosecutor said in response to that: "Your honor, the defendant is a disgraced former army officer who was court-martialed and dishonorably discharged less than two months ago. He held the highest possible security clearance while employed as a contractor for the Central Intelligence Agency and worked on some of their most sensitive projects. Even though he was specifically and repeatedly warned not to do so he discussed his work and these projects with his wife, who held no clearance at all, on a daily basis.

"Mr. Ludvick was paid exceptionally well for his service to the CIA. That money is all accounted for in U.S. banks. However, the government has located over $60 million dollars in offshore banks that the defendant has paid no U.S. taxes on. That money could only have been generated through a criminal enterprise. While we have frozen those assets we believe the defendant has millions of dollars more hidden overseas.

"Mr. Ludvick and his wife frequently travel to the Caribbean and maintain a sailboat in the Cayman Islands. That, coupled with his as yet undiscovered overseas wealth and the amount of prison time he is facing make him a serious flight risk."

What do you think the judge decided?

Chapter Thirty Five

After the arraignment Luis met with me again in jail. "Pete, this would probably be a good time for you to tell me everything you can that's not a national secret. Do you really have $60 million in offshore banks? Where did it come from? Did you really tell Jill everything about your work?"

This was the street kid coming out in Luis. No messing around with niceties and euphemisms, just straight talk. I liked him even more for it.

"Yes, I have all that in offshore banks, and quite a bit more they haven't found. Hopefully they never will. I earned every penny of that money. The CIA paid me two salaries, the official one through Mulvaney & Proust, and the unofficial one directly to my banker in the Caymans. The unofficial money came to about $30 million over the ten years. I made millions more from gambling winnings and investments. There is no criminal enterprise."

"If you can prove the provenance of your money the laundering charge won't stand up. Can you do that?"

"Sure. I signed contracts. It was all spelled out there. The casinos must keep records that will show my winnings. My accountants can show my investment income."

Luis was shaking his head. It's never a good thing when your lawyer is shaking his head. "Pete, I have copies of all your Mulvaney & Proust contracts. Jill gave them to me. They don't show any offshore money at all."

"That's because I signed separate contracts for the offshore money. The CIA classified them, so I had to keep my copies in my office safe at CIA headquarters. We just need to… crap. They've screwed me, haven't they?"

"Yup. I'll submit a formal request for copies of the classified contracts, but their response is sure to be, 'What classified contracts?' The burden of proof is on you to show you came by that money legally, otherwise any movement of the money into investments or other accounts will be considered laundering.

"Pete. I don't mean to make light of the tax evasion and money laundering charges. They're very serious, but they pale in comparison to the Title 18 charges. The government has way overcharged you, they always do. Even so, if they convict you on only ten percent of those charges you're still looking at about two hundred years in prison."

"I'm guilty, Luis, no doubt about that. I felt so betrayed by my boss on 9/11 that when I got home a few days later I told Jill exactly what I do for the CIA. After that, there was no reason not to discuss my work with her every day.

"I can't see them proving it, though. We were always home alone and never discussed my work anywhere else. And in July of this year the director himself gave me permission to tell Jill everything. Honestly, I'm more worried about the other charges."

"Your preliminary hearing is scheduled for two weeks from today. We'll learn a lot more about the government's case then, and I'll try to get the judge to reconsider setting bail. Otherwise, you'll be here until after the trial."

Each night in jail I *shifted* to North Korea to check on the American POWs. I also flew to my house to look in on my family. Jill knew I would so she left me notes under a light in the den. She knew my REM intervals, assuming I went to sleep at 10 PM as I had done for years. She was often awake with Adilyn between 5:30 and 6:00 AM and I got to see them together most mornings. Knowing I was watching Jill would sometimes mouth "I love you" and hug the air. Although my astral presence was in direct contact with her she never felt it, but it sure helped my morale.

******

At my preliminary hearing the judge again denied bail. The government had a bevy of forensic accountants in court. One of them testified to locating my offshore accounts. My tax records sufficed to show I had not paid taxes on the money. I had used some of the offshore money to purchase homes in the Florida Keys and Hawaii. Jill and I stayed in them only infrequently for scuba diving vacations. The rest of the year they were rented out. That was the foundation of the money laundering charge. I had discussed it all with Luis so we were expecting it.

The basis of the Title 18 charges was stunning. The CIA had hundreds of hours of digital audio recordings of Jill and me speaking in our house! The U.S. attorney explained that after the passage of the Patriot Act on October 26, 2001 the

CIA had obtained a secret warrant to record everything in my house. CIA technicians had installed all the electronics in my house when I first moved in. I suspect they installed listening devices back then. Maybe they had been listening to my private conversations for years, or maybe they were telling the truth in court. Either way, the invasion of my privacy was outrageous. Legally, my goose was cooked.

Luis had hired two other attorneys to assist him in my defense. One was an expert in tax evasion and money laundering cases and the other specialized in national defense cases. All my lawyers and the judge were in the process of getting security clearances. The government had already filed a slew of motions to exclude any mention of my classified operations. Essentially, they were saying, "We have recordings of Ludvick revealing classified information to his wife but we can't let you hear those recordings, just take our word for it." It was bizarre.

A trial date was set for April of 2003. The government claimed to need two months to complete the background checks and issue security clearances to my lawyers, and that was just for the lower level clearances. If the government lost its bid to exclude all the highly classified info then my attorneys would need to go through additional checks to receive higher clearances. The judge ordered a special master to be appointed to review all the classified recordings. The government was appealing his ruling. Basically, the government was signaling it was going to appeal every ruling and fight every adverse decision with tooth and nail. Meanwhile, I sat in jail.

Chapter Thirty Six

The preliminary hearing had been closed to the public for national security reasons. Even Jill was not allowed to attend. After the hearing Luis told Jill of the audio recordings made in our house and passed on my suggestion that she move into a hotel until we could have a private security firm sweep our house for listening devices.

Jill and Adilyn came to visit me in jail as often as allowed, which was once a week. As my attorney, Luis was allowed unlimited visits but he also normally came by once a week. Even though he did not yet have a security clearance I offered to tell him everything about my work at the CIA. He actually paled when I said it. "God, no, Pete, don't even think about it! Federal law prohibits the government from listening in on attorney/client conversations, but this is a national security case, so all bets are off. I'm assuming they're listening to everything we say, and so should you."

One month after the preliminary hearing I was escorted to the attorney/prisoner visiting room. When I arrived it was empty. A minute later a man I had never seen before walked in and sat down. He did not introduce himself. "I have a message from your former boss. Now that you've felt the stick maybe you'd like another bite at the carrot. It can happen. Come back to work for us and all this goes away, like a bad dream. You'll still get what the director offered. All your accounts will be unfrozen. Even your dishonorable discharge will be expunged. Talk to your lawyer about it."

Before I could even consider a response he got up from the table and waved a hand at the security camera. The door opened, and he was gone. I sat there dazed, wondering if this was real or if I was back in my cell asleep, having a lucid dream.

******

I discussed Jefferson's offer with Luis on his next visit. He was not surprised. "Pete, I'm convinced everything that's happened to you since you turned down the director's offer has been contrived to coerce you into changing your mind. I think the CIA set you up for this years ago, in anticipation of this exact eventuality. It's all been rolled out way too smoothly for them to have done this off the cuff."

"Yep, I agree. Susan warned me not to trust Jefferson, but I had no idea he would go this far."

"Susan? Is she someone you worked with? Perhaps she might be able to assist us in your defense."

"Ah, crap Luis, forget about her. I never should have mentioned her name. And no, I never worked with her and she wouldn't be able to help us anyway."

"Okay, Pete. I hope you realize you're in deep kimchee and need all the help you can get. As it stands now you're looking at a few hundred years in prison. Have you thought about accepting Jefferson's offer?"

"Not even for a moment! That'd be a deal with the devil if there ever was one. Once I knuckle under to those scumbags they'd know they own me. Why bother paying me all that money when all they have to say is 'do this or go back to jail?' Why give me weekends off when the alternative is prison? I'd be a virtual slave to those people. No thanks, as weird as it sounds I'd rather be a 'free' man in prison than a slave to them in the 'free' world."

"It's not just about you, Pete. You have to think about your wife and daughter. Especially your daughter. Every child needs a father."

"Arrrggghh! Stop it! Did Jefferson get to you, too? It's tearing me up inside to think about Adilyn growing up without me."

Luis wheezed out a mournful sigh. "I'm sorry, Pete. I'm your lawyer, and sometimes I have to tell you things you don't want to hear. This is one of those times. We're not going to win this one. The deck is stacked against us. You're paying me for my advice. My advice to you is to take Jefferson's offer. Get your life back. Be with your family."

******

During her next visit I discussed Jefferson's offer with Jill. She was sympathetic to my reasoning but she wanted me to come home. "I miss you, Pete, and I need you. More than that, Adilyn needs her father. Come home to us. Take the offer."

I couldn't believe it! My own wife turning against me! Had Jefferson gotten to my lawyer and my wife? Didn't they see I could never work for the CIA again? I felt my sanity slipping away.

Chapter Thirty Seven

My case went to trial on August 18th, 2003, almost a year to the day since I was arrested. The original trial date of April was apparently just an easily moved target date. My lawyer was angry with me for not taking the simple way out. My wife, well, my wife hadn't even visited me for the last two weeks. I guess that says it all right there. I was fighting on my own.

The trial lasted three weeks. Jill remained angry with me and did not attend. Right after jury selection was completed but before the trial itself started I received another visit from Jefferson's emissary. He told me in exchange for my freedom I would have to agree to work with the CIA for the rest of my life at whatever salary and conditions they decided. The director's offer was history. The messenger made it clear once I was convicted there was nothing anyone could do about it. This was my final chance. I told him to shove it and never even mentioned it to Luis or Jill.

The U.S. attorney had pushed hard for a non-jury trial but Luis had pushed back just as hard demanding I receive one. It was one of the few victories we achieved. As a result, rather than expose the CIA's secrets to twelve citizens the government dropped nearly all of the Title 18 charges, leaving me liable for only eight counts of unauthorized disclosure of classified information. Those eight counts were specific enough to convict me but not reveal any hint of what I actually did for the CIA.

When the trial was over I stood convicted of one count of tax evasion, one count of money laundering, and eight counts of unauthorized disclosure of classified information. The judge sentenced me to the maximum penalty of one hundred ten years in prison.

Luis immediately announced his intention to appeal the verdict. He asked the judge to allow me to remain in the Washington, D.C. Jail pending the appeal. His request was denied. A week later Luis informed me I would be transferred any day to the United States Penitentiary near Florence, Colorado, known as "ADX Florence" or simply "Supermax." It has a well-deserved reputation as the toughest, highest security federal prison in America. Only the most incorrigible inmates, the baddest of the bad, are sent to Supermax. Apparently I was one of them.

Jill and Adilyn visited me on my last day in the D.C. Jail. It was bittersweet, with much crying by all of us. Luis had passed on to Jill information on how she could safely access the approximately $20 million I still had in offshore banks that the government had been unable to find and confiscate. Our properties in Hawaii and the Florida Keys had been seized by the government as part of the supposed money laundering scheme, but we owned our home in Virginia free and clear. Jill and Adilyn would not be hurting for money, but they were hurting just the same. She couldn't bear to live in our Virginia home any longer and told me she would put it on the market and move far away. I found out through Luis they ended up in Coronado, California.

Chapter Thirty Eight

Time passes ever so slowly in prison, but it does pass. I always took advantage of my one hour per day outside my cell. Every night I escaped to wherever I wanted, but my nightly excursions always included a trip home to look in on Jill and Adilyn. I also checked daily on the POWs in North Korea. Their numbers continued to slowly but inevitably diminish.

In May of 2006 word swept through the Supermax of a newly arrived prisoner - Zacarias Moussaoui, the so-called "20th hijacker." On September 11, 2001 nineteen Islamic terrorists hijacked airplanes and changed our country forever. Moussaoui was supposed to have joined them onboard one of the doomed planes but for some reason he did not.

September 11, 2001 had forever changed my life as well, initiating the chain of events that led to me being imprisoned here in Supermax. How ironic that I end up sharing my fate with one of the would-be hijackers.

Not long after Moussaoui arrived I learned from Luis that my appeal had been denied. While there were still a couple of legal long shots left Luis held out little hope of prevailing. I told him not to bother, as his fees must be eating up a significant chunk of what I now thought of as Jill and Adilyn's money. To my great surprise I learned Luis had refused any payment for his appellate work. He was so incensed at what our government had done to me he vowed to work on until all possible avenues were exhausted.

With little to no possibility of me ever getting out of prison Jill told me she wanted a divorce. I still loved her and Adilyn with all my heart and because of that I immediately agreed. I wanted her to be happy and as much as it broke my heart to think it, Adilyn needed a father who would be there to nurture her and guide her as she grew up.

******

In January 2007, two weeks after our divorce became final I received a visitor. As soon as I learned he was a CIA man I should have demanded to be taken back to my cell, but the chance to be out of it was too good to pass up. It was a decision I would come to regret immensely.

Visitors of prison inmates never make small talk. Their time is limited and there is no point in asking about the usual inanities of food, health or weather - none of that matters in prison. My visitor got right to it. "Mister Ludvick, my name is Madison. I replaced Thomas Jefferson as head of the project. I'm here to offer you your job back."

The whole idea was so absurd I laughed out loud, startling myself. It was the first time I had laughed in years. As I was slowly recovering from what became an uncontrollable laughing jag Madison spoke again. "I assure you, sir, I am absolutely serious. If you…"

"Wait a minute. Madison is your last name?"

"Yes, it is. My full name is…"

"Let me guess. Your full name is James Madison, Jr., just like our fourth president. Or did you leave off the Junior?"

"No, you're correct. How did you know that?"

"At some point Jefferson told me he was the third director of the project. Even though he swore Thomas Jefferson was his real name it was just too much of a coincidence - Thomas Jefferson was the third U.S. president.

"James Madison is not your real name, is it? And Jefferson was not my boss's real name either, was it?"

"Jefferson told me you were quite astute, Pete. May I call you Pete?"

"No, absolutely not! And since I don't know your real name I'll just call you asshole. It's not a word I would have used a few years ago but prison changes a person. Jefferson lied to me from day one and kept on lying for ten years. Now Jefferson's gone and here you are, day one, lying to me."

The flustered CIA man tried to recover by telling a little bit of truth. "James Madison is not my real name. I am the fourth director of the project, hence my assumed name is Madison. My real name is not important. What is important is what I can offer you, which is your life back. If you agree to work for me I can have you out of…"

"My life back? My life is over. You took it from me. My wife divorced me. My daughter barely knew me and doesn't remember me. I earned every penny of the money the government stole from me, and you know it. All the charges against me were trumped up crap. I served my country with honor in wartime and you sullied my name forever with a dishonorable discharge. I've done nothing to deserve the horrors you've inflicted on me. I gave the CIA ten good years and in return you gave me the rest of my life in prison. If I wasn't chained to this chair I'd beat you to death with my bare hands. Get the hell out of here and stay out of my life."

Of course Madison did not leave. Instead he just calmly sat there, absorbing all my bile. Eventually I ran out of steam and sputtered into silence. "Yes, Mr. Ludvick, your life is over, but it doesn't have to be. We'll start you off with millions of dollars up front. All of it above board this time. Fully taxable, but fully legal. We'll call it a hiring bonus. With your gambling acumen you'll make many millions more, legally. Your wife has not remarried. In fact, she's not even dating yet. There's still time to recover from this. You served your country well in war. Your country is still at war, two wars now, and we badly need you. So much so the President of the United States is willing to issue you a full pardon. Your dishonorable discharge can be expunged as well. You can have it all back."

I wasn't buying any of it. "You people lied to me from beginning to end. The last word I got from Jefferson was an offer of lifetime slavery for the CIA in return for not being in prison. He said it was my final chance. Once I was convicted there was nothing to be done about it. Now here you are dangling a presidential pardon in front of me. A possibility Jefferson must have known about all along. It was all lies, from start to finish."

"You have to trust me, Pete. I'm not Jefferson."

I exploded, my face purple with rage. "Jefferson wasn't Jefferson! You're not Madison! Trust you? You're all liars. You're all Jeffersons. Him, you, the director, all of you. Find another slave. I'll never work for the CIA again."

Chapter Thirty Nine

Prior to Madison's visit, like all prisoners, I thought time passed agonizingly slowly. Now, knowing I could leave prison anytime simply by agreeing to work for the CIA again, every tick of the clock was exquisite torture. Surely Madison must have known how his offer would affect me. Known? He was counting on it. I was being manipulated all over again. Played like a fiddle. It made me hate him all the more.

I couldn't live without Jill and Adilyn, but I couldn't live with myself if I worked for the CIA. Suicide seemed to be the obvious answer and I spent countless hours seriously contemplating it. I was not considered a suicide risk so I had the means - bedsheets to hang myself, even the pen I was using to write this memoir. I could use it to rip open the jugular vein in my neck. I could place the tip against my eye and run face first into my cell wall. If I didn't quite have the gumption for that I could always pick a fight with one of the pumped up gorillas and let him beat me to death. If I was totally gutless I could just pay one of the hardcore crazies to kill me.

Alternatively, I could pretend to agree to work for Madison and be released from prison. Once free I could flee the country and go into hiding. Yeah, right, just abscond from CIA headquarters, as if they never imagined I might try such a thing. They'd be watching me more intently than a cat watches a canary. If by some miracle I got away then all I had to do was evade the combined might and focused efforts of the United States government for the rest of my life. Sure. The odds of me running this ballpoint pen through my eye and into my brain are higher. I was right back to square one: I could only get my family back by working for the CIA but I couldn't work for the CIA. A classic Catch-22 situation. Knowing it didn't make it any easier. I rued the day I stayed to listen to Madison's offer. Astral traveling every night allowed me some respite and checking in on Jill and Adilyn helped, but in some ways it made things even worse. I felt my mind slowly but surely slipping into the abyss.

******

Salvation comes to a few lucky prisoners, usually by way of finding religion. On June 12, 2008 my salvation came from a different source. I was so stressed and despondent by then it had affected my ability to go out of body. My dreams were filled with horrid nightmares from which I could not escape. Two or three times a month I would get a reprieve from them and fly gratefully into the astral plane. June 12th was such a night. Upon leaving my body I looked in on Jill and Adilyn, then *shifted* to North Korea to check on the POWs. They were gone! Their prison held no trace of them; in fact, it was completely devoid of both prisoners and guards.

I spent hours that night fruitlessly searching for the men I had come to know so intimately. Having endured years in prison myself I felt a special kinship with these unsung and forgotten heroes. I had to find them. I had last seen them nine days previously. They could be anywhere by now, perhaps even back in America, finally rescued from their incomparable hell, but I didn't believe that. They had been lost for thirty years before I found them and now they were lost again, due to my self-indulgent neglect. I had to find them. I remembered every one of their faces and each of the thousands of prisons I had searched. They could be in any one of them, or someplace completely new. Locating them became my passion, my mission in life. My quest to find them again dredged me up from the doldrums and saved my sanity.

Chapter Forty

On October 3, 2009 I received another visitor. Instead of me being escorted down to the visitors' area she came to me in my prison cell early that morning. It was Susan!

Our astral entities embraced and I was suffused with that incredible feeling of oneness. Susan insists it is not love but when in the throes of it I can think of no other word to adequately describe it. I was content to simply bask in the glow of the "not love" but Susan almost immediately started "talking" to me.

"Pete, I've been looking for you for three years. I'd just about given up hope."

"Three years? I've been behind bars for seven already."

"I didn't realize you were missing until five years ago, when I flew to your house in Virginia one night and found complete strangers occupying it. I asked Jefferson where you were and of course he lied to me. He said you had quit and gone into hiding. I occasionally fly through CIA headquarters and eavesdrop because I've never trusted them. Three years ago I overheard Jefferson say something about you being in prison. I started searching for you that day, but I'm not as adept as you are in directing my travel."

"That's right, you can hear sounds while astral traveling. My lack of hearing in the astral plane frustrated Jefferson to no end."

"Each astral traveler is unique, with different abilities, different strengths and weaknesses, just as people are. I'm glad I found you, Pete. I have much to tell you. I'll come back again soon, but my time tonight is ending. Goodbye for now." Before I could protest she was gone.

******

For the next few nights I went out of body but never left my cell, waiting for Susan. On the third night she returned. As our first order of business we agreed she would come to my cell every third night for the near term. Susan said she had other urgent business to attend to and her flying abilities had recently become less reliable. She had never told me where she lived and I never asked. I knew a lot about her but what I didn't know could fill volumes, and it was obvious she wanted it that way. Out of respect for her privacy I had not attempted to find out.

I told Susan all the things Jefferson had done to me since I tried to quit after the 9/11 terrorist attacks. She listened in silence, never doubting, never questioning. Not for the first time I wondered if it was even possible to lie to someone while mentally communicating in the astral plane.

On her next visit Susan did most of the talking. "I don't work for the CIA anymore, Pete. I had an arrangement with Jefferson, but now that he's gone my obligation is too."

"Obligation? He told me once you were a volunteer."

"My relationship with Jefferson was very complicated. Now that he's dead it doesn't matter anymore."

"Dead! I didn't know he was dead."

"Ah, yes, how could you know? He reached the mandatory retirement age and they shoved him out the door, kicking and screaming. Two months later he killed himself. The world is a better place for it. He was a great patriot, but he was not a good person."

"And the man who calls himself Madison? He says he will free me if I work for him. What do you know of him?"

"Nothing, except that he is CIA, so he is not to be trusted. You will never truly be free working for them, Pete. You know that, and that's why you're still here. Take heart, I have a plan to free you, but my time is up and it must wait until our next visit."

******

Those three days stretched out like an August afternoon in the desert. I spent my days going crazy, alternating between hope and despair. My nights were split between Coronado, California and various prisons in North Korea. Still no sign of the American POWs.

When Susan returned I was like a kid at Christmas, desperately hoping the puppy I wanted was inside one of the presents under the tree, but secretly knowing it just couldn't be there. "I don't know how long I can stay, Pete. Astral traveling gets harder and harder for me."

"I know your abilities are different than mine, Susan, but I don't understand what you mean."

"I'm dying, Pete. Soon now."

I was taken aback. Then I remembered how sickly she looked when I last saw her physical body fourteen years previously. As I struggled to gather my thoughts Susan interrupted. "I'm okay with it, Pete. Death is a part of life. There's life on earth and life here in the astral plane. Who's to say there's not something else? Please don't dwell on my situation, we need to address yours."

Despite my protestations she forged ahead. "Once I learned you were in prison I had two goals - find you, and find a way to get you out. I never for a moment believed you could possibly deserve to be in prison.

"You know at the CIA they called me the hitchhiker. My job was to find other astral travelers. I found many before you and many after you. None of them have all the gifts you have. I told Jefferson about some but not all of them. To my knowledge, no one has come close to replacing you.

"My plan to get you released from prison is a simple one. The CIA was extorting you to return to work for them. I decided to extort them to free you. Once I devised my plan I went back and studied the travelers I had not revealed to the CIA. Two of them may be the key to getting you out of prison. Both have the ability to direct their travel. Both are highly intelligent. One is an engineer for Lockheed Martin in Arizona. He speaks three languages. The other is a senior high honors student in Waverly, Iowa. She's a physics major. They are ideal candidates to work for the CIA."

I interrupted her. "And yet you never told Jefferson about them. I thought that was your job."

"I told you, my relationship with Jefferson was complicated. I never accepted money from the CIA. Unlike you, I had no contract. I did what I did for our country, and for my own more personal reasons. Pete, I'm exhausted. Please, let me finish.

"These two travelers are your ticket to freedom. Freedom from prison and also from the CIA. With your permission I will tell Madison of their existence, but I'll only tell him their names and addresses after you are released from prison via a presidential pardon. I no longer work for the CIA and I'm dying. There's nothing they can do to me. I'll give them these two travelers only on the condition that they release you and promise to let you live your life without interference."

I was stunned, but I could tell Susan was laboring to stay here with me so I hurried on. "Susan, I can't understand how you could even suggest such a thing. You'd be condemning these people to a life of slavery for the CIA. You know I'd never agree to that. What am I missing?"

She responded weakly, as if from a distance. "I was never a slave to them, only you, because they trapped you when you took their illegal money. I'll tell you where these travelers live and you can meet them in the astral plane. Warn them of all the pitfalls. Tell them of your experience with Jefferson, then let them decide, but only after you are free."

I was conflicted. I hated the CIA and didn't want anyone else to ever fall into their grasp again, yet I desperately wanted to be with my family and out of prison. Susan must have sensed my indecision.

"Pete, did you save lives at the CIA? Fight our enemies? Help our nation? For ten years your life was good, your work was critically important and rewarding. Only the lies ruined it. Forewarned, these new travelers can serve our country and protect themselves, and you can be free. You chose to work for the CIA with no knowledge of Jefferson's duplicity. If they choose, with full knowledge, you bear no responsibility for their decision. You can…"

Susan was abruptly gone and I was alone in my cell.

I knew from her weak presence and sudden departure something was seriously wrong with her. I hoped her declaration that she was dying soon was merely pessimism on her part.

Isolated in my cell I had plenty of time to consider her plan to extort the CIA into releasing me. The more I thought about it the better I liked it. Susan hadn't had time to explain the timing of her plan. I wasn't about to pull a bait and switch routine like a shady used car salesman. I would tell these other astral travelers my whole story up front. Even if they had no interest in working for the CIA perhaps, after hearing my story, they would be willing to feign an interest long enough for me to get my pardon. I was relying on my belief that there are no lies in the astral plane, only truth. They would know I was telling the entire story, warts and all. No good, decent person would allow another to rot in prison undeservedly. I was counting on their humanity.

It also occurred to me the CIA might eventually find these people without me, or they could reveal themselves. If I spoke with them first in the astral plane they would be fully prepared when Madison came knocking, offering his lies, half-truths and euphemisms. If Madison wouldn't take no for an answer all they had to do was flunk his tests. He had no way of proving otherwise, and I would be sure to tell them so.

******

Three nights later I waited anxiously and fruitlessly for Susan to return. For the three nights after that I went out of body but never left my cell, in the unfulfilled hope she would appear. Each night after that I *shifted* to CIA headquarters looking for her, regularly *shifting* back to my cell for brief periods lest I miss her there. It felt like a bizarre version of astral phone tag, but the longer it went on the more I was convinced I was the only player.

Eleven days after last seeing Susan she appeared in my cell. We embraced and I knew instantly she was in dire straits. Her presence was faint and fluttery, like a moth's wings, and just as fragile. Even her thoughts seemed forced, breathless. "You were right, Pete. This *is* love. I always loved you. Goodbye."

For only the second time in my life I heard a sound in the astral plane. A tiny, subtle popping sound as Susan left. Recalling my experience with the dying airman in Saudi

Arabia I knew Susan was dead. My best friend in two different worlds was forever gone, and with her my last chance for freedom. My grief was so intense I woke myself up, sobbing uncontrollably. A long time later a hideous thought flashed through my head: Was I grieving only for Susan or was I also selfishly lamenting losing my final shot at freedom? To my eternal shame I have to say I'm still not sure.

Chapter Forty One

A week after Susan's death (I knew she was dead as surely as I know my own name) my lawyer's representative came to visit me and collect the newly written pages of my manuscript. He was a local attorney so everything we said was protected by the attorney-client privilege, but I had long ago stopped believing that. Any government that would falsely imprison one of its own citizens would surely ignore all the other constitutional safeguards.

I told him I had to see Luis in person as soon as possible but refused to go into details. The attorney was frustrated by my insistence on not talking to him about it but I knew Luis would understand. He showed up two days later.

When we met I asked him for paper and a pen. I wrote out my instructions, carefully covering what I was writing with my other hand and body. I knew where the obvious security cameras were but there might be others. Once Luis put the paper in his briefcase I gave him further instructions by whispering in his ear. We communicated in that manner back and forth until he was satisfied he understood what I needed, then he left.

I had decided to carry out Susan's plan but I was lacking two essential ingredients - the two astral travelers she had discovered. My eidetic memory was still as good as ever, so I recalled almost exactly everything she had told me about them. It wasn't much, but I hoped it was enough. One was an engineer with Lockheed Martin in Arizona who spoke three languages. Susan had referred to him as "he" so I knew he was male. The other was a senior high honors student in Waverly, Iowa majoring in physics. Susan referred to that person as "she" so I knew she was female.

Lockheed Martin Corporation is a gigantic defense/aerospace company that employs thousands of engineers. But I knew the person I was looking for was located in Arizona, so that narrowed it down a lot.

Waverly, Iowa must be pretty small since I had never heard of it. There, I was looking for a female physics major, which implied she was in college. How many colleges could there be in a small Iowa town? And Susan said she was a senior and a high honors student, narrowing it down greatly. I felt I had an excellent chance of finding her.

My written instructions to my lawyer were to hire an investigative agency to compile a list of people fitting the descriptions of these two, which Luis would then deliver to me. That occurred in mid-December of 2009. For me, Christmas had come early. Always mindful that the CIA could have everything in my cell confiscated at any time, rather than taking the list of names from Luis I instead committed a portion of them to memory and he returned the list to the safety of his briefcase.

There was good news and bad news in the list. The good news - Waverly, Iowa had only one college, Wartburg College, a small, private school with 304 members of the senior class. Of that number, only 21 were female physics majors, all of whom were on the Dean's list.

The bad news - Lockheed Martin had three separate facilities in Arizona, all in the greater Phoenix area. They employed well over one thousand people in Arizona. 447 held the title of engineer of one thing or another and 402 of them were men. It was just another example of my bad luck that men overwhelmingly dominated the engineering professions.

The investigators told Luis without using extra-legal means such as breaking into the company's personnel files it could take years to determine which of the employees spoke three languages, since language skills were not part of an engineer's job description. I was stuck with all 402 names and addresses.

******

Susan had a special gift - the ability to see from long distances other astral travelers in the astral plane. She once described it as seeing cars on a mostly deserted highway. I had no such talent so I had to find these travelers a different way. I started with the female physics majors and *shifted* to the first address on the list. Upon entering the bedroom of a small apartment I found a young woman asleep. Throughout the night, for every minute of each of my REM periods I waited for her astral entity to appear. Nothing happened, so either she was not the astral traveler I was looking for or she was but had not gone out of body that night. If she had, I was certain I would have sensed her as I had sensed Susan in the past.

I visited two other young women the next two nights, also without success, but I was feeling confident. Already I was down to only eighteen candidates, which represented less than three weeks' time. On the fourth night I shifted to the listed address and discovered it was a four bedroom house. Two of the bedrooms held young women of college age. I hadn't thought of that possibility and didn't know if I would sense an astral traveler other than in close proximity to myself. I was forced to return to the same address the following night and stake out the other bedroom. I could only hope none of the listed addresses was a sorority house with a dozen bedrooms.

On my twelfth night staked out in a young woman's bedroom I got lucky. Okay, maybe there's a little double entendre there, but you know what I mean. I found her. I was at the very end of my twenty minute REM interval and about to leave when she went out of body. I sensed her presence but before I could do anything further I was involuntarily pulled back to my prison cell.

Ninety minutes later I entered my forty minute REM phase and immediately *shifted* back to her bedroom. Ten minutes later she left her sleeping body. Since this had to be at least her second REM period she would have twenty minutes or more out of body. I had no idea if she was aware of me, but she did not immediately *shift* or fly out of her house. I slowly closed the distance to her presence so as not to frighten her. Moments later we connected with the now familiar feeling of oneness. At least it was familiar to me. I found out it was Megan's first experience meeting another astral traveler. We "talked" for her entire twenty minute REM interval, getting to know each other. I tried my best to answer the dozens of rapid fire questions she threw at me.

It felt odd being the experienced traveler for a change. With Susan, I felt like a child at the feet of his grandmother, absorbing the wisdom she had gained over a long lifetime.

When Megan's REM period was almost over we agreed to meet in the next REM interval, which would give us forty minutes together. In fact, we met every REM phase for the next five nights. Megan never doubted my story for an instant. The feeling of oneness is so overwhelmingly powerful I had a much harder time convincing her she was not madly in love with me.

Without hesitation she agreed to help get me out of prison. She was curious about working for the CIA as an astral spy and intrigued by the potential to make millions of dollars. She wasn't sure she really wanted to work for them but even if not she was willing to fake an interest in order to get me released from prison.

Among many other things, I learned Megan could hear normally in the astral plane. Madison would certainly be thrilled about that. Megan wanted to meet with me nightly and astrally travel places together. I admit it sounded fascinating but I had to find the Lockheed Martin engineer. I didn't think Megan alone would be enough to get me freed. With 402 men to check out I might be at it for a year or more. Megan was disappointed but then she came up with a brilliant suggestion - she would help me find the engineer. It would cut the search time in half.

******

Megan and I coordinated our sleep routines so our REM phases would overlap as much as possible. Each night during our initial ten minute REM period I would give her two names and addresses of Lockheed Martin engineers. She did not have an eidetic memory and two at a time was all she could handle. After the ten minute REM period she would wake herself up, write down the info I had given her, and go back to sleep. It was pretty raggedy at first, but she soon got into a routine.

A week into our search when we met in the first REM interval Megan excitedly told me she had found another way to reduce our search time. When she *shifted* to an address on her list she found her target engineer awake and drinking bourbon. Alcohol! Megan had been a teetotaler all her young life but she recalled my story of regular alcohol use prohibiting out of body experiences. Any target we found drinking couldn't be eliminated entirely but instead of wasting a night watching him she suggested we move him to the back of the list as a low probability target. She went on to say we could search each target residence for signs of regular alcohol use such as beer cans in the trash or alcoholic beverages in abundance. If the target person lived alone the odds were high the alcohol was for his own use and he could be moved to the back of the list. This girl wasn't a physics major for nothing!

Each month I met with Luis to update him on my search and memorize another chunk of names and addresses. Even with Megan's help and moving less likely candidates to the bottom of the list it was still a long, slow slog. The fact that a young college coed was willing to spend night after night bored to tears watching sleeping men solely to help me out spoke volumes about her character. Two months into the search I broke from routine and asked Megan if she was interested in taking a night off to astrally explore together. She jumped at the chance. For some reason it had never occurred to her to try my favorite thing, astral scuba diving. We *shifted* to Hawaii where it was still light. Near the end of the night we *shifted* to the Bahamas where it was now mid-morning. She had the time of her life. We agreed to take one night a week from then on to explore together. It was the least I could do for this amazing young woman who was willing to do so much for me.

During this time I put my search for the American POWs on hold. My gut feeling was they had been moved to a new facility within North Korea. I couldn't search every building in the country and I couldn't search for the engineer and the POWs at the same time. I made the selfish choice.

In July of 2010, almost six months into our joint search Megan found the engineer. She "spoke" with him for her remaining REM periods that night as she did not know where to find me. The next night at the usual meeting during our first REM phase she broke the news to me. I actually thought she was joking with me, then realized it probably isn't possible to joke in the astral plane. On our next REM interval we met in my cell for a moment then together *shifted* to Robert Green's house in Goodyear, Arizona, where he was waiting for us.

When the three of us embraced in the astral plane it was an order of magnitude different than anything I had ever experienced. It wasn't fifty percent more intense, or even twice as much. More like quadrupled. I'm sure the physics major and the engineer could explain the math behind it, but I was content to simply luxuriate in it. The intensity of the feeling coupled with the knowledge my long search was finally over served to lull me into a stupor. When I reluctantly stirred from my lethargy my REM period was ending. We quickly agreed to meet at Robert's house during our next, longer REM interval.

I "talked" virtually non-stop during our next two meetings. Megan had briefly explained to Robert why we were searching for him when they initially met, but the engineer was astounded and greatly angered to hear my story. He was a U.S. Marine Corps veteran. He was involved with defense work for Lockheed Martin, held a medium level security clearance and considered himself a patriot. Before I could broach the subject of him possibly helping me he stated what a travesty it was that I was in prison and he would do anything he could to help me get out.

Chapter Forty Two

I spent several more nights meeting with Megan and Robert. We found it best to meet separately as the three of us meeting together produced such great synergy it was virtually impossible to accomplish anything.

After working out a plan I met next with Luis, who still did not know about my out of body abilities. After years of representing me, however, he understood I had some special mental ability the CIA needed, and he realized the people I had been searching for must have similar abilities.

I whispered to him I had found the people I was searching for and thought they might lead to me receiving a presidential pardon. Now I needed to meet with James Madison of the CIA to present him with my proposal. Luis was skeptical but agreed to contact Madison and set up the meeting.

******

Per my instructions Luis told Madison I was reconsidering his offer to go back to work for the CIA and wanted to discuss it with him in person, with my lawyer present. Of course, that was complete baloney but it worked to prompt the CIA man to meet with me.

The meeting got off to a bad start. Madison was angry Luis had misled him about the purpose of the meeting. When I started to tell Madison, in vague terms, the true purpose of the meeting he got even more upset, cutting me off and insisting Luis had to leave the room before we could discuss anything classified. He and Luis argued that for a while, eventually coming to an uneasy truce. Luis would leave the room while Madison and I discussed classified matters, then he would return to discuss the details of possibly getting me released from prison.

Using Susan's plan and following the script Megan and Robert and I had worked out I informed Madison of the existence of two astral travelers who were previously unknown to the CIA. I even told Madison Susan had found them and never told the CIA about it, hoping to provoke some reaction from him. Apparently he had gone to the same poker school as Jefferson because his face revealed nothing. However, when I told him both people had an ability to direct their travel equal to my own I saw a telltale flicker in his eyes and knew he was sniffing around the bait.

I told Madison about the assets these two possessed beyond being able to direct their travel. Their ability to hear sounds in the astral plane (my deafness while traveling seemed to be an oddity rather than the norm). Their formidable intellects. Megan's youth. Robert's language ability. Their ability to travel together. By the time I was finished and we called Luis back into the room Madison was practically drooling. He was so excited at the prospect of working with these two he couldn't possibly hide his interest behind a poker face. He didn't even bother to try.

When he returned Luis saw the smile on my face and immediately wanted to discuss the particulars of a presidential pardon. Madison was having none of it. "Not so fast, Mr. Hernandez. So far all I've gotten from your client is a story. It's a good story, and I'll admit I'm intrigued, but only a fool would buy a car without test driving it first. You understand me, Pete?"

"I do. I anticipated you'd want proof and I'm prepared to give it to you." Before I could say more Madison pointed at Luis, then at the door. With a muttered curse in Spanish Luis left the room.

I went on. "The younger of the two is prepared to participate in a test of her ability to direct her travel and also to prove she can hear sounds in the astral plane. That should be simple enough for you to arrange.

"I told you both travelers have expressed an interest in working for the CIA. The details of their contracts are between you and them, with one exception. After the first one passes your tests she will absolutely not begin any contract negotiations until I have received my pardon. If your offer isn't good enough to land her that's your problem, not mine.

"Once I have been pardoned and am out of prison I'll give you the name and address of the second traveler. Those are my terms."

Madison was already shaking his head. "I'd need proof both travelers can do all you say. You can't expect me to just take your word on something this important."

I smiled. "I can, and I do. If I gave you both their names I wouldn't have anything left to bargain with. You can't seriously expect me to trust you to keep your word after all

I've been through. The girl alone is worth it to you, even if the second traveler is a figment of my imagination. But he's not, he's real, and I think you're missing something monumental here, Madison."

"Really? What's that?"

"How do you think I know so much about these people?"

"Why, through Susan. You said she found them. She told you…" It finally dawned on him that I hadn't been in Susan's presence for at least the eight years I'd been in prison.

I made it plain to him. "That's right, I haven't seen Susan on earth in fifteen years, but I communicated with her regularly in the astral plane right before she died. I'm also communicating with these two new travelers the same way, just as they can talk to each other.

"Think about it, Madison. Two people who can be physically located on opposite sides of the planet yet speak to each other in the astral plane just as clearly and easily as I'm speaking to you right now. Instantaneous, absolutely secure communications that can never be compromised. It's the dream of every intelligence agency. Jefferson got a hint of it between Susan and I a long time ago and he was pretty excited about the possibilities. I bet you are, too."

Madison's brow was furrowed and he was chewing his lower lip. I revised downward his poker playing prowess. "How much does your lawyer actually know about what you did for us?"

I knew where he was going with this. "I've never told him, but he's been my attorney for the past eight years through my court-marital, trial and appeals, and he's a smart guy. He knows I have a special ability that you want, and he knows the two new travelers have a similar ability. He's a retired army full bird colonel. You can trust him to play along with your euphemisms and keep his mouth shut."

"I agree. Let's get him back in here."

Luis and Madison spoke for the next hour, jabbering back and forth in legal jargon as if I wasn't even in the room. Apparently Madison was also a lawyer by training, a fact he had conveniently failed to reveal until now. At times I felt like I was back in the astral plane eavesdropping on Boris Yeltsin talking to one of his lieutenants in the Kremlin, except this time I could hear. Not that hearing all the legal gobbledygook did me much good.

Eventually they wound down and Madison got up to leave. He started to extend his hand to me as if to offer a handshake, then thought better of it and simply walked to the door. After a moment a prison guard opened it and let him out, leaving Luis and I alone.

Luis held up one hand and spoke first. "I'm sure whatever listening devices they have in this room were turned off when Madison was here, and I'm just as sure they've already turned them back on, but I don't really care if they hear this or not.

"That was the just the opening round between Madison and I. He's going to extend his stay here in Colorado. He and I are going to meet tomorrow somewhere nearby and continue to hash things out. Whatever you said to him definitely got his attention, Pete. I'll do the best I can for you."

We whispered to each other for a few minutes more and then he left, promising to return when he had a deal to present to me.

******

After dinner the next evening Luis returned to see me. It was after normal visiting hours even for lawyers but we met anyway. I guess that was Madison's doing. As usual we whispered to each other with cupped hands to foil the ears we were certain were listening.

Luis explained to me he and Madison had relatively quickly agreed on the steps necessary to get me out of prison. The devil, as they say, was in the details. Madison argued for a presidential commutation of sentence for me. Luis held out for a pardon. Both got me out of prison but a commutation meant all my convictions would stand forever in my record. Basically, the president would reduce my sentence to time already served. A presidential pardon would make all of my convictions, including my court-martial, disappear. Luis prevailed. If Megan and Robert and I all agreed to the deal I would walk out of prison as if the whole thing had been a bad dream, all official records of it expunged.

Luis had negotiated a far better deal than I ever could have done. Basically, it went like this: If Megan proved her abilities and signed a one year contract to work for the CIA as an astral spy I would receive a presidential pardon. Ninety days after I was freed Luis would give Madison Robert's name and address. Robert must also agree to undergo a test of his abilities. The ninety day waiting period would allow me time to disappear. Luis was convinced that regardless of any deal struck with the CIA, witnessed and recorded by a dozen attorneys and ultimately approved by the President of the United States himself, the CIA would soon thereafter kill me. It would be made to look like an accident, of course, but dead is dead. Luis told me it pained him greatly to think his own government, representative of the country he had fought and bled for, would kill one of its own innocent citizens. Nevertheless, he felt certain they would do it, or at least attempt it. I had to disappear for my own safety. Whether Robert signed a contract or not was immaterial to the deal; only Megan had to sign on for me to go free. Luis's professional reputation was Madison's guarantee that Robert would present himself for testing.

Another coup on Luis's part - Madison agreed Luis could represent both Megan and Robert in their contract negotiations with the CIA. Everything would be legal and above board, all monies fully taxable. Megan's contract, if she signed one, would stipulate that I receive a presidential pardon or the contract would be null and void.

Some of the facets of the deal would never have occurred to me. As far as I could see it was airtight. All I could do was hope Megan went for it. I would present it to her just as Luis had explained it to me, but I wasn't about to twist her arm, even if meant remaining in prison. The same went for Robert.

Sadly, I found myself agreeing with Luis's assessment of my life expectancy if I was freed. Somehow I needed to disappear and remain hidden for the rest of my life from the best spy agency in the world.

Later that night I met with Megan and Robert in the astral plane, right there in my cell. It served to remind everyone of the stakes involved. Robert immediately agreed to the plan, which required no contractual commitment on his part, only that he participate in CIA testing.

Megan was more hesitant. She wanted to meet with Luis first to discuss it with him before committing to anything. She was fine with testing for the CIA but refused to agree to a one year contract in the blind. I couldn't blame her - I would have said the same thing myself. Luis had anticipated Megan wanting to meet with him and he asked me to pass a few things along to her in the privacy of the astral plane. Luis's paranoia about the CIA had grown exponentially over the years he represented me. He was certain the CIA had him under 24 hour surveillance in the hope of seeing Megan and Robert meeting with him. If the CIA could identify Megan and/or Robert they might approach them outside his presence, even though Madison gave his word that would not happen.

I told Luis my last contract offer from the CIA had been for fifty million dollars per year and came from the director himself. Armed with that knowledge he told me his initial negotiating position for Megan's one year contract would be twenty million dollars, with a floor of ten million. It was Luis's intention to complete all contract negotiations for Megan without her ever having to reveal her identity. If she liked the terms only then would she show up for the CIA test. After passing the test she would make the final decision whether to sign the contract or not. Luis would add contractual safeguards to ensure if Megan wanted to opt out after only one year she simply had to walk away. He assured me that with his law firm looking after her interests the CIA could not possibly screw her like they had screwed me.

Megan was flabbergasted when I conveyed to her the amount of money Luis said he could get for her. Frankly, she didn't believe Luis could do it. I didn't know what to say to that but Robert did. He pointed out that dozens of professional athletes make that kind of money every year and nobody thinks twice about it. Surely someone with as rare a talent as Megan was worth as much if not more. Robert went on to say if he signed a contract he would demand at least that much money.

I had promised myself I would simply present the facts to Megan and not attempt to persuade her to sign up. I didn't have to - Robert advocated strongly for her to sign on. "It's only one year, Megan," he said. "I did four years in the Marine Corps for peanuts and it went by in the blink of an eye. I did it for my country, not the money, but now we have an opportunity to serve our nation and get rich at the same time. As young as you are, think of what millions of dollars would mean to you. It's the opportunity of a lifetime."

I'm sure Megan is as patriotic as the rest of us, but it was the money that convinced her. She agreed to sign a one year contract if Luis could get her the kind of money we were talking about.

Luis and Madison finalized a contract offer for Megan contingent upon her successfully passing all the CIA tests. Her one year salary would be $12 million with an additional $3 million signing bonus. She would have to live within a twenty mile radius of CIA headquarters and work a flexible schedule as determined by the CIA. There was a lot more minutia in there but I focused on the clause requiring me to receive a presidential pardon prior to the contract becoming operative.

With the contract offer on the table Luis felt it safe for Megan to publicly meet with him. She flew to his law office in Virginia where they reviewed the contract and made a few changes at the margins. The CIA test of her abilities was ridiculously easy. She had to *shift* to the communications center of the American embassy in London and describe everything she saw and heard. For Megan it was the equivalent of asking her to go down the street to the 7-11 store and pick up a loaf of bread. She signed the contract and became an instant millionaire at twenty two years of age. Five days later, on August 14, 2010 I walked out of prison a free man, courtesy of the President of the United States of America. I had been behind bars almost eight years to the day.

Chapter Forty Three

Right up to the moment the last prison door clanged shut behind me I didn't believe it would really happen. Luis walked me out of prison and once we made it into the hot summer sunlight he nearly crushed my ribs with a bear hug. I started to thank him but couldn't seem to enunciate the words properly. It was only when Luis handed me his handkerchief did I realize I was crying.

Luis drove me off the prison grounds and headed for the airport. I still wasn't sure where I would go. I had peeked in on Jill and Adilyn in their Coronado, California home several times over the last few nights. Luis told me Jill had never dated anyone since I went to prison, despite the fact of our divorce. Even though she and I had not spoken in years it gave me hope she still cared for me and we might possibly get back together again.

I hadn't dared to speak to her about me possibly being freed. She had suffered far too much already due to my mistakes and I wasn't about to disappoint her again. Now that I actually was out I planned to call her from the airport. If she was interested in possibly rekindling our relationship I would fly to San Diego and take it one day at a time from there. If she was not, well, if she was not I had no idea what I might do or where I might go.

A few blocks from the airport Luis pulled off into a motel parking lot, stopped the car and got out. Holding up his cell phone he said, "I'm sorry, Pete, I have to make an urgent phone call. I'll just be a couple of minutes. Why don't you step out and stretch your legs, enjoy the sunshine?"

I was a little surprised but it wasn't like I had a plane to catch or someplace to be. I got out of the car and squinted in the brilliant daylight. Lost in thought, I didn't notice the woman walking up to me until she was almost upon me. It was Jill! My Jill!

I saw her arms open wide and threw myself into them. For the second time that morning I needed a handkerchief, not just for me but for Jill as well.

******

We spent the night right there in the motel. Luis had arranged it all, of course. He had been in regular contact with Jill over the years and knew she still had feelings for me. When it became clear to him I would be freed he broke the news to her and she eagerly agreed to come to Colorado to meet me. Adilyn was still in Coronado staying at a friend's house.

I didn't have to wonder anymore if Jill still loved me. We made love many times that night. As my high school girlfriend Melissa once infamously explained to me, there's a difference between having sex and making love. Jill and I most definitely made love.

******

The next morning I wanted to tell Jill all about Megan and Robert and my pardon, but she stopped me with a look. She explained that Luis had brought her up to speed on all the events as he knew them, placing special emphasis on those last three words while pointing to her ear and then circling her finger around the room. She was telling me Luis thought the room we were in might be bugged by the CIA! Her emphasis on things "as Luis knew them" was a warning to me not to discuss anything beyond the quasi-classified level of Luis's version of things. Madison had made it clear to Luis and me that all the non-disclosure agreements I had signed would remain in effect for the rest of my life and violation of any of them might land me right back in prison. "Pete, let's get out of here. We can discuss all that later. What we really need to talk about is Adilyn."

We grabbed a shuttle to the airport and got on the first flight leaving for San Diego. In the interim Jill gave me the Reader's Digest version of Adilyn's life since I went away. She had just finished third grade and would start fourth grade at Village Elementary School next month. Jill had told her I was in prison but it was all a mistake. She had last seen me in October of 2003 when she was not yet three years old. She didn't remember me at all. It broke my heart to hear that.

Jill picked up her car from the airport parking lot when we got off the plane in San Diego. Rather than go straight to her house she drove to Coronado Beach where we got out and walked. "Okay, Pete, I think we can finally talk here. Luis told me the motel where we met, the airplane, and especially my car might not be safe. I know you need to disappear. I agree with Luis about that. I've got plenty of your money left to make it happen. The only question is will Adilyn and I go with you or will you go alone?"

"What? Of course you're going with me! Don't you want to?"

"It's not that simple, Pete. Yes, I want to go with you, but it's not about me and it's not about you. It's all about Adilyn now. She's almost ten years old. She's got lots of friends here. She loves her school. And she doesn't know you from Adam. It isn't fair or right to think we can just rip her away from her friends, school and community, give her a new identity and start all over again."

That stopped me cold. I was so thrilled to know Jill still loved me I hadn't given a moment's thought to how disappearing might impact Adilyn's life. After focusing on getting out of prison for the last eight years I suddenly had a whole new set of problems related to *being* out of prison. Still, so far life on the outside was going much better than I ever dared hope. Jill still loved me, now I just needed my own daughter to like me, or at least tolerate me enough to agree to drop everything and start a new life.

Jill phoned the neighbor where Adilyn had spent the night and asked her to return Adilyn home. Jill had done quite a bit of internet research regarding father/daughter reunions after prison. The familiar surroundings of her own home were supposed to make Adilyn feel more at ease. I hoped it worked for her because I was as nervous as a long tailed cat at a rocking chair party.

Jill pulled her car into the attached garage and we entered the house through the kitchen. I could hear the television playing softly in the living room. The house was familiar to me from my many astral visits.

We walked into the living room to find Adilyn on the sofa. Jill said, "Adilyn, this is…"

"Daddy!" My little girl screamed and ran into my outstretched arms, smothering me with kisses. Jill was dumbfounded. I was delirious with happiness. Adilyn knew it, but she jokingly said, "Daddy, you're crying! Aren't you happy to see me?"

I tried to answer but my voice failed me. All I could do was hug my daughter harder. I think I had cried more in the last two days than in the rest of my entire adult life. When I stole a glance at Jill I saw she was crying as well.

Two hours later Adilyn was still bringing me up to speed on everything that had happened in her life since I last saw her seven years previously when she and Jill said goodbye to me at the Washington, D.C. Jail. There seemed to be no order to her anecdotes, no rhyme or reason. Her recollection of a visit to Auntie Doreen's house preceded a story of a naughty boy in school which was followed by the happy tale of a day at dog beach watching dozens of doggies frolicking in the warm Pacific surf.

It didn't matter what she said. The only thing that mattered was I was home with my family. Home. The word has a unique sound, a special feel, even if you only think it. Jill was still trying to come to grips with Adilyn's instantaneous acceptance of me as her father. We were sitting on a large couch, with Adilyn on one side, Jill on the other, and me in the happy middle. Ecstatically, elatedly, euphorically happy.

After Adilyn put forth a dramatic rendition of the time she fell off her bicycle and ended up at the urgent care clinic she showed me the small scar on her chin. I told her, "You're still just as beautiful as ever. It's a tiny scar, Angel, and it will get smaller as you grow bigger."

Adilyn replied, "I'm not an angel, Daddy. You're my angel. I remember you visiting me when I was a baby."

Jill and I looked at each other. I said, "Mommy and I are both surprised you remember me, sweetheart. You weren't even three years old when I went away."

"Not you, Daddy, the Daddy Angel. I don't remember you, but I remember the Daddy Angel visiting me at night in my crib and later when I was small and slept in the Snow White bed."

Frowning, Jill said, "I think those were dreams, honey. Daddy was gone when you slept in the Snow White bed."

Adilyn shook her head obstinately. "No, Mommy. I was asleep, but I wasn't dreaming when I saw the Daddy Angel. He was real, and he was soft and white and fuzzy and warm and would float around me, staring at me, loving me. I always felt safe when the Daddy Angel was with me.

"When I changed to the big girl bed I stopped seeing the Daddy Angel but I could still feel you, Daddy. I even went back and slept in the Snow White bed sometimes hoping I could see you again, but I never did."

Jill turned as white as a sheet. "I remember those times, Adilyn. I thought you said you were having nightmares."

"No, Mommy, I said I wanted to feel safer. I felt safest when I could see the Daddy Angel and I thought I could only see him in the Snow White bed, but it didn't work."

Again, Jill and I looked at each other, confounded by Adilyn's matter of fact assertions. Was it possible she actually saw my astral form when I visited her back then? Was she really saying she could still feel my presence when I visited her recently? She put that question to rest before I could ask it.

"You came to see me two nights ago, Daddy. It felt like you were especially happy. I was hoping it meant my real Daddy was coming home, not just the Daddy Angel, and here you are."

Jill shrugged her shoulders as she looked at me, as if to say, "I guess anything's possible."

I spoke to Adilyn. "Sweetheart, your mother and I were concerned you might not be comfortable around me since it has been so long since you last saw me, but you obviously are relaxed and happy to have me home. Is it because of the Daddy Angel?"

"Yes, Daddy, what a silly question. I don't remember you but I know you're my Daddy because of the Daddy Angel, which is a part of you. I can't see the Daddy Angel anymore but I can feel him when he comes at night, and I can feel him now inside of you. It's how I know you're you." Adilyn saw the look of astonishment on her mother's face and misinterpreted it as disbelief. "I guess I'm explaining it badly. Do you know what I mean, Daddy?"

"I do, sweetheart, and I think you're explaining it perfectly."

Chapter Forty Four

It took seven weeks for us to disappear. Four weeks of that was waiting for our new documents. While we waited we were taught how to live below the radar. Off the grid. Call it whatever you want. It's easier than you think, and actually kind of fun. You're probably thinking we're living in some foreign country that has no extradition treaty with the United States. Nope. First of all, the CIA doesn't want to arrest me, they want to kill me. At least we think they do. Maybe they don't really care and we jumped through all the hoops for nothing, but in my gut I know that's not true. Jefferson once compared me to a nuclear bomb. Do you think the CIA is happy with a nuclear bomb running around loose? A nuclear bomb with a photographic memory who worked for the CIA ten years and hates them?

Secondly, the CIA by law is not allowed to operate on American soil. If they need to do something in America they must ask another government agency to do it for them or hire an outside contractor. That costs money or favors, neither of which are in endless supply. So, maybe we're still in the good ol' US of A. Maybe.

I wrote previously that money may not be able to buy happiness but it can certainly make life easier. Well, it can also make disappearing a snap. I was able to recover well over $20 million dollars from overseas accounts the CIA never found. Dirty money, you say? Maybe, but I earned every penny of it, and spent a few of those pennies establishing new identities for all of us. Jill and I also had some cosmetic surgery. Not a lot, but enough.

We home schooled Adilyn for a couple of years before enrolling her in a school again. Jill is pregnant with our third child. Maybe we adopted one or two more to further disguise our family. Maybe.

I never saw Megan or Robert or Luis again. Losing good friends is the worst part of disappearing. I don't know if Robert chose to join the CIA but I suspect he did. I don't fly anymore, in airplanes or in the astral plane. Airplanes are too risky, requiring too much screening and ID. The astral plane is also too risky for me. I know other travelers are out there, and all of them may not be my friends. Maybe there is a new hitchhiker, or even a team of them, looking for me as I write this. If so, they'll never find me. Right after we decided to disappear I started drinking a glass of wine every night and a few beers on occasion. For a while I had to fight to keep myself from going out of body at night but within two months I had lost the ability entirely. It's a small price to pay for peace of mind. My biggest regret is the American POWs in North Korea, or wherever they may be. I made certain Megan and Robert knew about them, so perhaps they have been found again. I hope so.

The last thing my lawyer Luis did for me was to have this manuscript published. I sent him the final few pages through a series of cut outs that would have made the CIA proud. If you are reading it that means it has gotten past the government censors. You know by now I wrote the last parts of it when I was already out of prison. I suppose I could have gone back and changed the prologue, but why spoil a good story?

Sweet Dreams!

Peter E. Ludvick

Printed in Great Britain
by Amazon